P9-CLO-923

# THE GUSTAV SONATA

BY THE SAME AUTHOR

*Novels*

Sadler's Birthday
Letter to Sister Benedicta
The Cupboard
The Swimming Pool Season
Restoration
Sacred Country
The Way I Found Her
Music and Silence
The Colour
The Road Home
Trespass
Merivel

*Short Story Collections*

The Colonel's Daughter
The Garden of the Villa Mollini
Evangelista's Fan
The Darkness of Wallis Simpson
The American Lover

*For Children*

Journey to the Volcano

# THE GUSTAV SONATA

Rose Tremain

Chatto & Windus
LONDON

5 7 9 10 8 6 4

Chatto & Windus, an imprint of Vintage,
20 Vauxhall Bridge Road,
London SW1V 2SA

Chatto & Windus is part of the Penguin Random House group of companies
whose addresses can be found at global.penguinrandomhouse.com.

First published by Chatto and Windus in 2016

www.vintage-books.co.uk

A CIP catalogue record for this book is available from the British Library

HB ISBN 9781784740030
TPB ISBN 9781784740047

Typeset in Adobe Garamond 11.5/13.25 pt by
Palimpsest Book Production Limited, Falkirk, Stirlingshire

Printed and bound by Clays Ltd, St Ives plc

*To the memory of Richard Simon*
*1932–2013*

'If anyone should importune me to give a reason
why I loved him, I feel it could not otherwise be expressed
than by making the answer, "Because it was he, because it
was I".'

– Michel de Montaigne, *On Friendship*

# CONTENTS

*Part Three*

# Part One

# Mutti

## *Matzlingen, Switzerland, 1947*

At the age of five, Gustav Perle was certain of only one thing: he loved his mother.

Her name was Emilie, but everybody addressed her as Frau Perle. (In Switzerland, at that time, after the war, people were formal. You might pass a lifetime without *knowing* the first name of your nearest neighbour.) Gustav called Emilie Perle 'Mutti'. She would be 'Mutti' all his life, even when the name began to sound babyish to him: his Mutti, his alone, a thin woman with a reedy voice and straggly hair and a hesitant way of moving from room to room in the small apartment, as if afraid of discovering, between one space and the next, objects – or even people – she had not prepared herself to encounter.

The second-floor apartment, reached by a stone staircase too grand for the building, overlooked the River Emme in the town of Matzlingen, in an area of Switzerland known as Mittelland, between the Jura and the Alps. On the wall of Gustav's tiny room was a map of Mittelland, which displayed itself as hilly and green and populated by cattle and waterwheels and little shingled churches. Sometimes, Emilie would take Gustav's hand and guide it to the north bank of the river where Matzlingen was marked in. The symbol for Matzlingen was a wheel of cheese with one slice cut out of it. Gustav could remember asking Emilie who had eaten the slice that had been cut out. But Emilie had told him not to waste her time with silly questions.

On an oak sideboard in the living room, stood a photograph

of Erich Perle, Gustav's father, who had died before Gustav was old enough to remember him.

Every year, on August 1st, Swiss National Day, Emilie set posies of gentian flowers round the photograph and made Gustav kneel down in front of it and pray for his father's soul. Gustav didn't understand what a soul was. He could see only that Erich was a good-looking man with a confident smile, wearing a police uniform with shiny buttons. So Gustav decided to pray for the buttons – that they would keep their shine, and that his father's proud smile wouldn't fade as the years passed.

'He was a hero,' Emilie would remind her son every year. 'I didn't understand it at first, but he was. He was a good man in a rotten world. If anybody tells you otherwise, they're wrong.'

Sometimes, with her eyes closed and her hands pressed together, she would mumble other things she remembered about Erich. One day, she said, 'It was so unfair. Justice was never done. And it never will be done.'

Wearing a smock, with his short hair neatly combed, Gustav was taken each morning to the local kindergarten. At the door of the schoolhouse, he would stand absolutely still, watching Emilie walk away down the path. He never cried. He could often feel a cry trying to come up from his heart, but he always forced it down. Because this was how Emilie had told him to behave in the world. He had to *master himself.* The world was alive with wrongdoing, she said, but Gustav had to emulate his father who, when wronged, had behaved like an honourable man; he had *mastered himself.* In this way, Gustav would be prepared for the uncertainties to come. Because even in Switzerland, where the war hadn't trespassed, nobody yet knew how the future would unfold.

'So you see,' she said, 'you have to be *like Switzerland.* Do you understand me? You have to hold yourself together and be courageous, stay separate and strong. Then, you will have the right kind of life.'

Gustav had no idea what 'the right kind of life' was. All he knew was the life he had, the one with Emilie in the second-floor apartment, with the map of Mittelland on his bedroom wall and Emilie's stockings drying on a string above the iron bath. He wanted them always to be there, those stockings. He wanted the taste and texture of the knödel they ate for supper never to change. Even the smell of cheese in Emilie's hair, which he didn't particularly like – he knew this had to linger there because Emilie's job at the Matzlingen Cheese Co-operative was the thing that kept them alive.

The speciality of the Matzlingen Co-operative was Emmental, made from the milk of the Emme valleys. Sounding like a tour guide, Emilie announced to Gustav, 'There are many fine inventions in Switzerland and Emmental cheese is one of them.' But in spite of its fineness, the sales of Emmental – both within Switzerland and to all those countries outside it, still struggling to rebuild themselves after the war – were unreliable. And if sales were down, the bonuses paid to the cheese workers at Christmas and on National Day could be disappointing.

Waiting to see what her bonus was going to be would put Emilie Perle into a trance of anxiety. She would sit at the kitchen shelf (it wasn't a table, just a shelf on a hinge, where she and Gustav sat to eat their meals) doing her sums on the grey edges of the *Matzlingerzeitung*, the local newspaper. The newsprint always blurred her arithmetic. Nor did her figures keep to their columns, but wandered over the réportage of Schwingen Competitions and the sightings of wolves in the nearby forests. Sometimes, the hectic scribblings were blurred a second time by Emilie's tears. She'd told Gustav never to cry. But it seemed that this rule didn't apply to her, because there were times, late at night, when Gustav would creep out of his room to find Emilie weeping over the pages of the *Matzlingerzeitung*.

At these moments, her breath often smelled of aniseed and she would be clutching a glass clouded with yellow liquid, and Gustav felt afraid of these things – of her aniseed breath and the dirty glass and his mother's tears. He would climb onto a stool beside her and watch her out of the corner of his grey eyes, and soon, Emilie would blow her nose and reach out to him and say she was sorry. He would kiss her moist, burning cheek and then she would lift him up, staggering a little under the weight of him, and carry him back to his room.

But in the year that Gustav turned five, no Christmas bonuses were paid at all and Emilie was forced to take a second job on

Saturday mornings, as a cleaner in the Protestant Church of Sankt Johann.

She said to Gustav, 'This is work you can help me with.'

So they went out together very early, before the town was properly awake, before any light showed in the sky. They walked through the snow, following two frail torchlight beams, their breath condensing inside their woollen mufflers. When they arrived at the church, this, too, was dark and cold. Emilie turned on the two greenish strip lights on either side of the nave and they began their tasks, tidying the hymn books, dusting the pews, sweeping the stone floor, polishing the brass candlesticks. They could hear owls calling outside in the waning dark.

As the daylight grew stronger, Gustav always returned to his favourite task. Kneeling on a hassock, pushing the hassock along as he went, he'd clean the iron grating that ran down the length of the aisle. He pretended to Emilie that he had to do this job very carefully, because the ironwork had ornate patterns in it and his rag had to go round these and in and out of them, and she said, 'All right, Gustav, that's good. Doing your job carefully is good.'

But what she didn't know was that Gustav was searching for objects which had fallen *through* the grating and which lay there in the dust. He thought of this strange collection as his 'treasure'. Only hands as small as his could retrieve them. Now and again, he did find money, but it was always the kind of low-value money with which nothing could be bought. More usual items were hairpins, withered flower petals, cigarette stubs, sweet wrappings, paper clips and nails made of iron. He knew that these things were of no account, but he didn't mind. One day, he found a brand-new lipstick in a golden case. He designated this his 'chief treasure'.

He took everything home in the pockets of his coat and hid the objects in a wooden box that had once contained the cigars his father used to smoke. He smoothed out the sweet wrappers, liking the vibrant colours, and shook out the tobacco from the cigarette ends into a little tin.

When he was alone in his room, he would stare at the treasure. Sometimes, he touched it and smelled it. Keeping it hidden from Emilie – as though perhaps it was a present for her which he would one day surprise her with – was what excited him about it. The lipstick was a dark purple colour, almost black, like a boiled damson, and he found it beautiful.

He and Emilie had to spend two hours at the church, to get everything shipshape for the weekend services. During this time, a few people would come in, bundled up against the cold, and enter the pews and pray, or else go to the altar rail and stare at the amber-coloured stained-glass pietà in the west window.

Gustav saw that Emilie crept round them, as if trying to make herself invisible. Seldom did these people say 'Grüezi', or say Frau Perle's name. He watched them from his hassock. He noticed that almost all of them were old. They appeared to him as unfortunate beings, who had no secret treasure. He thought that, perhaps, they hadn't got 'the right kind of life'. He wondered whether the 'right life' might lie in the things which he alone could see – the things underneath some grating or other, over which most people heedlessly trod.

When the cleaning was done, Gustav and Emilie walked home, side by side. The trams would be running by then, and a bell chiming somewhere, and a scatter of pigeons fluttering from roof to roof, and the flower stallholder setting out her vases and buckets on the corner of Unter der Egg. The flower seller, whose name was Frau Teller, would always greet them and smile, even if snow was falling.

Unter der Egg was the name of the street in which their apartment block stood. Before these blocks had been built, Unter der Egg (Under the Harrow) had been a rural strip, where the residents of Matzlingen had been able to rent allotments and grow vegetables, but these were long gone. Now, there was just a wide pavement and a metal drinking fountain and Frau Teller's stall, which was the last reminder of green things growing in this place. Emilie sometimes said that she would have liked to grow vegetables – red cabbages, she said, and snow peas and marrows. 'But at least,' she would sigh, 'the place wasn't destroyed by the war.'

She had shown Gustav some magazine pictures of destroyed places. She said they were all outside Switzerland. Dresden. Berlin. Caen. There were no people in any of these photographs, but in one of these pictures there had been a white dog, sitting alone in a mound of rubble. Gustav asked what had happened to that dog and Emilie said, 'It's no use asking what happened, Gustav. Perhaps the dog found a good master, or perhaps it died of hunger. How can I possibly know? Everything, in the war, depended on who you were and *where* you were. And then destiny took over.'

Gustav stared at his mother. 'Where were we?' he said.

She closed the magazine and folded it away, like a soft garment she planned to wear again in the near future. She took Gustav's face in her hands. 'We were here,' she said, 'safe in Matzlingen. For a while, when your father was Assistant Police Chief, we even had a beautiful apartment on Fribourgstrasse. It had a balcony, where I grew geraniums. I can't see a geranium plant without thinking of the ones I grew.'

'Then we came to Unter der Egg?' asked Gustav.

'Yes. Then we came to Unter der Egg.'

'Just you and me?'

'No. At first there were the three of us. But not for long.'

After the cleaning of the church, Gustav and Emilie would sit at the folding shelf in the tiny kitchen and drink hot chocolate and eat black bread with butter. The long winter day stretched ahead of them, cold and empty. Sometimes Emilie would go back to bed and read her magazines. She made no apology for this. She said children had to learn to play on their own. She said if they didn't learn to do this, they would never cultivate an imagination.

Gustav would stare out of the window of his room at the white sky. The only toy he owned was a little metal train, so he'd set the train on the windowsill and shunt it backwards and forwards. Often, it was so cold by the window that Gustav's breath made realistic steam, which he puffed over the engine. At the carriage windows, people's faces had been painted on, all of them given expressions of blank surprise. To these startled people, Gustav would occasionally whisper, 'You have to *master yourselves.*'

The strangest place in the apartment building was the bunker underneath it. This had been built as a nuclear shelter, more usually referred to as an 'air protection cellar'. Soon, every building in Switzerland would be required to have one of these.

Once a year, the janitor summoned the residents of the building, including the children, and they descended all together into the shelter. Behind them, as they went down the stairs, heavy iron doors were closed.

Gustav clung to Emilie's hand. Lights were turned on, but all they showed were more stairs going down and down. The janitor always reminded everybody that they should 'breathe normally', that the air filtration system was tested frequently for its absolutely perfect functioning. It wasn't, he said, called an 'air protection cellar' for nothing. But there was a strange smell about it, an animal smell, as though foxes or rats had nested here, living off dust or off grey paint licked from the walls.

Beneath the countless stairs, the shelter opened into a large storeroom, stacked from floor to ceiling with sealed cardboard boxes. 'You'll remember what we keep in the boxes,' the janitor said, 'enough food for all of us for approximately two months. And the water supply will be in the tanks over there. Clean drinking water. Rationed of course, because the mains supply – even if it was functioning – would be disconnected, in case of radiation contamination, but sufficient for all.'

He led them on. He was a heavy man. He spoke loudly and emphatically, as though he assumed he was with a party of deaf people. The sound of his voice echoed round the concrete walls. Gustav noticed that the residents always fell silent during the nuclear shelter tours. Their expressions reminded him of the painted people on his train. Husbands and wives huddled together. Old people clutched at each other to steady themselves. Gustav always hoped that his mother wouldn't let go of his hand.

When they got to the 'dormitory' part of the shelter, Gustav saw that the bunks had been built one above the other in stacks of five. To reach the top bunks, you had to climb a ladder, and he thought that he wouldn't like this, to be so far from the ground. Supposing he woke in the night, in the dark, and couldn't find Mutti? Supposing Mutti was on the very bottom bunk, or in a different row? Supposing he fell out of his bunk and landed on his head and his head exploded? He whispered that he didn't want to live there, in an iron bunk and with cardboard food, and Mutti said, 'It will probably never happen.'

'What will never happen?' he asked.

But Emilie didn't wish to say. 'You don't need to think about it yet,' she told him. 'The shelter is just a place of safety, in case the Russians – or anybody at all – ever took it into their heads to harm Switzerland.'

Gustav lay in his bed at night and thought about what might happen if Switzerland were harmed. He wondered if Matzlingen would be turned to rubble and whether he would find himself all alone, like the white dog in the picture.

# Anton

## *Matzlingen, 1948*

Anton arrived at the kindergarten in the cold spring of the year.

He came into the schoolroom and stood by the door, crying. None of the children had seen this boy before. One of the teachers, Fräulein Frick, went to him and took his hand and knelt down and began talking to him, but he didn't seem to hear her. He just kept on weeping.

Fräulein Frick beckoned to Gustav. Gustav didn't particularly want to be the boy chosen to comfort this weeping child, but Fräulein Frick urged him to come towards her and said to Anton, 'This is Gustav. Gustav is going to be your friend. He will take you to the sandbox and you can build a castle together before we begin our lessons.'

Anton looked down at Gustav, who was slightly smaller than he was.

Gustav said to him, 'My mother says it's better not to cry. She says you have to *master yourself*.'

Anton appeared so startled by this that his sobbing stopped abruptly.

'There,' said Fräulein Frick. 'That's good. Go with Gustav, then.' She produced a handkerchief and wiped Anton's cheeks. The boy's face was a hectic pink, his eyes big pools of darkness. His body was trembling.

Gustav led him over to the sandbox. Anton's small hand felt burning hot. Gustav said, 'What kind of castle do you want to build?' But the boy couldn't answer. So Gustav gave him a spade and said, 'I like castles with moats. Shall we start on the moat?'

Gustav marked out a circle and they began digging. A few other children clustered round them, staring at the new boy.

Before Anton arrived, Gustav had had no close friends at the kindergarten. There was a girl who amused him called Isabel. She liked to climb onto the work tables and jump off again, landing like a gymnast with her feet together and her arms outspread. She always brought her pet mouse to school in a wooden cage and Gustav was one of the few children allowed to stroke the mouse. But Isabel was too exhausting to play with for long. She had to be the Queen of every game.

All his life, Gustav would remember vividly that first morning spent with Anton. They didn't talk very much. It was as if Anton was so exhausted by his weeping that he *couldn't* talk. He just followed Gustav around and sat very close to him at the work table and watched what he did and tried to copy him. When Gustav asked him where he'd come from, he said, 'From Bern. We had a house in Bern, but now we've only got an apartment in Matzlingen.'

Gustav said, 'The place where I live is very small. We don't even have a kitchen table. Have you got a kitchen table?'

'Yes,' said Anton, 'we've got a kitchen table. I was sick all over it at breakfast because I didn't want to come here.'

Later, Anton asked Gustav, 'Have you got a piano?'

'No,' said Gustav.

'We've got a piano and I can play it. I can play "Für Elise". Not the fast bit, but the first section.'

'What's "Für Elise"?' asked Gustav.

'Beethoven,' said Anton.

Perhaps it was the idea of Anton playing the piano with his small hands, or perhaps it was when Anton told him that his surname was Zwiebel, which was identical to the word for 'onion', and made you feel sorry for him; whatever it was, there was something about Anton which made Gustav feel that he had to protect him.

The following day, Anton was crying again when he arrived. Gustav saw Fräulein Frick coming towards him, but he stood in her way and said that Anton would be all right with him. He led him to the Nature Table and showed him the silkworms that were being reared in a grocery box with a perforated lid. He said, 'In the box we had before, the holes were too big and the silkworms climbed out of them.'

'Where did they go?' asked Anton through his tears.

'They went all over the place,' said Gustav. 'We tried to find them and put them back, but some of them got trodden on. Treading on a silkworm is disgusting.'

Gustav saw Anton smile, but then his tears welled up again and he put his face in his hands.

Gustav said, 'What are you crying for?'

Anton stammered that he was crying for the loss of his friends at his old kindergarten in Bern.

'Are they dead?' asked Gustav.

'No. But I'll never see them again. I'm in this place now.'

Gustav said, 'I think it's stupid to cry for them, then. Isn't your mother angry that you keep crying?'

Anton took his hands away from his face and stared at Gustav. 'No,' he said, 'she understands that I'm unhappy.'

'Well,' said Gustav, '*I* think it's a bit stupid. You're here now, so you just have to get on with it.'

The bell rang for the beginning of morning lessons. Anton followed Gustav to one of the work tables. Pieces of grey sugar paper were put in front of them and boxes of crayons and they were told to start the day by drawing a picture of anything they liked.

Anton's tears slowly speckled the paper, like fat raindrops, but after five or six minutes, he stopped crying.

'What are you going to draw?' he asked Gustav.

'I'm going to draw my mother,' he said.

'Is your mother beautiful?'

'I don't know. She's just my mother. She works at the cheese co-operative, making Emmental.'

Fräulein Frick rapped on her desk with a ruler. 'You know the rules,' she said. 'When we're drawing pictures, we're silent. We talk silently to our pictures, not to each other.'

Gustav wanted Emilie to be sitting at the kitchen shelf in his picture, so he drew the shelf first, a kind of oblong, resting on air. He coloured it brown. Then he began on Emilie's face, not a round thing, but a narrow kind of shape he didn't know how to make. He saw straight away that what he'd drawn was *too* narrow. He put his hand up and Fräulein Frick came over and Gustav said, 'This was meant to be a face, but it looks like an ice-cream cone.'

'Never mind,' said Fräulein Frick. 'Why don't you make it a cone? Put some nice strawberry ice cream into it.'

There was something amusing about this – that Emilie Perle could suddenly become a cornet. Gustav whispered to Anton, 'I was going to draw my Mutti but she went wrong. Now she's an ice cream.'

And this was the first time that he heard Anton laugh. And it was the kind of laugh that couldn't be resisted; you had to join in, and suddenly the two boys couldn't stop giggling. Gustav suspected that Fräulein Frick was watching them sternly, but she said nothing and when he looked up at her – mastering his giggling at last – her expression wasn't stern at all, but just rather sweetly amused.

Gustav selected a pink crayon and drew a scribble of ice cream on his cornet. Then he looked over to see what Anton was drawing. He was using only a black crayon. He'd laid a small ruler on the sugar paper and drawn a line all the way round it. Inside the perfectly ruled shape was a series of black lines of differing lengths. Gustav knew what the thing was meant to be: it was a piano.

Gustav told Emilie about Anton's laugh. He said, 'I like hearing it.'

In the night, he began trying to think up funny stories to tell Anton, so that he'd be able to hear his laughter all through the day. And then he had an idea which surprised him – he decided to show Anton the treasure in the cigar box. He would show him because he thought that Anton would see that it was a collection worth hoarding. But Gustav wouldn't risk taking it in to the kindergarten. He said to Emilie, 'Could we invite Anton Zwiebel for tea?'

'Zwiebel?' said Emilie. 'That's a very peculiar name.'

'He can't help his name,' said Gustav.

'No. But names are important. When I first met your father and he told me his surname was Perle, I thought how beautiful it was and how I would like to become Frau Perle.'

Gustav looked up at his mother. She was undoing her scraggly hair from the red handkerchief she tied it in for work, letting her hair fall round her face. Then, she smoothed it and patted it, as if, right then and there, she was preparing once again for that first meeting with a man called Erich Perle.

'On a Wednesday, we could invite him?' said Gustav. 'On your half-day off.'

'Anton Zwiebel. Well, I've never heard a name like that before. But yes, we can invite him – if his parents agree. I could make a Nusstorte, assuming I can get the walnuts at this time of year . . .'

'He might not like walnuts.'

'Too bad. If he doesn't like them, he doesn't have to eat the Nusstorte.'

It was late spring by the time the invitation to tea went out. It was agreed that Anton would walk from school to Unter der Egg with Gustav and that his father would collect him from Emilie's apartment at six o'clock. The father, it appeared, was a banker, who'd worked for a large national bank in Bern and now worked for a smaller branch of that bank in Matzlingen. The reasons for the move weren't explained. All Anton said was that everybody in the family missed living in Bern. Herr Zwiebel, the banker, missed his big bank; Frau Zwiebel, who was a housewife, missed the wonderful shops and Anton missed his old friends.

Every May, in the courtyard at the back of the apartment, a white cherry tree bloomed. In this spring of 1948, perhaps because of the steady rains that had fallen at the end of winter, the flowers on the cherry were so abundant that the branches of the tree hung low towards the stones of the yard.

Gustav's window, where he played with his tin train, overlooked the cherry tree, and he saw how the residents who went in and out of the building by that route, almost invariably paused and stood staring at the tree, with its cargo of beauty, and sometimes reached out to it, as they might have reached out, in yearning, to a lost person. Emilie said that there had once been cherry trees at the front of the building, all along Unter der Egg, but they'd been torn out and now there was just this one tree in the courtyard. She said, 'The tree is special for people, because it's lasted through all the upheaval – as certain things sometimes seem to do.'

'What things?' asked Gustav.

'Well,' said Emilie, 'like that white dog you pointed out in the rubble of Berlin. It had survived.'

'You said it might have found a good master or it might have starved to death.'

'I know I did. But the point was, when everything around it had been destroyed, it was still there for a while. It had hung on.'

So the Wednesday afternoon of the tea arrived. Gustav enjoyed walking home in the sunshine with Anton. He felt proud, in a way that he couldn't explain.

When Anton was introduced to Emilie, Gustav saw that his mother stared at him for longer than she would normally stare at people she met for the first time, and Gustav wondered what was going through her mind. She said, 'You and Gustav go and play in his room for a little while, then we'll have tea and Nusstorte. I hope you like Nusstorte.'

'I don't know what it is,' said Anton.

'Ah,' said Emilie. 'Well, Gustav will explain to you.'

They went to Gustav's room, where, at this time of the day, the sun was falling in a diagonal across the window, and Gustav said, 'Nusstorte is a sort of pastry thing, with caramel and walnuts inside.'

But Anton wasn't listening. They were standing at the windowsill, next to the metal train and Anton was staring down at the white cherry tree. He said, 'Can we go down there?'

'To play in the courtyard?'

'I want to see that tree.'

'It's just a cherry tree,' said Gustav.

'Can't we go down there?'

'We'll have to ask Mutti.'

Emilie said, 'All right, but I'll come with you. I don't want you making a noise on the stairs. You remember Herr Nieder is very ill, Gustav?'

'Herr Nieder is our neighbour,' said Gustav to Anton. 'He's dying.'

'Oh,' said Anton. 'Has he got a piano?'

'I don't know. Has he, Mutti?'

'A piano?' said Emilie. 'Why do you ask?'

'Well,' said Anton, 'if he does, I could play "Für Elise" for him.'

'He might not want you to play "Für Elise",' said Gustav.

'He would. Everybody likes me to play that.'

'Well, not now,' said Emilie. 'Let's go down very quietly, shall we?'

So they arrived in the courtyard and Anton stared at the cherry tree and his dark eyes widened. He ran to the tree and began to hop from one foot to the other and then to jump up and down, uttering little cries of joy.

Gustav stood very still, watching Anton. He decided that there was something connecting Anton's joy at the sight of the cherry blossom to his early-morning weeping at the kindergarten, but he couldn't say what. He went towards his friend and took his hand and together they began to skip round and round the tree, laughing until they were out of breath. Gustav had no idea exactly *why* he was skipping, but he knew that Anton knew and that seemed to be enough.

One or two of the apartment residents arrived in the courtyard and stopped to smile at the two boys dancing round the old cherry. Later, when Anton had gone home, Emilie said, 'I suppose there may not be any cherry trees in Bern. It's unlikely, but one can't say for sure. Perhaps he had never seen one before?'

'I don't know,' said Gustav.

'I think he is a nice boy,' said Emilie, 'but of course he is a Jew.'

'What's a Jew?' asked Gustav.

'Ah,' said Emilie. 'The Jews are the people your father died trying to save.'

# Nusstorte

## *Matzlingen, 1948*

At the end of the year, Gustav and Anton left the kindergarten. They were both six years old.

They were sent to the same school in Matzlingen, very near to the church Gustav and Emilie cleaned on Saturdays. The school was called the Sankt Johann Protestant Academy and it was in an old echoey building – stucco plastered over ancient stone – with shutters painted dark red and a heavy door, embellished with black ironwork. It had a steep roof, where doves sometimes roosted.

Gustav missed the kindergarten; the Nature Table, the sandbox, the children's pictures covering the walls. There had been a *lightness* about the place, a feeling of freedom in the classrooms, as though outside the windows there had been pastures and woods and wide rivers, instead of an ordinary street. In contrast, the Sankt Johann Protestant School was dark and the classrooms bare. Gustav felt cold there. Other buildings crowded in upon it. It was full of strange, lingering noise.

'In time,' Emilie said, 'you'll get used to it. That is the only option you have.'

He looked forward to Saturdays, when they went to clean the church and he could be with Emilie all day. Instead of reading her magazines, she would help Gustav with his homework. But this seldom went very well. She told him his work was *lamentable* – 'that's all I can say, Gustav. Lamentable.'

His maths was not too bad. There was something about numbers which he found reassuring. But he knew his reading was poor, his writing unsteady. Sometimes, she slapped his knuckles with a ruler. She said, 'If your father were here, he would have done far worse.'

He worked as hard as he could – for the sake of Emilie, for the sake of the 'high standards' expected of children in Switzerland – but he could see that his efforts fell short of what was required of him. He thought that already he mourned his early childhood, when all he'd had to do was *care for things*: feed silkworms with mulberry leaves and talk to the painted people on his train.

Several times, Gustav had asked Emilie if Anton could come to tea again and Emilie had said yes, but whenever he'd suggested a specific day, she had straight away decided that it wasn't convenient. 'The truth is,' she said eventually, 'this apartment is too small for two children.'

'It's not,' said Gustav. 'It wasn't too small last time.'

'Yes, well, why don't we invite some other boy? You have more friends than just this Zwiebel, don't you?'

Gustav stared at his mother. She was folding her apron after doing the washing-up, and she kept folding and folding until the cotton apron was a hard wedge in her hands.

'Anton is the only friend I really like,' said Gustav.

Emilie unfolded the apron and hung it up on a peg behind the door. She sighed and said, 'Very well. Did he appreciate the Nusstorte?'

'I think he did.'

'All right. Invite him next Wednesday. I'll make that again.'

Anton seemed pleased about the invitation. Then, on the day that Anton came to tea, the Nusstorte went wrong.

This was a delicacy which Emilie boasted she could cook 'blindfold'. But on that afternoon, the pastry was burnt at the edges and the caramel was too thick, like toffee.

Emilie didn't apologise. She just plonked the dish of Nusstorte down on the cramped kitchen shelf, beside the teapot, angrily cut a few slices, then lit a cigarette and turned her face away from Gustav and Anton to smoke it.

When she'd finished the cigarette, she looked directly at Anton and said, 'You didn't tell us anything about yourself last time. What does your father do?'

Anton was trying to eat his slice of Nusstorte, but was finding it difficult. He reached into his mouth and took out the lump of sticky pastry and stuck it onto his plate. 'He's a banker,' he said.

'That is very bad manners, you know,' said Emilie Perle, grimacing at the gob of Nusstorte. 'How long have you been in Switzerland?'

'What did you say, Frau Perle?' said Anton.

'I'm asking, how long has your family been in Switzerland?'

'I don't know.'

'Zwiebel is a name more German than Swiss. Perhaps you came over from Germany during the war?'

'I don't know. I don't think so.'

'Or from Austria? With the help of others, perhaps? I expect you know that a lot of people, like Gustav's father, enabled persecuted families from Germany to make a new life in Switzerland. Perhaps your family was helped in this way?'

Anton stared at Emilie. She was puffing on another cigarette, blowing the smoke towards the open window. Anton looked away from her and turned to Gustav. 'Can we go and play now?' he said.

'Do you remember Germany?' persisted Emilie.

Anton shook his head. Gustav saw that his face had turned red, like it did whenever he was about to cry. He knew, somehow, that this peculiar conversation about Germany had come about because of the failed Nusstorte.

In Gustav's room, Anton sat down on the narrow bed and looked at the wooden chest of drawers, the Biedermeier chair, the rag rug, the metal wastepaper bin and the map of Mittelland – the only objects the small space contained. He said nothing.

Gustav stood at the window, pushing his train back and forth. There was silence in the room for several minutes and this silence felt like a kind of suffering to Gustav. He opened the window, hoping to hear – as he sometimes could – the murmuring of the city doves on the roof. The sound of animals or birds could sometimes be consoling. But there was no sound of doves. Gustav went to the chest of drawers and took out the cigar box which contained his 'treasure'. He brought the box over to the bed and set it down beside Anton.

'Look at this,' he said. 'I was going to show you last time. It's my treasure.'

Anton turned his attention to the contents of the box. His face was still red and Gustav saw a tear slide down his cheek. He knew that something should be said, but he had no idea what.

Anton ran his hands through the collection of paper clips, flower petals and nails. Then he picked up the golden lipstick and swivelled it open and stared at it. He wiped his tear away with his hand, looked for a moment at the lipstick, and then slowly painted his lips the deep damson colour. The sight of Anton with these damson lips was so strange that all Gustav could do was laugh. It was a hectic laugh, high-pitched and afraid.

Anton smiled. 'Have you got a mirror?' he said.

'No.'

'I want to see what I look like.'

'You look peculiar.'

'I want to see.'

'We can go into the bathroom.'

They ran across the landing. Both of them were laughing now and the fear in Gustav's laughter had diminished. The laughter propelled them into the bathroom, which they were suddenly aware was full of steam, and visible through the steam was Emilie lying in the bath. Her eyes had been closed, her damp head resting on the rim of the bath. When Emilie was tired or angry, she liked to do this, run a bath so hot it filled the room with steam and lie there, naked in the warm mist. Now, when she saw Gustav and Anton come charging in, she screamed. She picked up the soap and threw it at the boys and it hit Gustav on the arm. He knew the pain of this wasn't very bad, yet it seemed, for a moment, like the worst pain he'd ever endured. Anton was staring at Emilie, at her thin arms resting along the rim of the bath and at her scant breasts, and Gustav knew that this was a terrible thing for his friend to be doing. He pushed him out and quickly followed, slamming the door behind them and rushing back to what felt like the safety of his room.

'I'm sorry,' he said to Anton. 'I didn't hear her running the bath.'

Anton was wiping off the lipstick with the back of his hand. Then he went to the window and gazed down at the cherry tree in the courtyard. Gustav rubbed his arm, where the soap had hit him. He thought of the soap slithering around on the bathroom lino and his mother captive in her bath, with no soap to wash herself with.

'What happened to the cherry tree?' asked Anton after a moment.

'What? What happened?'

'It's not white any more.'

'No,' said Gustav. 'Things are only white for a bit.'

Emilie didn't say goodbye to Anton at six o'clock, nor come out to greet his father when he came to collect him. She'd gone to her room and remained there, with the door locked.

'How is your mother, Gustav?' enquired the banker father politely.

'All right, sir, thank you,' said Gustav.

'She's not ill, I trust?'

'No. I think she's sleeping.'

'Oh, well, we must be quiet then. What's that all over your face, Anton?'

'Nothing, Father.'

'Well, it's a very colourful nothing!'

'It's my fault,' said Gustav. 'Shall I fetch a flannel to wash it off?'

'Yes. I think that would be a good idea. He can't go home looking like that.'

Gustav went into the bathroom and turned on the hot tap. The steam from Emilie's bath had evaporated, but there was a damp, unpleasant smell in the cramped space which made Gustav feel embarrassed to be there. He moistened a flannel and quickly returned to Anton and his father. The father took the flannel and scrubbed roughly at Anton's face. Gustav noticed for the first time the size of the gold signet ring Herr Zwiebel wore on his broad fourth finger.

'My wife and I were wondering,' Herr Zwiebel said after a moment, 'whether you might like to come to tea with us one day?'

Gustav felt a stab of joy, mixed with something else, which seemed like fear, but which he didn't want to admit was fear. 'Thank you,' he said.

'Will you ask your mother? You can walk from school with Anton and my wife will bring you back in the car.'

'Thank you,' said Gustav again.

'You can listen to me play,' said Anton. 'I can almost do the fast bit of "Für Elise" now. And I'm learning a Schubert lied. Schubert is difficult, isn't he, Father?'

'Yes, he is. But so are many things. Eh, Gustav?'

'Yes. But my mother says you have to go on until you master them.'

'Quite right,' said Herr Zwiebel. 'Absolutely right.'

Later that night, Emilie, with newly washed hair framing her serious face, said to Gustav that the whole afternoon – and not just the episode in the bathroom – had been very difficult for her.

'I'm sorry, Mutti. We didn't know you were in the bath,' said Gustav.

'I said *not only that*!' snapped Emilie. 'The thing is that the presence of that child here in this wretched little apartment is quite painful to me.'

'Why?' said Gustav.

'When you're older, I'll try to explain it all to you. But for now, please don't invite him here again. At least not for a while.'

Gustav stared at his mother. In front of her was one of her aniseed drinks and she was sipping it very fast.

Whenever he remembered this moment, Gustav knew that what he'd felt was a sudden, overwhelming tiredness – a tiredness born of all the things he didn't understand. He remembered closing his eyes. A vision of Emilie with her clean hair and her clouded glass came and went, came and went, as things did when he was on the threshold of sleep.

# Linden Tree

## *Matzlingen, 1948*

Emilie asked where the Zwiebels' apartment was and when Gustav told her it was on Fribourgstrasse, she said, 'Oh no.'

Gustav couldn't remember Fribourgstrasse – he'd been too young – but he'd been told about their flat there and about Emilie's geraniums, which she had loved so much.

'What number Fribourgstrasse?' she asked.

'Seventy-seven.'

'Oh well, at least it's not the same building. They may not have a nice balcony, like we had.'

Emilie was making rösti, Gustav's favourite dish, but she left the frying potatoes to go to the kitchen window and take deep breaths of air, so Gustav came to the stove to watch over them. He liked watching over things that were cooking. He thought that in his future life, which his mother called his 'right kind of life', he might become a chef.

He prodded the rösti with Emilie's steel spatula, but it was soon snatched out of his hand. 'Leave it alone!' she said.

Gustav was so used to Emilie's crossness that it didn't upset him very often. It was just part of how she was, like her thin hair was part of her and her cigarette smoking and her love of magazines. He left the kitchen and went to his room and sat on the bed, where Anton had sat to put on the damson lipstick. All he minded about was being allowed to go to tea with the Zwiebels. But he was almost certain that, now Emilie had been told they lived in Fribourgstrasse, she would find some reason to say no.

Gustav got up and found his cigar box and took out the lipstick, and remembered how the casing had shone so brightly in the dust underneath the church grating. He polished it a little on his shorts, then he took it through to the kitchen, where the rösti was becoming fragrant and crispy, and held it out in his hand. 'I've got a present for you, Mutti,' he said.

Emilie stared at the lipstick in Gustav's outstretched hand. 'Where did you get that?' she said. 'You didn't steal it, did you? Your life will never amount to anything, Gustav, if you begin stealing.'

'I found it in the church,' said Gustav. 'Under the grating.'

Emilie hesitated. She wiped her face, sweating a little from the hot stove, with the hem of her apron. Then she said, 'Don't you think you should have given it up to Pastor Sammlung?'

'No,' said Gustav. 'It was just lying in the dust. I got it for you.'

'I think you should have given it up to the pastor. One of his congregation might have come asking about it.'

Gustav ignored this and said, 'Look, Mutti . . .' He took the top off the lipstick and showed Emilie the beautiful purple colour.

'Good heavens!' she said. 'Who would wear a shade like that?'

'Don't you like it?'

'No, I don't. Now, the rösti's almost ready. Go and wash your hands. And when we go to the church on Saturday, take the lipstick back. Remember, your father was a policeman. He would never have countenanced small acts of pilfering.'

But later, consoled by her aniseed drink, Emilie said, 'If you go to tea with the Zwiebels, and the father is away, who will bring you home?'

'Anton's mother. She has a car.'

'And you would be home by six?'

'I don't know.'

'I don't want you spending too long there.'

'Why?'

'They live differently from us. I don't want you thinking that our life could be like theirs.'

'What d'you mean?'

'Cars. Pianos. Expensive food. That kind of thing.'

'I like our food. I like our dumplings and rösti . . .'

'Good. Because it's all we can afford. Home by six, then.'

The first things that Gustav saw when he went into the living room of the Zwiebels' apartment at Fribourgstrasse 77 were the big black grand piano and the window box of scarlet geraniums on the balcony overlooking the street. A part of him – the part which loved Emilie so much – pretended he hadn't seen the geraniums.

Anton's mother was standing by the window, holding a little watering can. She held out a soft, manicured hand to Gustav.

'Ah,' she said, 'Gustav. You're very welcome. You've been so kind to Anton.'

'How do you do, Frau Zwiebel?' said Gustav, bowing, as he had been taught.

'And such nice manners!' laughed Frau Zwiebel. 'Where did you learn those?'

'He didn't learn them. He's just like that,' said Anton.

'Even better,' said Frau Zwiebel. 'If only it were true of everyone! Now, boys, what would you like to do before we have tea?'

'I'm going to play for Gustav,' said Anton. 'I'm going to play "The Linden Tree".'

'Oh,' said Frau Zwiebel, 'do you know it well enough yet?'

'Yes, I do.'

'Well, would you like that, Gustav – for Anton to play "The Linden Tree"?'

'I don't know what it is.'

'It's what's called a lied. It's a song by Schubert.'

'Who's going to sing?'

'Nobody today. Sometimes, my husband sings a few bars of this, but mainly Anton just plays the piano part.'

'If you listen carefully and close your eyes,' said Anton, 'you can hear the leaves of the tree rustling in the notes.'

'What do you mean, hear the leaves rustling in the notes?'

'You'll see what I mean.'

'Come on then,' said Frau Zwiebel, taking Gustav's hand, 'you and I will sit on the sofa, Gustav, and Anton will play.'

The room was large, with a chandelier hanging from the

ceiling rose and the walls were hung with heavily framed pictures – too many to count. Near the fireplace stood a porcelain bear. Gustav sat down next to Frau Zwiebel, who smelled of pungent summer flowers.

He watched Anton fuss with the piano stool, turning it until it was the right height for his small frame. Then, he sat down and fussed with the music, lifting a page and putting it back, folding one corner down. He said, 'The piece is in the key of E major. Most of the lieder in this cycle are in minor keys, but this one isn't. I can't remember why.'

Gustav stared at Anton. It was difficult to imagine this boy on the piano stool as the same boy who had cried by the kindergarten sandbox. He looked older. His eyes were dry and bright. It was almost as if Anton had gone away from him into another life, into a place where he, Gustav, was too young – or too afraid – to follow. He wanted, then, to stand up and say, Don't play this 'Linden Tree', whatever it is. I don't want to hear it.

But the playing had already begun. Frau Zwiebel clasped her hands together in passionate appreciation and she now whispered to Gustav, 'The tree talks to a sad man. The tree whispers to the man, come and lie down here, under the leaves, and rest. Can you hear the leaves talking to the man?'

Gustav didn't think that he could hear this, or else that perhaps he heard it somewhere in him but couldn't concentrate on it because of that feeling he had that Anton had run on far ahead of him and that he might never look back. But he knew he had to be polite to Frau Zwiebel, so he whispered that yes, he could hear the tree talking, and he thought then that if music could be the leaves of a tree moving in the wind, then perhaps it could also be the man, and he began to expect that there would be a chord – was that what it was called, a *chord*? – which would sound like a human voice. But the song just ended.

Anton got down from the piano stool, smiling, and bowed to his mother and bowed to Gustav. And Gustav knew he was expected to clap, so he clapped and Frau Zwiebel clapped and said, 'Well done, Anton. That's coming along very well.'

'Did you like it, Gustav?' asked Anton.

'Yes,' said Gustav. 'But why didn't the man talk back to the tree?'

Anton burst out laughing. 'Talk back to the tree? You can't have that! He's not really there. He's quite old and sad. He's just remembering, isn't he, Mother?'

'I think that's it, yes. He's remembering. I think he heard the leaves of the tree rustling like that when he was very young, perhaps as young as you boys: "*Und seine Zweige rauschten / Als riefen sie mir zu . . .*" And perhaps he used to lie down under the tree and dream. But he can't go back.'

'Why can't he?' asked Gustav.

'Because that's how life is. You can never go back once things are past.'

'Like we can't go back to the kindergarten?'

'Exactly. You have to go forward. Never back. Now, Anton, what else are you going to play?'

'I'm not going to. I'm going to show Gustav my new train set. I just wanted him to hear "The Linden Tree".'

There was so much that had been confusing about 'The Linden Tree' that Gustav almost wished Anton hadn't played it. It wasn't just the business about the notes sounding like rustling leaves (and yet they didn't, not quite), or the sad man who was and was not there; it was the fact of Anton *being able* to play this complicated song. How could he have learned it? When?

And then Gustav had another thought which he found disturbing. He imagined that at the very time when he and Emilie were on their hands and knees cleaning the Church of Sankt Johann, on Saturday mornings, Anton was with his piano teacher. He and Emilie were scrubbing and dusting and polishing while Anton was playing music by Schubert.

He decided: I won't tell Mutti. Mutti doesn't need to know about the geraniums, and Mutti doesn't need to know about Anton playing 'The Linden Tree'.

While these thoughts distracted Gustav, Anton was asking him to look at his new train set. The boys knelt down beside the little steel rails set out in a circle on the carpet in Anton's spacious room. The train on it, smartly painted and with brass fittings and realistic coal in the furnace box, had a winder key. You wound it up and set it on the rails, and it clicked slowly along. There was a signal set up over the track and Anton put his hand on the train, so that it would stop here. 'That's what trains do,' he said, 'they stop at signals. And this makes my mother afraid. I don't know why. She always asks, "Why are we stopping?" and Father says, "I expect we're stopping at a signal, dear. Nothing to worry about."'

Perhaps Anton thought that this would amuse Gustav, this little imitation of his parents, because when Gustav didn't laugh he asked, 'Are you all right? You're a bit quiet.'

'I'm all right,' said Gustav. 'But your train's better than mine, isn't it?'

'I like yours,' said Anton. 'I like those people painted on the windows. Mine's got nobody in it – just coal.'

# Ice

## *Matzlingen, 1949*

This was the new, wonderful thing: skating.

Frau Zwiebel, whose first name was Adriana, had once been a 'hopeful' in the skating world. At fifteen she'd won a competition in Bern. She told Gustav that this had been one of the happiest moments of her life. She'd expected to go on and win more prizes, but at sixteen she moved into 'a different category' and the girls she was competing against were what she called 'full-blown professionals, with dragons for mothers and steel for sinews'. And so no more prizes came her way, but she still loved skating, for its own sake, and when she heard about the new rink opening in Matzlingen – a covered rink with smooth, manufactured ice and a huge gramophone which played Swiss folk music and American jazz, and a café counter which sold drinks and pretzels – she said to Anton, 'Let's go on Sunday afternoons. We can take Gustav. I'll pay for us all.'

She had a beautiful glide. And she could still gather momentum for a perfect lutz and land with grace. Adriana Zwiebel dressed herself in woollen leggings, a short tartan skirt and a green leather jacket. The eyes of the men at the rink followed her as she made her elegant turns, with her arms held out like a dancer's and her dark hair tied in a ponytail flicking and flouncing as she moved.

Seven-year-old Anton and seven-year-old Gustav watched her, too, not so much because she was beautiful, but because they knew they could learn from her. Anton was naturally good at skating and Gustav was not, but Gustav set himself to master everything Anton could do and, in time, everything that Adriana could do – however distant this goal might be. He fell over frequently, but he never cried, though the ice was hard, the hardest surface his bones had ever met. He taught himself to laugh instead. Laughing was a bit like crying. It was a strange convulsion; it just came from a different bit of your mind. The trick was to move the crying out of that bit and let the laughter in. And so he'd pick himself up and carry on, laughing.

At the end of the afternoon, he and Anton would do one circuit of what they called their 'mad dash'. They would hold hands and skate in synchronisation as fast as they could round the rink's outer edge. They came to be known by the rink regulars as 'the laughing boys'. At this time, Gustav was one inch shorter than Anton.

It was at the skating rink, where Anton and Gustav were allowed to buy hot chocolate, that Gustav learned about something 'nobody ever mentions'.

Anton told him that he had once had a baby sister, named Romola. He said, 'I can't remember her very well. She just stayed being a baby and then she died.'

'Why did she?' asked Gustav.

'That's what nobody talks about.'

'Was she killed by some robbers?'

'I can't remember any robbers.'

'They could have come with a hatchet, or something?'

'I don't think they did. I was three. I would have remembered robbers, wouldn't I? I think my sister just died in her cot and then she was buried, and some time after that my father got ill and was put into a hospital. My mother told me he was ill because Romola had died and he had to be left in peace, to recover.'

Gustav and Anton looked out at Adriana, still on the ice, still turning and leaping, as if she would never weary of her own wonderful grace.

'What about her?' asked Gustav. 'Wasn't your mother ill, too, after the death of baby Romola?'

'No,' said Anton. 'My mother is never ill. She's never even tired. Except when we had to leave Bern. She said she was tired then. I expect it was the thought of moving all the furniture. We couldn't leave it behind, because my parents are very fond of furniture.'

'So why did you leave Bern?'

'Something to do with my father's job. I think the bank in Bern thought – after he'd been ill for a long time because of my sister dying – that he'd be happier in a smaller bank, and so we came to Matzlingen.'

'And you cried at the kindergarten.'

'And you drew your Mutti as an ice cream!'

They laughed then, but Anton stopped laughing suddenly and said, 'You must never, ever tell anybody about Romola, Gustav. Swear in blood.'

'What d'you mean, swear in blood?'

'You have to. We have to cut our arms with our skate blades and mix the blood together and then you have to swear.'

'All right.'

All his life, Gustav would recall that it's difficult to make a cut in your arm with an ice skate. The blades look sharp, but they're not sharp enough for easy cutting. 'We made a hash of it,' he would tell people. 'We couldn't get the blood to come. But then it did because we made the cuts too deep and we were both in pain, but we had to cover this up.'

Then, one day after school, Gustav was summoned to see the headmaster. Laid out on the headmaster's desk were some of Gustav's work books. There, for anyone to see, was how poor Gustav's writing still was. Even his attempts at drawing and map-making were weak.

'Well?' said the headmaster. 'What are we to make of these?'

'I don't know, sir,' said Gustav.

'No. Precisely. And nor does your mother. She's in despair. Aren't you, Frau Perle?'

Gustav turned and saw Emilie, sitting very still in a green chair. He hadn't noticed her when he came in. He didn't know how she'd got into the headmaster's study so silently. He thought she looked like someone in a painting.

Emilie said, 'The thing is, Headmaster, I really want Gustav to succeed in his life. I want him to do something his father would have been proud of, and if his education amounts to nothing –'

'No, no,' said the headmaster, 'his education will not amount to nothing. Gustav is not yet eight. We have time. But what I am going to suggest is some extra coaching, so that he can catch up in certain subjects. His maths are satisfactory, quite good, even, but the rest is poor. I have a young teacher in the school, Herr Hodler, who would be willing to come and tutor him, for a small consideration, on Sunday afternoons.'

'No!' Gustav burst out. 'Not Sunday afternoons! I go skating then.'

'Be quiet, Gustav,' said Emilie.

'The only time Herr Hodler has available is Sunday afternoons,' said the headmaster. 'It's up to you, but personally I feel this would be of great benefit. Otherwise, we may have to keep Gustav down a class, to repeat the year's work.'

Gustav turned imploringly to his mother, but she was looking past him at the headmaster.

'What will the tuition cost?' she asked.

'Not more than a few francs an hour. I don't know what entry fees you pay at the ice rink, but I've heard they're expensive. It may come to little more than that.'

Gustav wanted to tell the headmaster that it was Adriana Zwiebel who paid for the rink, and for the skate hire and the hot chocolate and pretzels, but Emilie had her finger pressed to her lips, warning him to say nothing.

They walked home in silence.

By the time they got to Unter der Egg, it was raining. Gustav went straight to his room, hoping to be left alone, but Emilie followed him there. She sat on the bed and he stood at the window, holding on to his tin train. He was praying she wouldn't speak. Because he knew that if Emilie told him he was going to have to give up his skating with Anton and Adriana, he was probably going to cry.

# Coconut

## *Matzlingen, 1949–50*

That was it, then: no more skating. No more 'laughing boys'.

Gustav hit the walls of his room. He smashed his train. He screamed at Emilie. She cuffed his head to silence him. She picked up the broken train and threw it into the rubbish bin.

Herr Hodler was a thin, pale young man, with eyes that were pink-rimmed, like the eyes of a white rabbit. At the apartment on Unter der Egg, these rabbit eyes looked about, in vain, for a table on which the required work might be done.

'There is no table,' said Emilie Perle.

She showed Herr Hodler the hinged kitchen shelf. He stared at it. He wasn't being paid well for this tuition and the sight of this inadequate space made him sigh with frustration. He told Emilie he would do his best, but that he didn't think Gustav's concentration would be helped by these 'cramped work conditions'.

He hadn't been told that Gustav had had to sacrifice his skating, so he was further dismayed by the boy's anger and resentment at being there with him. When Gustav deliberately knocked to the floor the storybooks and history books which had been placed on the shelf, Herr Hodler swore.

'*Scheisse!*'

The swear word seemed to echo around the silent kitchen. It had always been part of Emilie's credo of self-mastery that swearing was an unpleasant indulgence, never to be allowed. And now the schoolteacher had transgressed this sacred edict.

It made Gustav want to laugh. He felt better. He apologised to

Herr Hodler and helped him to pick up the books and rearrange them on the shelf. When he saw that one of the books was entitled *A Short History of Switzerland*, he said to Herr Hodler, 'I don't know anything about the history of Switzerland. All I know is the war didn't come here. It went to Germany and Russia and other places and all the buildings were bombed. Is that right?'

'Yes,' said Herr Hodler. 'More or less. Except millions of people died, too. What we believe in Switzerland is that we should avoid conflict, especially being drawn into the conflicts of others. We call it "neutrality". Do you know what this means?'

'No.'

'It means we *believe in ourselves.* We protect our own. And you know, this is a good way to be in your life, Gustav. Have you ever eaten a coconut?'

'What?'

'You know coconuts have a very tough outer shell?'

'I've never eaten one.'

'Well, the shell is hard and fibrous, difficult to penetrate. It protects the nourishing coconut flesh and milk inside. And that is how Switzerland is and how Swiss people should be – like coconuts. We protect ourselves – all the good things that we have and that we are – with hard and determined yet rational behaviour – our neutrality. Do you understand what I'm saying?'

'That I've got to be like a coconut?'

'Yes. Then you will not be hurt, Gustav.'

'I am hurt.'

'In what way?'

'I used to go skating on Sunday afternoons. Skating was my favourite thing in the world. Now, I can't go any more. I've got to do lessons with you.'

Herr Hodler's pink, flickering eyes looked anxiously at Gustav. 'I didn't know this,' he said.

'I was getting quite good at skating. I could do small jumps. Now it's all over. That hurts me.'

'I understand. All I can suggest is that we get on with the lessons as quickly as we can. That way, you will make progress, and then perhaps in a few weeks' time, you can resume your skating?'

*

After that, Gustav and Herr Hodler became friends – or at least not enemies.

Herr Hodler permitted Gustav to address him by his first name, which was Max. Gustav saw that Max Hodler had very beautiful handwriting and he asked him to teach him how to write like this.

Lines were ruled. Along these lines, Max supervised the slow beat-beat, like distant music, of Gustav's letter formation: a a a a a a, b b b b b b, c c c c c c.

He said that Gustav should pretend he had never learned to write, because somehow he had learned all wrong and now he had to start again. Sometimes, Max drew very large letters for Gustav to copy and together they examined the forms and shapes of the letters, how they turned and curved, like patterns on the ice. And so this is what Gustav thought about now, when he was forming letters. He pretended his pencil was a skater.

'Good,' said Max. 'There is improvement.'

Gustav wanted to take the improved letters to show Emilie, but he suspected that Emilie was asleep and, besides, Max said they couldn't waste time showing anybody half-formed work. There was far too much to do. Gustav's reading was still poor and to help him concentrate, Max Hodler brought along one of his own favourite books, *Struwwelpeter*. In this book, disobedient children brought doom upon themselves in a variety of ways. A little girl, who loved playing with matches, set fire to her dress and was burned to a pile of ash. A boy called Konrad who sucked his thumb had the thumb cut off by a great red-legged scissor-man.

*Weh! Jetzt geht es klipp und klapp*
*mit der Scher die Daumen ab,*
*mit der grossen scharfen Scher!*
*Hei! Da schreit der Konrad sehr.**

* The first English version of *Struwwelpeter* by Heinrich Hoffmann was published in Leipzig in 1848. This very free translation, by Alexander Platt, has remained the most popular. Here, these lines are rendered as follows:
Snip! Snap! Snip! The scissors go;
And Conrad cries out 'Oh! Oh! Oh!'
Snip! Snap! Snip! They go so fast,
That both his thumbs are off at last.

These stories thrilled Gustav. Partly, they were able to thrill him and not frighten him too badly because the children in the drawings wore old-fashioned clothes, so he assumed that everything that happened to them was safely in the past and couldn't happen now, when it was almost 1950. He asked Max if he could borrow *Struwwelpeter* and read it in bed at night. Max hesitated. He warned Gustav that the stories might give him nightmares.

'No, they won't,' said Gustav. 'I'll just learn to read better, if I read them over and over.'

He took Max to see his little room, with its map of Mittelland, but with no toys and no books in it, and when Max saw this room he relented and said Gustav could keep *Struwwelpeter*, provided he took care of it. When he asked Gustav why he had no toys, Gustav said, 'I had a train. But I smashed it and Mutti threw it away.'

Drawing was something else Max Hodler was gifted at. He drew – very fast, with swift, bold pen-strokes – a picture for Gustav of three men standing in a field of flowers, wearing robes and carrying swords. He explained that these men, from the forest cantons of Schwyz, Uri and Unterwalden had lived a long, long time ago at the end of the thirteenth century. It was they who were the true founders of Switzerland. They had defied their powerful Habsburg masters to swear an allegiance and, from this allegiance, the country slowly came into being. Every year, on August 1st, this historic moment, in what was known as the Rütli Meadow, was remembered as Swiss National Day.

He told Gustav that not many people 'in the wider world' had any knowledge about the history of Switzerland. 'This,' he said, 'is because Switzerland is just an *idea* to them – clocks and chalets and banks and mountains. But we – you and I, Gustav – who are part of it, know that we are not just an idea. And we also know about neutrality, *about the concept of the coconut*, so we must learn our history and be proud of it.'

He wanted Gustav to try to copy his drawing, or even one small part of it, like a sword or a flower, but Gustav broke in to tell him about the posies of gentians Emilie arranged round the photograph of Erich Perle on Swiss National Day and how Emilie said that he had been a hero.

Max put down the fine pen he had used for his drawing and turned to Gustav.

'Tell me about that,' he said. 'Who was your father?'

'He was a policeman. Assistant Police Chief at Matzlingen Police Headquarters. He died when I was very little.'

'How did he die?'

'I don't know exactly. Mutti says it was the Jews.'

Silence fell in the small kitchen. Max Hodler shook his head and sighed, then got down from his chair. 'I'm going out for a short breath of air,' he said. 'See if you can copy something from the Rütli Meadow drawing, Gustav. Anything you like. A face. A hand. The stones among the grass. Don't hurry. Just work slowly and carefully.'

It was winter again, just past the new year, 1950. Gustav had been working with Max Hodler every Sunday for three months.

Alone in his cold room, Gustav missed his train. He'd given names to the painted people and used to whisper to them as they journeyed up and down the windowsill. The thought that he'd crushed them and killed them made him feel ashamed.

When he told Anton about this, Anton said, 'Sometimes, you have to break things. I broke a metronome. I was trying to play a Chopin waltz and it kept going wrong, so I broke the stupid metronome. My father hit me on the bottom with his belt. He asked me if I wanted to make him ill again.'

'How could you make him ill again?'

'By breaking the metronome; I told you. So, anyway, get your Mutti to buy you another train.'

But Emilie had no money.

More and more, in the late evenings, she drank her aniseed drinks and fretted over her sums on the edges of the *Matzlinger-zeitung*. Late one night, she told Gustav that rumours had begun circulating that the cheese co-operative was failing, that demand for Emmental had fallen now that the French were once again making so many different varieties of cheese, and that it was only a question of time before the Matzlingen Co-operative would close. 'And then,' said Emilie, 'what are we going to do?'

Gustav went and fetched the work he'd been doing with Max Hodler – pages of nicely formed letters, paragraphs of careful writing, drawings of swords and helmets and flowers and of girls setting their dresses alight with matchfire – and put this down in front of Emilie, covering up her mathematical scribbles on the newspaper.

She stared down, wide-eyed. She put on her spectacles.

'Is this your work?' she asked.

'Yes,' said Gustav, 'of course it's my work.'

'Well. It's not bad.'

Gustav let his mother take in the pictures of the girls setting themselves on fire, but before she could say anything about them, Gustav said, 'You can save money now, Mutti. Because I don't need Herr Hodler any more. My work is better.'

Emilie took a long swig of her aniseed drink. She fumbled for a cigarette and lit it with shaking hands. Gustav wanted to put his arms round her and lay his head on her shoulder, but he knew she didn't want this; all she wanted was her drink and her cigarette.

'We'll have to see,' she said. 'Some of this is still a bit messy. We'll have to hear what the headmaster says.'

Herr Hodler stayed until the spring came. By then, Gustav had learned most of the stories in *Struwwelpeter* by heart and could terrify Anton by reciting them.

*Weh! Jetzt geht es klipp und klapp*
*mit der Scher die Daumen ab,*
*mit der grossen scharfen Scher!*
*Hei! Da schreit der Konrad sehr.*

He had a sketchy idea of how his country had come into being. He could make 'sensible' drawings of churches with roofs like witches' hats and of the bear of Bern, symbol of the great city Anton still talked about.

And it was possible to say that Gustav had become fond of Max Hodler. It was possible to say that the single swear word, *scheisse*, had opened the door to a friendship. When the moment came for Max Hodler to leave, Gustav felt sad to be parted from him.

'I'll see you from time to time in school,' said Max.

'Yes,' said Gustav.

'You must keep working hard.'

'Yes.'

'Make your mother proud of you.'

'Yes.'

As a leaving present to Max Hodler, Gustav had made a copy of the map of Mittelland in his room. He'd coloured the land green and the rivers blue. Here and there, on the green ground, wandered a few animals, which might have been ibex or which might have been grey sheep. Bern was a black circle, with its brown bear keeping watch. By Matzlingen was the circular cheese with the slice cut out of it. Near this, Gustav had written *Herr Max Hodler lives here.*

What Gustav didn't know was that Emilie Perle hadn't paid Max Hodler his tuition fees since February. He didn't know, either, that Max had – just once – gone to ask for them, but that Emilie had been repelled by his rabbit eyes, damp and pleading, and had sent him away with nothing. By the time he left, the fees had still not been paid. All Max had from Emilie was a scribbled IOU. The tutor felt this to be unfair. He had worked hard with Gustav and was proud of the results. But Emilie Perle was too overwhelmed by her own troubles to give this any consideration.

The cheese co-operative remained open, but had cut back its production by 40 per cent and put all its workers on half-pay. Now, Emilie worked only three days a week. On the days when she had nothing to do, she walked around Matzlingen looking for new employment.

But light seemed to be arriving once again in Gustav's life. It was the bright, glittery light that had fallen on the Elysian Fields of the ice rink.

By the end of April, he was able to say to Anton, 'I can come skating on Sundays again.'

'Oh,' said Anton. 'Well, it doesn't matter now.'

'What?' said Gustav.

'It doesn't matter any more.'

'What d'you mean?'

'Well. We take Rudi Herens skating with us now.'

'Who's Rudi Herens?'

'He's a boy in our apartment building. He's a really good skater. He can do double-toe loops.'

'You mean you don't want me to come?'

'I do, Gustav. But three boys would be too many for Mother. She said that to me the other day: three would be too many.'

They were in a school passageway when this conversation took place. Gustav left Anton and walked away. He didn't know where he was walking to. It was time for a geography lesson, but it was not towards this that Gustav was going.

When he reached the end of the long passage, he went into the lavatories, a high barn of a room, which always felt cold, even in summer. He opened a cubicle and locked the door. He sat, not on one of the toilets, but on the tiled ground, with his knees drawn up to his chest. He thought about the things Max Hodler had said about coconuts – their hard outer shell protecting the flesh inside. He tried to imagine such a shell growing round him, an impenetrable shield. He examined his soft, white arms.

# Views of Davos

## *Matzlingen, 1950–51*

Sometime after this, when Adriana Zwiebel came to pick up Anton from school, she saw Gustav on the school steps, playing with some jacks, given to him by Max Hodler. She got out of her car and came, smiling, towards him. She was wearing a summer dress, patterned with coral-coloured tulips. Her hair was loose and shone in the sun.

Gustav gathered up the jacks and ran towards Adriana and she bent down and hugged him. 'How are you, Gustav?' she asked.

'All right, thank you, Frau Zwiebel,' said Gustav.

'Good,' said Adriana. 'But Anton told me about your mother losing some of her hours at the cheese factory. That's most unfortunate.'

'Yes,' said Gustav.

'I would like to help.'

Gustav wasn't sure what Adriana Zwiebel expected him to say. It was difficult for him to imagine how she could 'help' Emilie. Perhaps she didn't know how she could, either, because she abruptly changed the subject and said, 'How is your tuition going?'

'It's finished,' said Gustav. 'I'm better at writing now. And I can draw the men at the Rütli Meadow. Herr Hodler gave me these jacks as a present for my work.'

He held out the jacks, still shiny and new-looking, despite the dust from the schoolyard.

'Oh,' said Adriana, 'what fun! They say, in the old bad times, when Switzerland was a poor country, children used to play this game with knuckle bones.'

Anton came running out then and embraced his mother. Gustav watched them cling together. He expected that, now, something might be said about the skating, but the two of them were silent, just sweetly hugging each other. Gustav stared at them. What he wanted was to leave with them and go back to the apartment on Fribourgstrasse and eat cherry tart and listen to Anton's playing. But Anton was now tugging his mother away towards the car.

'Wait a moment, Anton,' said Adriana. 'I was saying to Gustav, we must try to find new work for his mother. I'm going to ask around. Would she consider leaving the cheese factory to work full-time elsewhere?'

'I don't know,' said Gustav.

'The thing is, I know that part-time jobs are difficult to find. Do you think she might like to work in a flower shop? The place where I buy my geraniums, they told me they would soon be looking for someone . . .'

A flower shop. The scent of roses. Everything fresh and damp. And no more smell of Emmental on Emilie's clothes. Gustav thought she might be happy at this suggestion. He nodded, on her behalf.

'Good,' said Adriana. 'I'll go and see them and ask. Anton will let you know.'

'Let him know what?' asked Anton, who hadn't been listening, but searching the deep pocket in his mother's dress for sweets and finding only a half-smoked packet of French cigarettes.

'If there might be a job for Frau Perle in Valeria's flower shop.'

'Why would she want to work there?' said Anton. 'I hate going into that shop. It's always cold.'

Adriana smiled. 'I don't think you know very much about it,' she said. 'People who work with flowers are usually happy.' Then she took Anton's hand and they walked away.

When Gustav got home, Emilie was cooking a vegetable stew. The small kitchen was scented with leeks. She had told Gustav they couldn't afford meat any more, not even the bratwurst on which he doted.

Gustav went to the kitchen widow and stared out at Unter der Egg. He could see Frau Teller packing up her stall and he thought about what Adriana had said about the vacancy in Valeria's flower shop, but he knew better than to mention it at this moment.

'I was looking at some photographs today,' Emilie said brightly, 'of your father and me, when we went on holiday to Davos. Would you like to see them?'

'Yes,' said Gustav. 'Was I there?'

He wasn't there. He was in some other *before-life* life.

The first photograph was of a wide balcony with snowy mountains in the background.

'Our hotel balcony,' said Emilie. 'Look how spacious it is. It was such a nice establishment. Hotels are wonderful places.'

Then there was a picture of Emilie in a wickerwork chair on the same balcony. The sun was on her face, and her hair looked fresh and clean and she was laughing.

'You look nice, Mutti,' said Gustav.

'Do I? Well, that was long ago, 1938, before the war. Now, here's your father. We thought we were going to have a good life.'

Erich was standing up, framed by the mountains, smoking a pipe. He was wearing a white shirt and his trousers were held up by braces. His face looked dark with sunburn.

The other pictures were mainly what Emilie called 'views of Davos'. She explained to Gustav that it had once been the most famous place in the world for the curing of tuberculosis, because the air was so good and there were so many hours of healing sunshine. People came from thousands of miles away to Davos, and were cured. Huge sanatoria were built there to accommodate all the people suffering from TB, which was also known as 'consumption' because the disease eats away the lung tissue. Some still came, because Davos would be forever known as a place of healing.

Gustav returned to thumbing through the 'views of Davos', looking for another picture of Erich. And here he was now, smiling, sitting at a café table, with a flagon of beer in front of him and a waiter in a long white apron standing behind him.

'You see the kind of places we were able to go to?' said Emilie. 'You see the waiter, very correctly attired? We felt so spoiled and happy. Your father didn't want to leave Davos. He rebooked our train tickets, to stay an extra two days. And on our very last night, I said to him, "Don't worry, I'm sure we will come back." Davos was the most perfect place we'd ever known. The sun shone every day, every single day. But we never went back.'

'Why not?' asked Gustav.

'Time,' said Emilie. 'When you're young, you think you're always going to have lots of time ahead of you, in which to do the things you planned. You don't notice time passing, that's the trouble. But it passes just the same.'

At the end of the year, the cheese co-operative closed its doors for good. The milk from the valleys around Matzlingen was shipped elsewhere, to Burgdorf or Lyss, or even as far as Bern. The great vats and churns, over which Emilie and her colleagues had sweated, were dismantled and moved outside to a rickety shelter, where the wind and rain began to rust them and where goats sometimes clambered, smelling the dregs of the curds in the corroding metal.

Emilie went to see the pastor of the Church of Sankt Johann to ask for more work and was given a job on Monday mornings, cleaning up after the Sunday services. But she hated it. She told Gustav, 'You'd be surprised what a mess people make in church. Sometimes I find communion wafers, half chewed and spat out onto the floor. And piles of confetti in a mush, like vomit.'

It was then that Gustav dared to mention the possibility of the job in Valeria's flower shop.

'How d'you know about it?' asked Emilie.

'From Frau Zwiebel.'

'Oh,' said Emilie, 'I suppose she buys her geraniums there?'

'Yes, I think she does.'

'Well, you can tell her, I'm not looking for charity.'

'What's charity? This is just a job. Someone else may have got it by now.'

At this, Emilie softened. She said, 'Well, beggars can't be choosers, I suppose. Perhaps you can ask Frau Zwiebel about it – if you ever see her.'

Gustav said he would ask. He liked to imagine his mother among scented greenery and roses and lilies. He thought that, when August 1st came round again, Valeria might let her have her posies of gentian flowers for nothing and how, when Emilie set these out beside the photograph of Erich Perle, she would be able to say to him, 'I'm working in a nice place now. My clothes don't smell of cheese any more.'

But Emilie Perle never took the job in the flower shop. She fell ill.

# Ludwig

## *Matzlingen, 1951*

For days, Emilie remained in bed in the apartment on Unter der Egg, sweating, shivering and coughing. Gustav had to tell her that there was no food left in the larder, so she sent him out with a few francs to buy cheap vegetables. She said, 'Just peel them, Gustav, and put them in the pot of water and boil them. Then bring me a cup of the broth.'

He was quite proud to be able to do all this – shop for leeks and carrots and onions and then peel and chop them and light the gas and set the heavy pot on the stove. He tied one of Emilie's aprons round himself. He turned on the radio and found a jazz programme, and attempted to beat time to the riffs of the saxophone with a wooden spoon.

'What's that awful noise?' cried Emilie from her bed. 'Turn it off!'

He sat by her, trying to spoon broth into her mouth. He saw that her lips were dry and cracked. She told him the broth was too hot, and closed her eyes. He stared at her, perplexed. A familiar, acrid smell, which Gustav didn't want to think about, filled the room. He didn't know whether he should try again with the broth, or tiptoe away, to let his mother sleep. He knew that, more and more in her life, sleeping was the thing she liked best.

He stirred the broth, round and round. He saw a wasp crawling up and down the window glass and hoped that it wouldn't come over to the bed and sting Emilie, trying to drink the moisture that was beading on her face. He touched her shoulder gently, to wake her and she gulped in a little more of the broth. Then she waved it away and said, 'I can't. I'm too ill. Go and find Frau Krams, Gustav. Tell her to call an ambulance.'

Frau Krams was the concierge of the building on Unter der Egg. She had a peculiar son called Ludwig, who was old enough to work at a full-time job, or to be sent into the Citizen Army, but who hung around on the stairs and corridors most of the time, humming a little private tune and doing odd jobs for the tenants, in return for small sums put into a palm outstretched like a street beggar's. Emilie Perle said Ludwig Krams was 'a disgrace to Swiss values'. He liked children, however. Whenever he saw Gustav he would ruffle his hair and say, 'How's it going, little man? Come and talk to me. Tell me what the world is doing to you.'

Gustav knocked at Frau Krams's door and Ludwig appeared, smoking a skinny cigarette. 'How's the universe?' he said.

'Not very good,' said Gustav. 'My mother is ill. She needs an ambulance.'

'Oh,' said Ludwig, 'ambulances, hospitals ... let's not mention those. Shall we play a game of jacks?'

'I haven't got the jacks,' said Gustav.

'Too bad,' said Ludwig. 'Too bad, manikin. Can't you fetch them?'

'Not now. We have to get an ambulance for Mutti.'

Gustav waited. Ludwig sucked on his cigarette. Gustav could see Frau Krams inside their parlour, winding wool from the back of a chair. She got up and came to the door, pushing Ludwig out of the way. 'Ambulance, Gustav? Did I hear that word? What's happened?'

Gustav described how his mother lay in bed and was too weak to move and perhaps had wet her bed more than once. Frau Krams put her plump hands over her mouth. '*Mein Gott!*' she said.

She followed Gustav up the stairs. Ludwig wanted to come with them, but Frau Krams sent him down again.

When they got to the apartment, the largeness of Frau Krams, the way her body seemed to fill up a doorway, was suddenly reassuring to Gustav. As he showed her into Emilie's room, he realised that he was very tired, as though some of Emilie's illness had passed into his blood and made him weak.

He watched as Frau Krams bent over Emilie, and stroked her burning cheek. The stench of urine was very strong. Frau Krams now took the green eiderdown off the bed. Then she threw back the rest of the bedclothes and lifted Emilie, light as a child in her arms, and sat her in the armchair, tucking the eiderdown tightly round her.

'I'm sorry . . .' said Emilie.

'Nothing to be sorry about,' said Frau Krams.

She took the stained sheets off the bed and opened the window. She told Gustav to run a bathful of water, then tip disinfectant in it, and soak the sheets in that. 'When you've done that, come and sit with your mother. I'm going down to call an ambulance. This could be pneumonia.'

'Or it might be TB,' said Gustav.

'What?'

'I know about TB. Then Mutti would have to go to Davos.'

Frau Krams stared at Gustav, who was now holding the bundle of urine-soaked sheets. She shook her head. 'No, no,' she said. 'I don't think so, pet. Now, wait here for me. I'll bring the ambulance people up.'

Gustav ran the hot water and found the disinfectant Emilie used to clean the toilet and poured it all in. The water jumped and bubbled, as if it were acid. Fumes rose from the bath and made Gustav gag. He waited till the bath was full, then he went back to Emilie, who had fallen sideways in the chair, with her head lolling on her chest. Now, she looked very peculiar, trussed up in the green eiderdown. She reminded Gustav of a silkworm. Her face was blank white, but with two hectic spots of red on her cheeks, like the bruises a silkworm might have suffered falling to the kindergarten floor.

There was one other chair in Emilie's room, a hard Biedermeier chair that had come with her to Unter der Egg from her former life on Fribourgstrasse. Gustav tugged this towards Emilie's armchair and sat down on it and stared at his mother. He saw in this moment how thin she had become, and how angry. And he wondered whether he was to blame for these things in some way that he didn't understand. He reached out and touched Emilie's shoulder, just visible, in a pink nightdress, above the rim of the eiderdown. He stroked this gently, feeling the hard collarbone under his hand. He wished she wasn't ill, so that he could climb onto her lap and be held in her arms until he fell asleep.

When Frau Krams came back with the ambulance men, Emilie was lifted into a wheelchair and manoeuvred into the tiny elevator. Gustav helped Frau Krams to pack a suitcase with clean nightdresses and shampoo and a toothbrush and Emilie's broken handbag and the photograph of Erich Perle. Frau Krams told Gustav that she would go to the hospital with Emilie and be back at Unter der Egg by supper time. She told him to come down to her flat and stay there with Ludwig until she returned.

Ludwig was drinking.

He said, 'Vodka is cool. But don't say a word, eh, Gustavus?'

Gustav sat on a hard sofa in Frau Krams's parlour. He took off his shoes and swung his legs onto the sofa and lay down and in moments had fallen asleep, to the sound of a little gas fire popping and sighing as the dusk came on.

When he woke, it was morning.

A soft blanket was covering him, red and white, like the Swiss flag, and he pulled this blanket tightly round himself, remembering that he needed protection.

He could hear Ludwig's humming, coming from the kitchen. The gas fire was out and there was sunshine at the small window. He knew now that his mother was in the hospital and that he was in the Krams's apartment. He wondered if it was time to go to school.

Ludwig came in and bent over Gustav and began tickling him and laughing and with the gusts of laughter came the smell of stale vodka.

'Get up, terrible boy!' said Ludwig. He reminded Gustav of some punishing character out of *Struwwelpeter.*

'I'm not terrible,' he said.

'Yes, you are. I'm going to tickle you until you scream!'

'I never scream.'

'I can make you scream.'

'No, you can't.'

'All right then. Take that blanket off. It's my blanket anyway, my favourite one, but I let you have it. Wasn't that kind of me? Now, we're going to have hot chocolate and bread and pickles.'

Ludwig and Gustav sat in the parlour at a table covered with a yellow oilcloth. Ludwig had boiled milk for the hot chocolate and set out a plate of bread, with butter and pickled onions. Gustav began gulping all this down. He would have liked to eat a huge plate of bratwurst with boiled potatoes. At last, he said to Ludwig, 'Why isn't your mother back?'

Ludwig shivered. 'Hospitals,' he said. 'They kidnap you. I was kidnapped. I was strapped down to a bed and they gave me electric shocks to my head.'

'Why?' asked Gustav.

'Who knows? That's the thing about the world, Gustavus: you just don't know why the things that happen happen.'

Gustav drained the dregs of the hot chocolate. 'Your mother said she'd be back by supper time, but now it's breakfast.'

'Yes. I hope she's not having electric shocks to her head. Shall we go to my room? I can show you some of my toys.'

'Toys?'

'Yes. The things I play with.'

'I think I'd better go to school.'

'If you do that, I'll be lonely, little man.'

The room was almost as small as Gustav's and it was choked with some of the things the tenants of the building had thrown out, but which Ludwig had decided to save: faded deckchairs, pictures of Jesus, a broken rocking horse, rusted garden shears, plant pot holders, a Moses basket, a picnic hamper, a sweet jar, magazines, two watering cans, a kiddy car, a set of brocade cushions . . .

Gustav stared at all this. There was barely room for Ludwig to get in and out of his narrow bed, so closely did the tide of found objects nudge against its side.

'What would you like to play with?' asked Ludwig. 'The rocking horse?'

'Yes.'

Ludwig clambered over the deckchairs and the picnic hamper to get to the horse. As he lifted it up, something fell out from a wedge of cushions: it was Gustav's broken tin train.

The sight of it filled him with wonder. 'That's my train! That's my train!' he cried. 'Give it to me, Ludwig.'

Ludwig picked up the train. 'It's mine now,' he said. 'I found it in the rubbish bin.'

'Mutti threw it away, not me. I didn't mean to break it. I was just angry about something. Please let me have it back.'

'No. You can't have it.'

'Please! *Please*, Ludwig!'

Ludwig held the train upside down in the air. If the people in the carriages had been loose and not painted on, they would have fallen out. Then Ludwig stared hard at Gustav. His thin white face seemed suddenly to curdle with a blotchy blush. He put the train down slowly, out of Gustav's reach.

'I've got a cool idea,' he said.

'Give me back my train!'

'I will if you go along with my idea,' he said. 'OK?'

'No. I don't know what it is.'

'Well, it's cool. You'll see. Lots of people do it. We did it at the hospital, where they gave me electric shocks. People are doing it all the time.'

'What?'

'Here,' said Ludwig. 'Feast your eyes on this, little man.' Then he opened his fly and brought out his penis, which he began stroking.

'You can have the train *if*. . .' he said.

Gustav gaped. 'If what?'

'Come here. Touch my prick. Stroke it like this, like I'm doing.'

'I don't want to.'

'You won't get your train, then. Come on, put your hand here. I've told you, it's the cool thing. We could have fun with it. Nobody would know. And I'm a sex superman! That's what they called me in the hospital. Just touch me a bit and I'll come.'

Gustav felt himself go very cold. He looked away from Ludwig to his train, lying on top of the upturned Moses basket. Ludwig, whose face was getting redder, reached out and tugged Gustav roughly towards him. Gustav fell over the rocking horse, bruising his shin. Ludwig had gripped his hand now and was guiding it towards his penis, which had grown longer and larger, but at this moment, Gustav heard the sound of a key in the outer door and he knew that this must be Frau Krams returning at last.

'*Scheisse!*' muttered Ludwig, and turned away from Gustav to rub himself more violently. 'Get out of here! Go to my mother,' he hissed. 'Close the door!'

Gustav wanted to grab the train, but he didn't dare. He left Ludwig's room and came into the parlour, where the remains of the breakfast were still on the table. Frau Krams had straight away begun clearing these away, but when she saw Gustav, she sat down.

'Why aren't you at school?' she said.

Gustav found that he couldn't speak. He was shivering. The bruise on his shin sent waves of pain down his leg. 'How's Mutti?' he managed to ask at last.

Frau Krams reached for her handbag, found a cigarette and lit it. Her eyes looked bruised with tiredness. She sighed as she said, 'It *is* pneumonia, Gustav. As I feared. I stayed all night because it seemed to be touch and go with her, touch and go for a long while. I wanted her to feel that someone was there.'

'That was very kind of you, Frau Krams. Is she going to come home?'

'No, pet. Not for a good while. She has to get much stronger before she can come back. So, listen to me. We have to make a plan for you. Do you have a grandma or an auntie you could go and stay with?'

'No,' said Gustav.

Frau Krams rubbed her eyes. 'I suppose I can look after you for a bit,' she said. 'We could try to clear Ludwig's room of some of that junk and put a mattress in there with him.'

Gustav shook his head, no.

'I don't blame you,' said Frau Krams. 'You don't want to share a room with watering cans and deckchairs. So tell me, what's to become of you?'

# Solo

## *Matzlingen, 1951*

Gustav sat beside the bathtub, staring at the disinfected water and the soiled sheets. Frau Krams had told him to take them down to the cellar, where the communal washing machine stood in a small concrete space, but he knew that the damp bedlinen would be too heavy for him to carry. He wondered how strong – at almost ten years old – he was supposed to be.

He left the bathroom and went to the kitchen and found the remains of the vegetable stew on the hob, but it didn't look like anything he might want to eat. The floating white leeks reminded him of the horrible long penis he'd seen in Ludwig's hand. He poured the stew down the drain, trying not to gag when he saw a large leek blocking the run-off. He thought that if he'd been some other boy, he would have begun crying or at least whimpering by now, but he wasn't: he was Gustav Perle. He was going to *master himself* – for the sake of his Mutti, for the sake of his dead father, for the sake of Anton, who cried too often, for the sake of a few beautiful things in the world, like the sun on a balcony in Davos. He took the slimy leek in his hands and threw it into the bin.

He washed his face and hands and changed his clothes and set out to walk to school. He didn't know what time it was, so he asked Frau Teller at the flower stall to tell him the time, and she said, 'All I know, Gustav, is that it's Wednesday.'

When he got to school, he found that lessons were only just beginning. He went into his classroom and sat down at his desk and the feel of the familiar wooden desk was comforting. It was as if it were the one thing in what Ludwig called 'the universe' which hadn't altered in the last twenty-four hours. Holding onto the desk, he decided that after school he would borrow money for the tram fare and go to see Emilie at the hospital. He hoped he would find her in a clean bed, with her hair washed and combed.

He whispered to Anton, 'Mutti's got pneumonia.'

'What's pneumonia?'

'It's like TB. She almost died in the night.'

'Do you really mean "died"?'

'Yes.'

'What would you do if she died?'

'I'd be alone,' said Gustav.

At break time, Anton told Gustav that his piano teacher, Herr Edelstein, had entered him for a Children's National Piano Competition, in Bern. He was going to play Debussy's 'La Cathédrale Engloutie'.

'When?' asked Gustav.

'In the summer. Before we go on holiday to the mountains. But there are heats first.'

'What are "heats"?'

'It's like a first round and then a second round. You have to go to Bern and play for two of the judges. Then if you're good enough, after two rounds, you get to go in the competition.'

'And what happens if you're not good enough?'

'I will be good enough, Gustav. Maybe you can come to Bern and hear me perform?'

Gustav liked to imagine Anton onstage in a huge concert hall, alone with the black grand piano, open like an enormous heart, about to gather him in. He hoped he would be able to persuade Emilie to take him there, so that she, too, could hear Anton playing.

It was cold in the schoolyard. Gustav wanted to tell Anton about the thing that Ludwig had done, so that the repulsion of it could be shared and not just remain burrowing through his brain, like a worm burrowing through the earth. But the thought of trying to describe it made him feel sick. He also wondered whether Anton would *blame* him, in some way, and then shun him. It was easy to imagine Anton walking away from him and telling the other boys that Gustav Perle had done a disgusting thing. So it came to him then that he would have to keep it locked away inside him and tell no one – *ever*.

He listened instead to Anton's excitement as he talked about the piano competition. Anton said, 'It may be a bit frightening, to play in front of so many people. My mother says there's a pill I could take to stop me getting nervous. She also says I'd better get used to it, because that's probably going to be my career in life, being a concert pianist.'

'How does she know?'

'Because I'm a "prodigy". That means I'm more brilliant at playing than almost everyone else of my age. So by the time I get to eighteen, I could be performing in huge concerts in Paris and Geneva and New York. You see?'

'Huge concerts?'

'Sure. Even at our age, my mother says, we have to think about what we're going to do later on in our lives. What are you going to do, Gustav?'

Gustav turned his face away. Into his mind came the image of himself, on his hands and knees, in the Church of Sankt Johann, searching for pitiful 'treasure' under the metal grating. And it was easy to project this forward into the future – as though there *were* no future for him, but only this: a man crawling along, growing older year by year, searching for things which other people had cast aside.

'I don't know what I'm going to do,' he said.

He went to see Herr Hodler after school. Max Hodler was wearing spectacles now and these spectacles shaded his pink-rimmed eyes and made him look older and slightly more handsome than he'd been before. When he was told about Emilie Perle's pneumonia, he said, 'Heavens, Gustav. That's very frightening.'

He gave Gustav a toffee and popped one into his own mouth. They sat in the book-crammed staffroom, chewing the toffees and saying nothing.

At last, Max Hodler said, 'Who is looking after you?'

'I'm all right,' said Gustav. 'If you could just lend me a bit of money for the tram fare, then I can go and see Mutti.'

'Certainly,' said Max. 'Are you going now? Let me come with you.'

Gustav shook his head, no. 'Mutti might not want to see anyone,' he said, remembering the urine-soaked sheets and the oily sweat on Emilie's face.

'That's all right,' said Max. 'I can just wait in the corridor.'

'I can go alone,' said Gustav. 'It's the number 13 tram.'

It was difficult to find where Emilie was in the big hospital. Gustav wandered from ward to ward, staring at all the sick people. He was beginning to feel tired again, and very hungry. When he saw a food trolley being pushed along, he asked the orderly if he could take a piece of bread. Without waiting for an answer, he reached out for the bread, but the orderly slapped his hand and said, 'Get away from my patients' rations! What are you doing here, anyway, boy? Are you from the children's ward?'

He was sent back, through all the rooms he'd already visited, to a desk staffed by a matron, wearing a starched white hat, like some kind of weird Swiss National Dress.

'Well?' she said. 'What do you want?'

He gave Emilie's name: Frau Perle – never Emilie to strangers. A young nurse was called by the matron and Gustav followed the nurse, retracing his steps through the crowded wards, past the food trolley, till they reached a dark and silent corridor and the nurse opened the door to a tiny room, lit with a shaded blue lamp.

Gustav went in. In the blue light, he could hardly make out Emilie's form on the metal bed. Tubes were attached to her arms, joined up to a bag upside down on a pole. Another tube had been pushed up her nose. Her eyes were closed and her breathing was very loud, like snoring.

There was a chair by the bed and Gustav sat down on this. He wanted to take hold of Emilie's hand, but he was afraid to dislodge the tubes, so he sat with his hands in his lap. He said, 'Mutti, can you hear me?'

She couldn't. She was in that place, like a dark and silent lake, where people go when they're asleep. Now and again, Gustav could hear footsteps going by in the corridor, but nobody came into the room. He sat very still, bathed in the blue light. The blueness of everything made him feel lonely. Heavy on his mind weighed the thought of the sheets in the disinfected bath and the task of dragging them down to the washing machine in the cellar.

He wondered how many other tasks Mutti performed in the space of a day to ensure that they lived a properly mastered life, where floors were cleaned and mice kept away and pillows were soft and dry. And he decided that was his mission now, to learn what to do to keep the apartment in a state of readiness for Emilie's return. He'd understood how to help clean the Church of Sankt Johann. So perhaps it was just as simple as that? He'd clean the apartment like the church nave and pews, with a mop and wood polish and a carpet beater. He'd ransack his treasure box for the low-denomination coins he'd amassed in it, and hope to buy food with these, and a bunch of violets to put in Emilie's room when she returned.

Of Ludwig he refused to think. But then he remembered, with a lurch of his heart, that Frau Krams had a key to the apartment. Ludwig could just take the key and come up in the middle of the night, holding his penis in his hand. Gustav wished he was the owner of a fierce dog, which would bite the penis off – like the red-legged scissor-man had snipped off Konrad's thumbs (*klipp und klapp!*) leaving Ludwig screaming like a bat and leaching gouts of blood onto the lino.

Before he left the blue hospital room, he found a chart with a pencil hanging from it on the end of Mutti's bed. On this he wrote:

DEAR Mutti, Dont worry about me. The Zwiebels will take care of me. Gustav x

When he got back to the apartment, he began searching for food. He found a tin of tomato soup – the last tin in Emilie's cupboards – and heated this up. He knew he should save some for breakfast or supper tomorrow, but he was so hungry that he drank it all.

He counted the money in his treasure box. It came to three

francs and twenty centimes. He wondered if anyone sold a bratwurst for less than this. Then, he wondered if he could survive on just one meal a day, his school dinner, which was usually dumplings with a little meat and gravy. He remembered how Max Hodler had told him that the country of Switzerland had come into being *by an act of will.* Switzerland was a *Willensnation*, and Max had said that all Swiss children should remember this and try to be as strong and as persevering as the men in the Rütli Meadow and then – hundreds of years later – the generals at the time of the war, who had defended Swiss neutrality. But Gustav had already learned that his will, when it came to hunger, was weak. He didn't understand how it could be any other way.

He had promised himself that, before he went to sleep, he would try to drag the disinfected sheets down to the basement. He let the water out of the bath, then climbed into it and stamped on the sheets to get more dampness out of them. He felt a burning in his feet.

In Emilie's broom cupboard, he found a folding metal pushchair in which she used to wheel him about when he was small. He manoeuvred this into the bathroom and tugged the sheets out of the bath and dumped them in the chair and wheeled the chair to the elevator. All the way along the tiled floor, the sheets left little drips and puddles.

When he got to the basement, it was dark. The light switch was too high for him to reach. He stood in the blackness, smelling the dank of the place and the acrid smell of the sheets. He knew that, if it hadn't been for Ludwig, he would have gone and knocked on Frau Krams's door and asked for her help, but he was afraid to do this.

He stood there a long time. Then he became worried that Ludwig might come and close the cellar door, with both of them locked inside. He didn't know what more to do except to wheel the sheets near to the washing machine and leave them there till morning.

Now, he was making a barricade behind the apartment door.

He used the Biedermeier chair, slammed up against a wooden shelf that Emilie had taken out of her wardrobe. Then, he carried all the pots and pans, one by one, from the kitchen to the door and heaped them onto and round the chair. He knew the door might still be pushed open, but at least he would hear the pans clinking and crashing, if Ludwig tried to get in. Then, he would run to the lavatory and lock himself inside.

By the time the barricade was finished, Gustav felt so tired that he thought he might fall over. He wanted to run a bath, to wash himself clean of all that had happened to him in the last twenty-four hours, but he was afraid that if he did this, he might slip under the water and drown. So he just took off his clothes and crawled into his bed. He said a prayer for Emilie and fell asleep.

# Pharma

## *Matzlingen and Bern, 1951*

Gustav got used to surviving on school dinners and on the parcels of food given to him by Max Hodler. Almost invariably, Max included a tin of bratwurst and this Gustav would cradle to his body before opening it. He thought Max Hodler was probably the kindest man in Switzerland.

Sometimes, he was invited to tea with Anton and Adriana at Fribourgstrasse 77, where he would stuff himself with cherry tart and Florentine biscuits and listen to Anton practising for the piano competition. He told Anton that he couldn't concentrate on Debussy very well, like he couldn't concentrate on history lessons any more, nor even on mathematics. All his mind could think about was food. Perhaps he hoped, as he said this, that Anton would say, why don't you come and live with us, then?

But Anton just swivelled round on the piano stool and said, 'Well, you know, in the war, millions of Jews were put in camps where they starved to death. At least you're not starving, Gustav.'

'Why were they starved to death?'

'Because Jews are hated. That's what Papa says. They are hated all round the world.'

'I don't hate them.'

'I know you don't. But lots of people do. Your mother does.'

It was a Saturday morning in early summer when Emilie Perle walked back into the apartment. She stood at the door to the parlour, looking all around her in surprise. 'It smells nice and clean,' she said. 'I suppose Frau Krams got everything sorted out for me, did she? I must be sure to thank her.'

'No,' said Gustav. 'She helped me do the washing and ironing, that's all. I did the mopping and the dusting and everything. I put clean sheets on your bed.'

Emilie sat down and looked at Gustav. 'You've got thin,' she said.

'I'm all right.'

'I didn't worry about you. You told me in your note that the Zwiebels were taking care of you.'

'Oh yes, they did,' lied Gustav. 'And now something exciting has happened to Anton. He's been chosen to go in for a children's piano competition in Bern. He had to get through "heats", but he passed them. He's going to play Debussy at the Kornhaus.'

'Ah,' said Emilie. 'Well, that's nice.'

'You could come with me to Bern, to hear him play.'

'I don't know about that. First things first.'

She began to walk about in the apartment. Her hair was freshly shampooed and clipped back in a girlish tortoiseshell slide. She said to Gustav, 'When you've been ill for a long time, everything looks strange, as though you've never seen it before.'

'Would you like something to eat, Mutti?' asked Gustav.

'What have we got to eat?' said Emilie.

'A tin of bratwurst and a tin of sauerkraut. And a slice of cherry tart that I saved from tea at the Zwiebels'.'

'That sounds very nice,' said Emilie. 'All they seemed to give us in the hospital was soup and more soup.'

Gustav selected a tray and put a clean tea cloth on it and placed a glass of water by the plate of bratwurst and sauerkraut. He added a clean table napkin. He wished he had a little posy of flowers to put beside it. But still, the sight of the tray of food gave him pleasure.

Emilie smiled as she took the tray from him. This was the first time Gustav had seen her smile in a long time. He wanted to ask her if everything was going to be all right now, if she would find a job and get money, if things were going to be as they'd been before, with her stockings hanging on the string over the bath, and fresh knödel made for supper on Mondays. But he guessed that Emilie didn't know the answer to this.

Emilie began to tuck into her food. Between mouthfuls, she looked up at Gustav. 'Your hair's too long,' she said.

She got a job in a pharmacy in the centre of the town.

She was given a pale blue uniform to wear over her faded blouses and skirts. She said to Gustav, 'Swiss pharma is the most advanced in the world. We sell medication that can't be found anywhere else.'

She explained that she couldn't sell any of this herself. She didn't have the 'requisite knowledge'. Each request had to be checked with the pharmacist. She could sell soap and aspirin and cough lozenges and bandages and disinfectant, but not much else. 'But my job is important,' she said. 'I'm the person who double-checks that the shelves are correctly supplied – that we don't run out of anything vital. And I help people to find things.'

When Gustav went into the pharmacy after school, he felt proud of Emilie. She held herself very upright in her blue uniform. She walked about the shop at a fast pace, in clean white shoes, instead of dragging her feet, like she did around the apartment or when she'd worked at the cheese co-operative. She smiled at the customers.

The pay was mediocre, but it was enough. Emilie and Gustav never went back to cleaning the Church of Sankt Johann. There was Nusstorte, sometimes, for tea, and small cuts of roast meat on Sundays.

The piano competition took place at the end of June.

It was agreed that Gustav would be driven to Bern with the Zwiebels the evening before and they would stay in a hotel and the boys would be allowed to stay up for supper in the hotel dining room. There was no mention of Emilie being invited.

Anton was competing in the 'Age 8–10' category. These children would play during the morning. There would be four other contestants in this section of the contest, three boys and one girl. When Anton explained this to Gustav, he said, 'It's only now that I realise I may not win.'

Gustav had heard his friend playing 'La Cathédrale Engloutie' many times, but he was unable to say whether another boy – or the lone girl – would turn out to be in some other class of 'prodigy', more prodigious than Anton's, and it would be they who were presented with the silver cup and had the Winner's sash draped round their narrow bodies. Yet he feared that this would probably be the case.

'What will you do if you don't win?' asked Gustav.

'I don't know,' said Anton. 'I might break a metronome.'

Gustav had persuaded Emilie to buy him a new jacket to wear on the trip to Bern. He'd imagined Bern, the capital city, to be like a picture he'd once seen of the Hanging Gardens of Babylon, with minarets and domes and birds of paradise roosting in the trees. He didn't want to look like a beggar boy in such an exalted place.

When they arrived there in Herr Zwiebel's car, he saw that it wasn't as he'd imagined it. It was a city of tiled roofs and tall stone buildings, grand portals, painted statues and a thousand flags shivering in the brisk June breeze. Along its streets, everything hurried – cars, trams and people – as if impatient to be somewhere else. The air was filled with traffic noise and the sound of bells. It was the kind of place it was difficult for Gustav to understand. All he'd known of the world until then was Matzlingen.

As they drove up a narrow street that was leading them to their hotel, Gustav looked over at Anton and saw that his friend's face was very white and that there was sweat on his lip.

'Frau Zwiebel,' Gustav said, 'I think Anton is going to be sick.'

Adriana turned from the front seat and looked at Anton. 'Stop the car, Armin!' she shouted. They jolted to a halt outside a hairdresser's salon. Adriana got out and ran round and opened the car door for Anton and he stumbled out and threw up onto the pavement. Adriana held his forehead tenderly. Armin Zwiebel turned his face away from the little disturbing scene. 'Well done, Gustav,' he said. 'You saved the interior of my car. We used to have a dog, which was sick in my old Mercedes, and we never quite got rid of the stink.'

Anton seemed to go on puking for quite a long while. A woman came out of the hair salon, newly coiffed, and recoiled in horror and hurried away as fast as her high-heeled shoes would permit. Herr Zwiebel lit a cigarette. 'I expect it's nerves,' he said. 'My wife has brought along something for that.'

'Is Anton going to win?' said Gustav.

'No,' said Armin Zwiebel.

'How do you know that, sir?'

'I just know it. He's very talented, but he is too fragile for competitions. His character is too anxious.'

'He got through the heats.'

'Yes. They were in a small practice room. Not on a grand stage. He will not manage to play well in the Kornhaus.'

Gustav somehow felt relieved that Herr Zwiebel wasn't expecting Anton to win. He felt that this formed a moment's bond between them – the Jewish banker and the dead policeman's son – because he knew now that he himself had decided, in his own mind, that Anton was going to fail. He'd been ashamed to think this of his friend, but now that he knew Herr Zwiebel was thinking it too, the shame vanished. They sat silent in the car. They both knew that what they had to do now was to help Anton though the next twenty-four hours.

The dining room of the hotel was like a tall glass cage, filled with palms and flowers. The bars and roof of the cage were white iron latticework. Above the glass, a full moon slowly traversed the sky and sank behind a ridge of cloud.

Armin Zwiebel ordered roast veal with mashed potato for Anton and Gustav, while he and Adriana were served great plates of oysters on crushed ice. Almost hidden behind palms, a pianist played Cole Porter tunes. Raising his head to listen for a moment, Anton commented, 'His left hand has no reach. The chords are too simple.'

'Hush, darling,' said Adriana.

'No, I won't hush,' said Anton, 'because he's playing for the public, isn't he? Isn't he getting paid to do this? They should have got somebody better.'

'I like Cole Porter,' said Adriana.

'So do I,' said Armin.

'That's not the point,' said Anton.

'We know. But eat your meal, sweetheart. Is the veal good?'

'Yes. But I'm not hungry.'

Gustav had almost cleaned his plate, so delicious was the roast meat and creamy potato, but Anton had pushed everything aside. His face was now very red, Gustav saw, as though it might have been burning hot in the glass-cage dining room, when in fact it was so cool in the draughty space that some of the diners were wearing their outdoor coats.

Adriana looked at her husband. He was sucking down an oyster, but he caught her eye.

'Anton,' he said, when he'd swallowed the oyster, 'when Gustav's finished his supper, you should both go to bed. Don't fret about the food. Your mother will come up with some medicine to help you rest. Gustav, did you bring any books? You might read to Anton to calm him before you go to sleep.'

'Yes, sir,' said Gustav, 'I brought *Struwwelpeter*.'

'Oh that, indeed! I remember that. Do you want Gustav to read *Struwwelpeter* to you in bed?'

'Yes,' said Anton. 'I like the one about the boy who floats away into the sky and is never seen again.'

Anton seemed relieved to be led away from the glass dining room. He held onto Gustav's arm as they went up the stairs to their room. They undressed silently and Anton got straight into bed, without washing or cleaning his teeth. Outside the window, the complicated sounds of the great city seemed to be tuning up for the night, getting slowly louder as the moments passed. The room was cold.

Emilie had packed Gustav's woollen dressing gown and he tied it tightly round his body. When he looked over at Anton, lying very still and straight in his bed, he thought about his friend's first day at the kindergarten and how he had stood at the sandbox, crying. He wanted to say to him, I'm here, Anton. I'll help you to bear whatever's going to come.

Adriana came in and sat on Anton's bed and gave him a pill to take. She stroked his head. 'This will help you sleep,' she said. 'In the morning, I'll give you another one to calm you. Now, you lie still, sweetheart, and Gustav will read to you.'

Anton nodded. He touched his mother's hand. 'Suppose I'm not the best player?' he said.

'Well,' said Adriana, 'then you're not. You mustn't think it's the end of the world.'

'I want to be the best. I want to win.'

'I know you do. But if you don't, we'll still be proud of you, won't we, Gustav?'

'Yes. We will.'

'Now, I'm going down to have coffee with Papa. You get the book, Gustav, and sit here. Anton will soon be asleep.'

Adriana went away, leaving behind her a fragile waft of perfume. Gustav breathed this in.

'Why are you sniffing?' asked Anton.

'I'm not. Now, which story do you want?'

'I told you, the one about the boy, "Head-in-Air", who's whirled away into the sky.'

Gustav showed Anton the illustrations. The boy, Hans, walks about the world never looking where he's going. One day, he collides with a brown dog. Another time, he falls into the river and has to be pulled out with a fish hook. Then, he goes out into a storm with his umbrella and the wind lifts him up and carries him away.

'And he's never seen again?' asked Anton.

'Yes. That's it.'

'I'd like to be him,' said Anton. 'I'd like to disappear into a rain cloud and not have to play Debussy tomorrow.'

But there he was now, walking onto the stage, to applause, like a sudden shower of rain, from the audience. The Zwiebels and Gustav were in the second row of the big auditorium, yet even from this position Anton looked small.

He wore a navy jacket and grey trousers. Instead of moving in a straight line towards the piano, he veered towards the edge of the stage, then stopped and looked around him, with an anxious kind of wonderment. He gave an awkward bow. Gustav didn't think he was meant to do this. The previous two contestants hadn't bowed. Eventually, he turned and made his way to the piano.

It had been hard to wake him in the morning. The pill Adriana had given him had put him into a slumber so deep, he was still reeling from it as they went down to breakfast in the glass dining room. Gustav had heard Herr Zwiebel whisper to Adriana that 'the pharma was too strong' and Adriana had looked at Anton with a worried frown creasing her smooth forehead.

They'd given him coffee and bread. A bright sun had shone through the glass and onto Anton's pale and sickly face. He rolled tiny pellets of bread in his hand and put them slowly into his mouth, like pills. He looked around him at the other guests. It had seemed to Gustav that he didn't quite know where he was. Gustav buttered his own slice of bread and spread it with apricot jam and gave it to Anton. 'Eat this,' he said. 'The jam will wake you up.'

Now, in the Kornhaus, Gustav was hoping that the bread and jam and the breath of air they had all taken in the hotel garden had lifted Anton out of his torpor. When he at last reached the piano stool, and began his usual fussing with the height of it, he appeared less confused. The applause subsided, waiting for the first great chords of 'La Cathédrale Engloutie' to sound. Anton rubbed his palms on his trousers, to get the sweat away, then he lifted his hands . . .

In the apartment on Fribourgstrasse, when Anton played the piano, his concentration seemed such that his body and the music he was conjuring from the instrument became one. You forgot the boy, Anton. There was just the gift of the music, bathing you, moment by moment. But here, in the echoing Kornhaus, as the piece began, Gustav could barely *hear* the music. Was Anton's left foot on the soft pedal? Was his touch so light or weak that the keys weren't being fully depressed? Or was it that such a clamour of agitation for his friend had begun in Gustav's own head that all exterior sound was muffled?

Gustav felt himself to be far away – in some other place, both near to and yet oddly distant from the place where he actually was. He wondered if he was going to lose consciousness. He dug his fingernails into his knees. He looked down at the stone floor, remembering that this Kornhaus had once been filled with sacks of grain and farmers' carts and the sound of men bargaining and exchanging silver coins. And this image of time past became so vivid to him that he clung to it and forgot the music, forgot the agony that Anton was going through, and only concentrated on this – on the smell of grain and horse manure and dust and the sound of money.

Then, quite suddenly, the music ended. Gustav raised his head and saw Anton get up from the stool and hold onto the piano and bow again. The organiser of the competition, a large man with a shining bald head, strode onto the stage. He took Anton's hand and raised it, like the referee raises a boxer's hand at the end of a bout.

'Ladies and gentlemen,' he said, 'I think we are all agreed that this was a very nice performance from our third competitor of the morning, Anton Zwebbel. Please show your appreciation with another round of applause.'

Later, when the winning places were announced and it was revealed that Anton had come last in the group of five, all he could say to Gustav was: 'The man got my surname wrong. He couldn't stand to say the "onion" word. If I'd had a different name, I might have won.'

# Magic Mountain

## *Davos, 1952*

When Emilie Perle was told that Gustav had been invited to go with the Zwiebels to Davos for a two-week holiday, she said, 'I don't think so, Gustav. You fell behind again with your work while I was ill. I think you'd better spend the summer studying. I will get in touch with Herr Hodler and hope he can give you some of his precious time.'

Gustav went to his room. He was ten years old now. He'd learned that arguing with Emilie only strengthened her resolve.

He stared at his map of Mittelland, faded where the sun had touched it, so that swathes of the green pastures appeared barren. He was looking for Davos, but all the while knowing that he wouldn't find it. Davos wasn't in Mittelland. It was far to the east, in the mountains, in a place where the sky was so blue, it could damage your eyes.

If he'd thought that Emilie would understand, he would have said to her, Anton needs me to be with him in Davos. I can invent games we can play that will take his thoughts away from the stupid piano competition. If he's alone with his parents, he'll keep returning to it in his mind.

But he knew that Emilie was indifferent to Anton. She would probably have preferred it if the Zwiebels moved back to Bern and were never seen in Matzlingen again.

In the evening, when Emilie called him for supper, he could see that she had been crying. She'd made a cheese pie. When she and Gustav were seated at the kitchen shelf and she'd served up the pie, she said, 'I was looking at my photographs of Davos again this afternoon. I was looking at how beautiful it is in the summertime. It makes me weep to see it. And I thought that it would be unkind of me to prevent you from going there.'

'You mean, I can go with the Zwiebels?'

Gustav waited. But Emilie didn't reply. She just kept eating the pie. It was as though the word 'yes' was buried in her throat, deep beneath the mouthful of pie. At last, she said, 'Davos really has a climate all of its own. The valley is sheltered from the north. When the north wind blows, you barely feel it. You'll see.'

The chalet the Zwiebels had rented stood at the top of a lush meadow, facing south, high above the village of Davos itself. At its back was the treeline, scenting the air with pine. At the base of the meadow was a small dwelling, inhabited by an elderly man who came to be known simply as 'Monsieur', because he spoke Swiss-German with a French accent. Monsieur kept a herd of skittish goats and a few chickens, whose will it was to range up the meadow each day, moving slowly, like a search party, with a careful, dainty step, looking for worms and blown seeds.

The chalet was old, with a steep shingled roof weighted down with stones and walls of pitch-blackened pine. The windows were small and decorated with yellow shutters. On a wooden veranda, a mossy drinking trough had been filled with scarlet geraniums. When the Zwiebels and Gustav arrived and saw the scarlet flowers basking in the sun and heard the breeze gently sighing in the pines, they all stood very still.

'Magic,' said Adriana.

The place was large. The boys each had a room to themselves. In the salon was a monumental oak table and two commodious sofas covered in rough-weave woollen cloth. On the wooden floor, in front of a wide fireplace, was a sheepskin rug and a box full of ancient toys. When Armin saw this, he said, 'How thoughtful of the owners – baby playthings for the children!' Everybody laughed. But Gustav wasn't ashamed to believe that the toy box would contain objects that could inform the games he and Anton would play. He knew that, at ten, they were both considered too old for children's toys, but his own life had been so devoid of them that they had remained alluring in his mind.

They unpacked the car. Adriana commented that Gustav's suitcase was very light. He said, 'I told Mutti that I might need bathing trunks, for the swimming pool, but she forgot to buy any.' And Adriana laughed. Then she sat down on Gustav's bed and said, 'I think we're going to have a lovely time here. Don't you? The air is so wonderful. We can buy you bathing trunks. And Anton is going to put the piano competition behind him.'

Gustav said nothing for a moment, looking at the brightly coloured curtains at his window and the blue, empty sky beyond, then he said, 'Perhaps Anton shouldn't go in for any more competitions?'

'You may be right. Anton's father is more or less of that opinion. But music will always be important to Anton. It's the thing he cares most about.'

'Competitions make him sick.'

'Yes. They seem to. But if you want a future as a concert pianist, you have to enter them. I'm not sure what we should decide.'

Gustav looked up at Adriana, dressed that day in a white linen blouse and narrow grey slacks, worn with white canvas shoes. He said, 'At least you and Herr Zwiebel are thinking about it. My mother never thinks about my future.'

'I expect she does, Gustav.'

'My father might have wanted me to go into the police.'

'Would you like that?'

'I don't know. Mutti says he was a hero. I don't think I could be a hero.'

'I'm sure you could. Or perhaps you wouldn't need to be.'

To get to Davos village, instead of taking the car, they walked down the meadow to the lane which ran by Monsieur's house, beside which stood a rusting harrow, a deserted dog kennel and an untidy heap of firewood. Monsieur came out and touched his hat to them and asked if they wanted fresh eggs. The goats, each with a bell tied round its soft neck, clustered at the fence of their compound, regarding the strangers. 'Or,' said Monsieur, 'if you want a good dinner one night, invite friends, I can kill a goat. Cheaper for you than buying lamb from the butcher, and far more tasty.'

Armin Zwiebel thanked Monsieur. Adriana said they would buy eggs on their way back.

'Or,' said Monsieur, 'your boys can go looking for them in the meadow. They lay all over the place. Would they like to do that?'

'I'm sure they would,' said Adriana.

'*Or*,' said Monsieur again, 'would they like to come hunting with me? There are wild boar up there in the forest. Then, we could all have a feast!'

Anton turned round from petting the goats. 'I don't want to kill anything,' he said. 'And boar are pigs, aren't they? We can't eat that.'

They followed the lane down to the village, which seemed half asleep in the sun of midday. A group of luggage porters lounged in the shade, beside their huge St Bernard dogs which pulled the luggage carts for those visitors arriving by train. Shutters were closed on the shopfronts, but several cafés were open. Gustav wondered if he would recognise the hotel where Emilie and Erich had once stayed – where the balconies were decked with flowers and where the waiters were 'correctly attired'.

Anton announced that he was thirsty, so Armin looked at his watch and said, 'Well, why don't we choose a café and have lunch? What d'you think, Gustav? Are you hungry?'

'Gustav's always hungry,' said Anton.

Adriana selected a quiet place called the Café Caspar, with a wide, gravelled terrace shaded by a wisteria, just past its flowering. The sunlight fell in brindled patterns on the white tablecloths and the polished glassware. Armin ordered grilled chicken and rösti for them all, and a carafe of German wine for him and Adriana. She lit a cigarette, stretched her arms wide and announced that she was 'in paradise'. Gustav and Anton drank lemonade and played jacks on a corner of the table, while waiting for the food to arrive. Inevitably, the jacks jumped about and fell into the dusty gravel.

'Try to sit still, boys,' said Armin.

'We're on holiday,' said Anton. 'Can't we do what we like?'

'Within reason,' said Armin.

Later in their lives, they asked themselves, was it 'within reason', the game they chose to play in Davos? They knew it was strange. But in the strangeness of it lay its fascination and its beauty.

It was on the second day that they found the stone path leading up through the pine trees into darker forest. The path was wide but overgrown. Wild strawberries were growing at its edge: tiny points of red, like beads of blood among the bandages of green leaves. Gustav and Anton stopped to gather a few of these and eat them. The texture was rough, but the taste was sweet.

They knew the path was leading somewhere. There were narrow ruts in the stone surface, as if, long ago, carts and carriages had passed this way. Overhead, the firs crowded out the light and they felt the air become colder. A wind got up and began sighing in the trees.

'Are you frightened?' asked Anton. 'Shall we go back?'

'No,' said Gustav.

They were high up now. At moments, there were glimpses of Davos village, far below. Then the path opened out and became a plateau and on the plateau was an enormous building.

It was ruined. Part of its roof was missing and the glass in most of the windows was broken. Along its southerly edge ran a wooden veranda, cracked and faded by the sunlight. At its back, pressed against the forest, was a brick outhouse with a vast chimney stack rearing up into the sky.

Gustav and Anton stood still and stared. A rusted chain, attached to wooden posts, had been strung across the path – a token attempt, it seemed, to keep people away from a place which had so obviously fallen into dereliction. Gustav listened for the bark of a guard dog, but everything was silent, except for the movement of the trees, like the sound of laboured breathing.

The boys climbed over the chain. All that remained of the entrance to the building was a stone portico with the words *Sankt Alban* engraved above the place where the door had been. They passed underneath this into a small, dark space and then through this space into an enormous room, filled with light. In ranks, along the back wall, facing towards the light, were twenty or thirty iron beds.

'Hospital,' said Anton.

'Sanatorium,' corrected Gustav. 'Where people came to recover from tuberculosis. Or to die.'

'Maybe they all died,' said Anton. 'That's why it was abandoned.'

They walked slowly along the light-filled room. They began to notice other things: rusty oxygen cylinders clamped to the walls, coils of rubber tubing, oxygen masks, buckets, kidney bowls, stained mattresses, a nurse's trolley still set out with brown glass bottles, a stethoscope lying in the rubble.

Anton picked up the stethoscope, dusted it against his Aertex shirt, and hung it round his neck.

'Doctor,' he said. 'You're my nurse, Gustav. Fetch the trolley.'

'We haven't got any patients,' said Gustav.

'Yes, we have. Can't you see them?'

'No.'

'On the beds. We're going to bring them alive again.'

So that was how it began, the game of choosing who, among the sufferers of Sankt Alban, lived or died. They gave the patients names: Hans, Margaret, Frau Merligen, Frau Bünden, Herr Mollis, Herr Weiss . . .

Hans and Margaret were children. Doctor Zwiebel and Nurse Perle were going to have to work especially hard to bring them back to the world. They found the best mattresses for them, those least eaten away by mould. They searched the rest of the building for things that might comfort them: pillows and torn blankets, chamber pots and hot-water bottles.

'And,' said Anton, 'we can bring them toys from the box in the chalet.'

'Yes,' said Gustav, 'except . . .'

'Except what?'

'Won't your parents think this is odd? They might not want us to play here.'

'We won't tell them,' said Anton.

'Where will they think we are?'

'Just "exploring". On holidays, when she doesn't want me around, my mother's always saying "Why don't you go *exploring*, Anton?" We'll tell them we're building a camp in the forest. And anyway, they'll be fucking.'

'What's fucking?'

'It's what they like to do on holiday. They go to bed and take their clothes off and kiss and scream things out. It's called fucking.'

Gustav thought about this. He said, 'I don't think my mother's ever done that. She just goes to bed and reads magazines.'

They forgot about time. To get back to the chalet for lunch, when they heard a midday bell chiming in the village, they had to go racing through the sunlit rooms, down the steps and back onto the steep path. Not stopping, now, to collect strawberries, they ran fast under the canopy of sighing trees, down and down towards the slender pines, until they emerged behind the house and saw Monsieur in the meadow, scattering grain for the hens.

They found Armin and Adriana, sipping wine on the terrace, beside the trough of geraniums. On the table was a dish of meats and pickles and cheese.

'You're out of breath,' said Adriana, as Anton and Gustav sat down. 'Where have you been?'

'Exploring,' they both said together.

'Exploring where?' said Armin.

'In the forest,' said Anton. 'We're making a camp.'

'A camp?' said Adriana, frowning. 'What kind of *camp*?'

'Just a den. It's not finished yet.'

'Can your father and I come and see it?'

'No.'

'Why not?'

'It's not finished. And anyway, it's ours.'

'Good for you,' said Armin with a smile. 'Now have some meat.'

'That time. That Sankt Alban time . . .' they would say, later in their lives. 'That was a thing we've never forgotten.' And sometimes, they would add, 'We've never forgotten it, because we thought we really had power over life and death.'

On the first day, they made sure that Frau Merligen, Frau Bünden, Herr Mollis and Herr Weiss were comfortable, while they took the pulses of Hans and Margaret and gave oxygen to Hans, who was dying faster than the others. They found some old bamboo and wickerwork recliners and pushed the sick children out onto the veranda, where the sun was strong and where there was shelter from the wind. From the chalet box, they'd brought a rag doll for Margaret and a tambourine for Hans. They told Hans to rattle the tambourine if he felt that death was coming near.

'What shall we do if Hans dies?' asked Gustav.

Anton thought for a moment, then said, 'That outhouse with the chimney – it's probably where they burned dead people. We'll put him in there.'

'I don't want him to die,' said Gustav.

'No. I don't either. I tell you what. Shall I be him? You can have the stethoscope and I'll lie on the recliner. If I feel I'm dying, I'll bang the tambourine and you have to come and give me resuscitation.'

'All right. I'll stay with Frau Bünden for a while. She's not looking good. Then you bang the tambourine and I'll come.'

Gustav decided that Frau Bünden resembled Frau Teller, who kept the flower stall on Unter der Egg. She was too young to die. He sat on her bed and told her to think about all the flowers she was going to return to: roses and lilies, tulips, daffodils, edelweiss and blue gentians. He said, 'You're safe in Davos now, Frau Bünden. It's the best place in Switzerland for you. What you have to do is *concentrate* on getting well. Don't think about the TB, right? Think about flowers.'

Frau Bünden said, 'I'm very weak, Nurse Perle. My lungs are full of blood.'

'I know they are. I'm not Nurse Perle now, by the way, I'm Doctor Perle. Doctor Zwiebel and I are going to save you. You just have to believe us. All right? This is Davos.'

Then he heard the rattle of the tambourine and said, 'Forgive me a moment, Frau Bünden, I have to go and look after Hans. I've got to make sure Hans doesn't die.'

Gustav adjusted the stethoscope round his neck and went out onto the veranda. Hans was lying very still, with his eyes closed. The sun shone on his dark hair and on his soft limbs, curled on the recliner. Doctor Perle knelt down beside him and stroked his arm. 'Hans,' he said, 'are you dying?'

'Can't you see I'm dying?' said Hans. 'Put your lips on my lips and revive me, Nurse Perle . . .'

'I'm not Nurse Perle, I'm Doctor Perle now,' said Gustav, 'and I'm not putting my lips on your lips.'

'You have to,' said Hans, 'or I'm gone. You'll have to burn my body in the outhouse . . .'

'I'm not doing that lip thing.'

'Gustav,' said Anton, sitting up suddenly, 'don't be a baby. This is how you revive someone. You put your mouth on their mouth. We learned it in school. Don't you remember? So, go on.'

Hans lay down again. He began to moan.

'Hush,' said Doctor Perle. 'I'm going to revive you now. Here.'

Anton turned his face towards Gustav. Slowly and reluctantly, Gustav brought his mouth to Anton's and lightly touched his lips. He felt Anton lift his arm and put it round his neck and bring his head nearer, so that the two mouths were now pressed hard against each other and Gustav could feel Anton's face, burning hot against his own. He'd thought he would pull away at once, but he stayed there. He liked the feel of Anton gathering his head in his arm. He closed his eyes. He felt that no moment of his life had been as strangely beautiful as this one.

Then he pulled away. 'Are you all right, Hans?' he whispered. 'Are you going to live?'

'Yes,' murmured Hans. 'Thanks to you. I'm going to live, thanks to you.'

Sankt Alban took over their minds.

The time they spent with Adriana and Armin – going for walks, swimming at the pool, taking the cable car higher up the mountain towards the Schatzalp, shopping for souvenirs, collecting eggs for Monsieur, lying in the sun, eating meals on the chalet terrace – all these things, enjoyable as they were, became infected with ordinariness. At every moment, they longed to be back at the sanatorium, back in the beautiful pretend world of the dying.

One day, they decided that Frau Bünden had died. They carried her, wrapped in a torn rug, on a wicker recliner, to the outhouse. Its door was hanging on one hinge and they pushed this and went in. They put Frau Bünden down. The space in which they found themselves was black with coal dust. At the far end of it was a metal door, and when they opened this, they saw that it was the door to an enormous oven, still choked with ash.

'I told you,' said Anton. 'This is where they burned the dead. I suppose they had to burn everything, to stop the infection spreading.'

'Are we going to put Frau Bünden in there?'

'Yes,' said Anton. 'And burn her.'

'We haven't got any matches.'

'We can bring some from the chalet.'

They came back the following day with matches and newspaper. They fetched logs from an old, rotting woodpile. Before they put Frau Bünden into the oven, Anton said, 'Wait, Gustav. You know there's going to be smoke from the chimney if we make a fire? Then, Monsieur or somebody might come and send us away.'

'We can't leave her to rot,' said Gustav.

They stared at the recliner not knowing what they should do. After a few moments, Anton said, 'Listen! Hans is rattling his tambourine. He needs us. We'll burn Frau Bünden some other time.'

'I know what,' suggested Gustav. 'Let's burn all the dead ones on our last day. We can light the fire and then just run back to the chalet.'

'How many dead ones are there going to be?' asked Anton.

'We haven't decided,' said Gustav.

They went out onto the veranda, glad to breathe in the scent of the firs and feel the sunlight on their faces. They stood looking down at the village far below and Gustav thought with dismay of the scant time remaining in Davos, and of his miserable return to the apartment on Unter der Egg. On an impulse – not knowing that he was going to do this – he turned to Anton and said, 'I don't want to go home. Something bad happens there.'

'What happens?'

'It's a secret, right? I've never told anyone and you must never tell a single other soul.'

'I won't. Don't look so panicked, Gustav.'

'All right. *Swear* you won't tell?'

'I swear.'

'OK, it's this, then. There's a man in our block, Ludwig, who tries to make me touch him.'

'Tries to make you touch him?'

'Yes. Touch his penis. I hate him. It makes me feel disgusting.'

Anton looked hard at Gustav. 'Did you do it?' he asked. 'Did you touch his dick?'

'No. I never would. I wish he was dead.'

'All right,' said Anton. 'Let's kill him. What's his name? Ludwig? We'll give him TB and let him die and then burn him.'

'Promise you won't tell, Anton?'

'Of course I won't. I've sworn, haven't I? But Ludwig's got to die.'

They selected another recliner. They put a badly stained mattress onto it and threw down a torn piece of grey fabric, which might once have been part of a curtain.

'There you are,' said Anton. 'Ludwig.'

Anton put the stethoscope in his ears and bent down towards Ludwig, to listen to the murmur of his lungs. 'Ah,' he said, after a while, 'I'm sorry to tell you, Ludwig, there is no improvement. Doctor Perle, is there any of Ludwig's special medicine left?'

'No,' said Doctor Perle. 'None. I can order more from Geneva, but I'm afraid it will arrive too late.'

'Did you hear that, Ludwig?' said Doctor Zwiebel. 'What we suggest is that you prepare yourself for death.'

At this moment, the sun went in. The rag covering Ludwig became a dark shadow, seemingly without form.

Gustav shivered. 'If we're going to kill Ludwig,' he said, 'I think Hans should be saved.'

On their last day, they lit the fire in the oven. They tried to put Frau Bünden into the oven, lying dead on her bamboo recliner, but the recliner wouldn't fit through the oven door, so they took her off the bed, wrapped in her rug, and threw her in. The wool rug seemed greedy for the flame and hissed and crackled like a firework.

Then Anton took an axe they'd found near the woodpile and began to break up the recliner.

'Why are you doing that?' asked Gustav.

'You'll see. It's clever. The bamboo stalks will look like human bones, then we'll have proper bodies to burn.'

It was hard work. They took it in turns to heft the axe. Then they arranged the bamboo pieces, still joined here and there to the wickerwork threads, into skeletal patterns. They looked strangely real, with their sad sinews of wicker hanging off them, representing all that remained of their emaciated flesh.

'They're good,' said Gustav. 'Very good, Anton. Except they've got no heads.'

It was at this moment that they heard, still some distance away, the sound of a fire engine's siren.

'*Scheisse!*' said Anton. 'They'll find us and cart us off to prison. Never mind about the heads. Let's call this one Ludwig and put him in, and then we'll run.'

They took up the bamboo skeleton and hurled it in, piece by piece.

'Die, Ludwig!' cried Anton.

'Die, Ludwig!' repeated Gustav.

The siren sound was very near now. Anton and Gustav ran out of the Sanatorium of Sankt Alban and down the forest path, then catapulted themselves into the undergrowth of the woods and hid there, waiting for the fire engine to pass. They clung together, afraid, yet filled with exaltation. They could hear each other's hearts beating.

It was only after a while that Gustav remembered Hans, still lying on the veranda. 'What about Hans?' he whispered.

'We can't go back,' said Anton. 'We have to pretend Hans just walked out of there.'

'Without his tambourine?'

'Yes.'

Gustav was silent for a moment, then he said, 'We didn't say goodbye to him, Anton. And I know I'm going to think about the tambourine. Aren't you? I'm just going to imagine it being there for evermore.'

# Part Two

# Schwingfest

## *Matzlingen, 1937*

Europe is moving, slowly, almost blindly, like a sleepwalker, towards catastrophe. But in the villages of Mittelland, the calendar of feast days and festivals unrolls through a fine untroubled summer. The valleys, with their plainchant of cowbells, lie half sleeping in the sun. The rivers, fed by snowmelt and spring rain, bubble innocently along, in their eternal, gossipy conversations.

Emilie Albrecht, twenty years old – not yet Emilie Perle – goes with her friend Sofie Moritz to a Schwingfest, held on National Day, outside Matzlingen. A great crowd has gathered here. Tables are set out with jugs of beer and sausages are grilled over wood fires. A band plays, the musicians already sweating in their smart uniforms. Some of the crowd, wearing their National Dress with pride, dance in little preordained circles, to soft applause. But it is the Schwingers, men of strength and substance wrestling in a makeshift arena, surrounded by gentle grass slopes, who are the main attraction, the heroes of the day.

Emilie and Sofie wear long, full skirts with embroidered aprons and gauzy blouses. Their smooth skin is tanned and freckled by the August sun. Their blue eyes shine with laughter as they watch the Schwingers slugging it out in the sawdust, shoulder to shoulder, thigh pressing against thigh, faces and arms streaked with sand and sweat. They cry out with delight as one of the Schwingers pounces on his opponent and lifts him by his linen shorts and swings him up into the air, with the seeming power of a prehistoric beast, and lets him fall sideways, pinning him to the ground with all his magnificent weight.

A cheer goes up. Emilie and Sofie clap and laugh. How sweetly foolish and yet how strong, how determined, how *male* the Schwingers are! And how magnificent it might be to be enveloped by their arms, to breathe their sweat, to discover an animal lust in their faces. The young women look at each other and nod, yes, we would like this one day, to be lifted out of our virgin lives, to be carried off as a giant might carry off a princess in the old fairy tales, and then to know, at last, the unspeakable thing.

Another bout begins. The scores are marked up by the judges. The two wrestlers writhe and lunge in the dust, each with his crowd of supporters to cheer him on. The August sun is so high in the sky, there are almost no shadows; the scene is pure colour and movement and unquantifiable human joy.

It's well known in Switzerland that a Schwingfest clutches at the heart, that it invariably sends everybody a little crazy for a brief afternoon. Who invented this sport? Nobody cares. It's older than time, and time has packed it with patriotic significance and sexual charge. Its excitement is a contagion that will grow throughout the day and explode at dusk with fireworks. Only a few will resist.

Now, Emilie and Sofie hold their breath, waiting for the next lift, the next swing, the next annihilating fall. They want it never to end. They've bought beer and sausages, wrapped in red-and-white-chequered paper. They are drunk on the beer, on the August sunlight, on the thrill of Swiss National Day, on the knowledge of their own youth and prettiness. They don't care if their lips are oily with sausage grease. They don't care, either, if their underwear, in that place between their legs – a place they have been told never to speak of – is damp. They lean in together and whisper. They speak, shockingly, of that forbidden place, and this excites them further. They have to mask their wickedness with laughter.

So she is ready, then. She is ready when, as the sun tilts, Erich Perle, crowned Schwinger Champion of the afternoon, comes towards her, carrying a jug of beer. He's a well-built, good-looking man with thick brown hair and kind eyes. She is ready, exactly where she sits now, on a grassy bank, a little drowsy, but still full of her dreams. She is ready for all that is going to happen.

She tells him her name is Emilie Albrecht and he tells her his name is Erich Perle and that he is Assistant Police Chief in Matzlingen. For some reason – and this moves her more than she can express – he tells her his age: thirty-four.

Erich Perle.

She looks up at him. She wants to be his wife. She wants to be Frau Perle. She wants to lie on a white bed with him. She wants his children. All this she knows, almost before he has sat down beside her and poured beer for her and Sofie.

But then, it seems – and this is surely wrong and wasn't meant to happen? – it is Sofie he keeps looking at. Sofie and Emilie both work at the Gasthaus Helvetia in Matzlingen and Erich says to Sofie, 'Oh, what a coincidence. We have our annual Police Department lunch at the Gasthaus Helvetia. I think I may have seen you there.'

'I don't think so,' smiles Sofie. 'Emilie and I are only maids.'

'Ah, maids . . .' he says with a twinkle in his eye. 'And are you maidens, too?'

'I don't know how you can dare to ask us that!' says Sofie. 'It's very impertinent, you know.'

'Of course it is. But – didn't you hear – the Schwingfest Champion is allowed to do anything he likes on this day, just until dusk.'

'Do anything he likes? We didn't know that, did we, Emilie?'

'No. Does that mean you could kill someone, if you wanted to?'

'I suppose I could. But then I would have to arrest myself.'

They laugh. Sofie is gazing at his laughing mouth. She asks him to tell them what it's like, wrestling in sawdust, lifting another man into the air and hurling him down.

'Oh,' he says, 'it's enthralling. Ninety per cent of police business is very dull. We all long to lift other men into the air and hurl them down!'

'Don't you like being a policeman, then?' asks Sofie.

He swigs beer. A faint line of white foam remains on his lips. Emilie lies back on the grass and closes her eyes. She imagines Erich Perle leaning down to kiss her, the scent of him becoming stronger and stronger until at last his mouth is on hers.

But he doesn't lean down. He starts talking to Sofie about his work. He says, 'The task of a police officer in Switzerland isn't really very onerous.'

'What's "onerous"?' asks Sofie.

'Burdensome or difficult. The reason police work isn't very onerous is because the Swiss *enjoy* obeying the law. On the whole, unless a law is felt to be unjust, they prefer to obey it. When I joined the force, I was told in one of the lectures that Switzerland is a country where people *have mastery over themselves.* In many other countries, this mastery doesn't obtain.'

Emilie opens her eyes. Squinting against the bright sunlight, she can see Erich's profile and Sofie's beyond it. It makes her smile to think that she has no *mastery over herself* when it comes to this man. Virgin though she is, she would go with him to the woods, now, this moment, and let him do the act, the act complete that she has been warned never, never to do until she is married. She knows it would hurt, but that the pain of it, with him, would be a beautiful kind of pain.

But then she sees something dismaying: Erich Perle has put his arm around Sofie. Emilie knows that Sofie is prettier than she is. And Sofie's voice has a little crack in it that men find irresistible. The manager at the Gasthaus Helvetia is ridiculously smitten with her, and it seems that Erich Perle might be going to fall for her, too.

*Mastery*, Emilie thinks. That was the word he used. I must master the situation. I must save it. On the next few minutes depends the rest of my life.

With her eyes still closed, she says, 'Herr Perle, you said that you, as the Schwinger Champion, could do anything you liked this afternoon, didn't you?'

'Yes. I did.'

'Could that *anything* include kissing me?'

She hears Sofie's shocked intake of breath. Silence from Erich

Perle. Emilie opens her eyes. Erich has turned away from Sofie and is looking down at her.

*Troubled*, Emilie thought afterwards. That was how he looked after she'd said these brazen words.

She waits.

'It could include it,' he says in a soft voice.

'Or,' says Emilie, 'perhaps you don't want to?'

'On the contrary . . .'

'Emilie,' says Sofie, 'you've had quite a lot of beer . . .'

'I know,' says Emilie. 'I have. Otherwise I probably wouldn't have had the courage to say what I feel, but what I feel is that I would like Herr Perle to kiss me. Men say what they feel; why can't women?'

She knows that the kiss will be fleeting, just a courteous touch of Erich's lips on hers. But what she does, when she feels him come near, is to reach up and pull him towards her and when his mouth reaches hers, she opens it. So then she feels him respond, excited, perhaps, by her shocking, unmaidenly behaviour. The kiss becomes long and deep and hard. She holds him to her, never wanting to let him go.

Later in the evening, there are fireworks. A little drunk, tired now by the thrills of the day, some staggering about, some huddled together in maudlin embraces, the crowds tilt their faces and send gasps of wonder into the air. Children who have fallen asleep are woken for the spectacle. Schwingfests in Matzlingen seldom happen except on Swiss National Day. A year will pass before all this joy can be shared again. The children are being asked to remember it.

The fireworks are impressive. Proper money has been raised. This is a small town showing the people its coffers and its civic pride. And how much, how violently, Emilie would like to have Erich Perle, Assistant Police Chief, by her side as the starbursts of violet and yellow explode across the fading sky. But Erich has had to leave. It may be Swiss National Day, he has told her, but the police rota has to be kept and he is on evening duty.

As he left, taking her hand and kissing it very formally, he said to Emilie, 'Perhaps I will see you again, Fräulein?'

She didn't like 'perhaps'. And she wanted him to say her name, not call her 'Fräulein', like the thoughtless and condescending guests, whose rooms she cleans at the Gasthaus Helvetia. She turned to Sofie and clutched at her arm as Erich walked away from her into the dusk. 'I know this sounds far-fetched,' she said, 'but I know I'm going to die if I can't have Erich Perle.'

'Have him how?'

'As my husband.'

Sofie faced her friend. 'Don't be ridiculous, Emilie. He's thirty-four. Do you think he doesn't have a girlfriend already? He might even be married.'

'No,' said Emilie. 'If he was married, he wouldn't have said he'd see me again.'

'He said he *might* see you again.'

'And I could feel it in his kiss. Passion.'

'He was just fired up by winning the Schwinger Competition. Men love winning things. But also, he had no option, the way you tugged him down. I thought that was quite shocking, if you want my opinion.'

'I don't want your opinion. All I want is a future with Erich Perle.'

Emilie knows the Police Headquarters in Matzlingen, an old stuccoed building in the centre of the town, its windows in need of painting, its entrance door heavily reinforced with ornamental metalwork, a huge Swiss flag above the portal. And she decides now that, if Erich doesn't turn up at the Gasthaus Helvetia in the coming week, she will go to the police building to find him.

Go to find him? Go brazenly in and call this man, this *stranger*, to her? And then what? Take him back to her tiny maid's room in the attic of the Gasthaus Helvetia? Open her body to all that he might wish to do?

Emilie doesn't recognise these schemes as belonging to the person she has been for twenty years – obedient, virginal, an innocent with soft blonde hair and the small breasts of a girl – a maiden. She knows that she has been transfigured.

Is this transfiguration visible? Emilie takes off her clothes and looks at herself in the narrow mirror, in front of which she puts on her maid's uniform each morning. She touches her pubis and is in an instant aroused by the sight of her hand there. Surely, she thinks, if she can arouse herself so easily, she can become an object of desire?

# Fribourgstrasse

## *Matzlingen, 1937–38*

It seems that Erich Perle *does* already have a girlfriend. The girlfriend is a librarian. Sofie has found this out.

It's difficult, then, for Emilie to concentrate on her work as a chambermaid. She feels her lowly state, her lack of education and knowledge about the world. She has difficulty eating and sleeping. It's as if she has been bereaved.

Then, one evening in September, there is a knock at the door of her room. Emilie is lying on her bed, wearing a white nightdress, reading her magazines. When she opens the door and finds Erich Perle standing in the narrow corridor, she bursts into tears.

He comes into the room and takes her in his arms. He smoothes away her tears with his wide, tobacco-scented hand. He lays her gently on the bed and begins to kiss her. She doesn't want him to speak.

By the time they are married, in December 1937, Emilie is pregnant. They tell no one yet. They plan to name the baby Gustav, after Erich's father, who worked in a sawmill and severed his own hand in the machinery and died in 1931 before he could reach hospital. In their whispered night-time conversations, 'baby Gustav' is held tenderly in their minds; baby Gustav will be born into the world on the tide of their passion, baby Gustav will be a breathing embodiment of their human love.

Married now, Erich Perle has the right to a larger apartment, under Police Rules. So they move into Fribourgstrasse, number

61, an airy first-floor flat with iron balconies and French windows and a back kitchen large enough for a dining table. There is a second bedroom, which will be baby Gustav's room and Emilie buys a crib for him and a rocking horse she finds in the Matzlingen Saturday market, and a family of toy penguins. She and Erich stand at the door of the room and sigh with pride. They look forward to the months passing and the arrival of June, when baby Gustav will be born. Erich strokes Emilie's breasts, now plumped out and sacred to him, both as an object of his continuing desire and as the source of the life-giving milk that will nourish his son.

So sweet has Emilie Perle's life now become that she has no wish to think about the things that are happening outside Switzerland. She knows that, sometimes, when a great storm appears on the horizon, it doesn't break, but gradually moves away and is forgotten. She hopes that all the rumours people are spreading about German aggression will subside – like the storm that never breaks – and everything and everyone will be left in peace. She spends her days knitting baby clothes, planting flowers in tubs on the balconies, learning recipes for meat dishes which will please Erich.

When Erich comes home one day in March 1938 and tells her that the Germans have annexed Austria and sent in Wehrmacht troops to enforce the Anschluss, she looks confused and asks, 'Is that going to matter to us?'

Erich is tired, often irritable. He's been telling her that 'political tensions' are affecting police work. The hours he spends at Police Headquarters have lengthened. Perhaps she hasn't given this enough attention, because now, to her horror, he turns on her. He asks her why she's so ignorant, why she never looks beyond her own needs and comforts, why she alone, in Switzerland, seems unaware that a war may be coming. He stands by the fireplace, shouting at her. He – who has always been so gentle to her and only demonstrated his male power, at her urging, in their passionate lovemaking – now attacks her with words she never, ever thought to hear.

She stands, shivering, by the window. 'Ignorant?' she says. 'Am I?'

'You know you are!' he says. 'At least you've never tried to hide it. But you've got to wake up now, Emilie. Europe is being broken apart. You've got to open your eyes! I refuse to be married to a blind woman!'

*A blind woman.*

What does he mean?

'I'm not blind!' she says.

'Yes, you are. You'll say that you're too young to see the world clearly, perhaps, but I won't accept this as an excuse.'

'I didn't say that –'

'The work I do is very important, Emilie. It affects many, many lives, and it's about to get a lot more difficult. But you never try to understand it, never ask me about it. If someone told you to describe my job, I expect you'd say, "Oh, well, I don't know really . . . I suppose he stands at a road junction directing traffic."'

'No, I wouldn't –'

'Or some such rubbish. Some of my colleagues . . . their wives understand only too well what their jobs entail, and they offer proper support, but you – you don't even try to comprehend it. You never look at a newspaper; you just read your stupid magazines. You bind yourself up in your own ignorance!'

She runs to him, a sob rising in her throat. 'Erich!' she cries. 'Erich! Don't say these things!'

She throws herself into his arms, but instead of catching her and holding her, he casts her away from him. He, who, in the dawn sometimes, needs her so badly that he pushes into her from behind, before she is scarcely awake, now hurls her aside so violently that she staggers and falls backwards onto a low table, then collapses, screaming in pain, onto the floor.

In the hospital, the labour cramps begin.

But it's only March. Baby Gustav isn't ready to be born into the world on a tide of passion. He's a half-formed thing. His little head, with its bright arteries and veins, is no larger than an orange. The ends of his tiny fingers are still blunt.

They take the foetus away – to be burned in the hospital incinerator. Emilie is sedated and arrives back in the ward with a foolish smile on her face and her eyes swollen with weeping.

Erich sits in a chair by the bed, his hands folded, like a

penitent. Emilie doesn't look at him, but up at the ceiling, as though she believes that something lies hidden there, within the fluorescent light. A nurse hands Erich a folded piece of paper. On the paper are written four words: *It was a boy.*

Erich knows that a moment's loss of control, a fearful moment's loss of *self-mastery*, has brought tragedy on his household and that his life will never be the same.

He has gone down on his knees to Emilie, begging forgiveness. But she will not forgive him. She asks him, 'How can such a thing ever be forgiven?'

He buys her presents: a soft shawl, a silk bedjacket, a blouse like the one she wore to the long-ago Schwingfest. She thanks him politely and puts them away in a drawer. Then she asks him to take the rocking horse and the toy penguins to the bric-à-brac market and sell them.

He does this obediently. He offers to take Emilie out, to a picture gallery or a tea room, but she doesn't want to go. She knows that, somewhere inside her, is a residue (this is the word she finds – *a residue*) of love for him. But it's as if the people they were only last week – the people who clung together at the door to their baby's room – belonged in a different life and can't be brought back.

In bed, they lie apart. When Erich thinks about the passion they shared such a short time ago, he wants to cry.

Sometimes, he gets up in the middle of the night and dresses himself in his police uniform, then drinks tea and goes out into the dark and walks to Police Headquarters, where the lights are still burning.

Police Chief Roger Erdman is sometimes to be found there at this hour also, poring over stacks of paperwork. Matzlingen is far from the Austrian border, but, since the Anschluss, more and more Jewish refugees are arriving, fleeing west, fleeing a persecution which they believe could follow them deep into Switzerland. The Jewish Refugee Assistance Organisation (the Israelitische Flüchtlingshilfe, or 'IF') is trying to work with police departments all over Switzerland, to ensure that these people, who have often escaped across the Austrian-Swiss border with almost nothing, are supported.

But how are they to be supported? The IF (funded in its turn by well-off Jews living in Switzerland) will pay for their subsistence and the police will try to find families to take them in. Without visas, they're not allowed to work, yet work is sometimes found for them. Men, who may have been engineers or doctors in Austria, find themselves digging roadside ditches; women, who once had maids and cooks to order about their comfortable homes, are given public toilets to clean, or matches to sell at street corners.

Police Chief Roger Erdman and Assistant Police Chief Erich Perle toil at their administrative tasks, smoking, pacing the lino floor, trying to keep tiredness at bay, until the dawn comes up. Coffee is brought to them. As the door to their offices opens for the secretary carrying in the coffee tray, they can see beyond the door to the dingy foyer where, on hard benches, the Jews sit and wait. They're not in rags. They're mostly dressed in clothes that were once stylish and of good quality and the women have done their best to comb and pin up their hair, but there is such fear and exhaustion in their eyes that Erich says to Roger Erdman one morning, 'I find it difficult to look at them.'

'I agree,' says Roger. 'Because it could be us on those hard benches. And that's what we're most afraid of – to look out there and see ourselves.'

Back in Fribourgstrasse, Emilie wakes and finds the bed empty. She doesn't care. She hopes Erich has gone out so that she can be alone. She is happiest when alone – if 'happy' can describe her condition. It can't; it is just less exhausting to be by herself.

She lies in a hot bath, looking down at her stomach, once grown large with baby Gustav, now shrunken and flat, and at her breasts, still sometimes leaking milk, and sore and aching. She thinks of things she might do with her day: read her magazines, listen to dance music on the radio, eat some rich cake, lie down again to sleep.

Sometimes, she wonders whether she won't leave Fribourgstrasse, leave Erich, leave Matzlingen and go to live with her mother in her old, isolated chalet in a valley near Basel. But she remembers what life was like there – with no running water, only a handpump in the yard – and how she longed to escape it.

She longed, too, to escape her mother's furious devotion to the Church – her widow's black clothes, her silver crosses, her print of Holbein's *Christ in the Tomb* above the fireplace, her fasts and sorrows, her excoriating bad temper. To go there would be to travel backwards in her life, even to become infantile again, when what she is – the wife of an Assistant Police Chief – still makes her marvel. And yet there is something about this marvellous present tense which no longer feels truthful. The present is gone. She is no one again. She's an ignorant girl. She might as well be making beds and cleaning washbasins in the Gasthaus Helvetia.

Even now, she seldom thinks about the war. Erich – on that terrible day when baby Gustav was lost – shouted at her to 'wake up', but she doesn't want to wake up. Why should she confront more sadness than she already has to endure, hour after hour, day after day? Hasn't she already lost everything that was dear to her? When the news comes on the wireless, she always switches it off.

She thinks about forgiveness.

Somewhere, buried deep inside her, must lie the power to relent, a willingness to take the man she thought she loved so much back into her heart. But she can't find it. She doesn't even know how or where to begin to search.

On the dresser is a photograph of Erich in his police uniform, taken just before she met him. Next to it is a photograph of their wedding. In both pictures, Erich Perle still strikes her as a handsome man. She traces his features with her slender hand. His son, little Gustav, would have inherited this fine and noble face, but Gustav is dead. His limp, half-formed body was burned in the hospital incinerator. How can that ever be forgiven?

# Tea Dance

## *Matzlingen and Davos, 1938*

At the far end of Fribourgstrasse, a new café is about to open. It is called the Café Emilie.

Emilie notices it on her way to the magazine kiosk and she stops for a moment to stare at it. A truck is parked outside it. Men are carrying in bentwood chairs. She tells them her name is Emilie.

'That's nice, Fräulein,' they say. 'Got your own little place, then!'

She peers in. She can see signs that read: *French and Swiss Patisserie. Käseschnitte. Cheese fondue. Ice Cream. Best coffee and hot chocolate. Tea Dancing Saturdays, 15.00h–18.00h.*

'We thought Matzlingen was a backwater,' says one of the men, resting for a moment from his task with the chairs. 'That's what we'd been told in Bern – a town where nothing ever happened. But look at this: tea dancing! Very *à la mode*, as they say in Geneva.'

'Is it?' says Emilie.

'So I heard. I expect you'll be coming along, won't you? D'you think you drink your tea with one hand and hold your partner with the other?'

'I suppose you do.'

'Might be fun, eh? Lots of spilt tea! You could find yourself a nice husband in a smart little café like this.'

Emilie is about to say that she's got a husband, that she seduced him with a kiss at a Schwingfest and they were married five months later, but she doesn't want to think about Erich. She nods to the man and walks on.

Erich has seen the Café Emilie, too. He wonders if his salvation might reside in this place.

One Saturday afternoon, he comes to Emilie and says, 'Put on that new blouse I gave you. We're going out. We're going dancing in the new café.'

Emilie says she doesn't want to go dancing.

'No,' says Erich, 'I know you think you don't. What I promise is that if, after half an hour, you're unhappy and want to come home, we'll come home.'

Emilie tries on the new blouse. But it's too tight. She's been stuffing herself on cake. Her breasts are larger than they were when she was carrying baby Gustav. Her hair is dirty. At twenty-one, she reminds herself of her fifty-year-old mother. She takes off the blouse and throws it on the floor. She locks the door of the bedroom and climbs into bed and closes her eyes. When Erich calls to her, she shouts at him to go away and leave her alone.

Erich asks Roger Erdman, who also has a wife, Lottie, much younger than he is, what can be done to mend Emilie's broken heart.

They are in Roger's office, on their twentieth or twenty-first cigarette of the morning. Outside, more Austrian Jews are waiting to be 'processed' and Roger Erdman wants to say that, really, they haven't got time to discuss Emilie at the moment. There is a meeting scheduled with an IF representative in one hour. Word has come from the Chief of Foreign Policy at the Justice Ministry that the flow of Jewish refugees has got to be 'stemmed by some means' or Switzerland will be over-run. Fear of what is known as *Überjudung* (an over-concentration of Jews, for whom Swiss society has little use) is growing throughout the country. 'But what can we do in Matzlingen?' Roger Erdman has asked. 'We're at the end of a long string. It's up to the Border Police to stop people coming over. But people forget that policemen have human feelings and sympathies. We're not counting machines.'

And now, Roger Erdman's sympathies are touched by how weary and how sad his colleague appears. He knows the story of how Emilie fell and how the baby was lost. He puts down his pen and looks at Erich. He tugs a diary towards him and turns to the month of June. He says quietly, 'Erich, I think I am going to let you have some leave next month. What you must do is take Emilie to the mountains. If anything can help her recover, that will be it.'

Erich thinks for a moment. Then he says, 'How can I take leave now, Roger, when we have all these new responsibilities? I'll be letting you down.'

'Well,' says Roger, 'have you looked at yourself recently? If you don't take some leave, you're going to be ill – and then you really will be letting me down.'

Once, as a young child of about five years old, Emilie went to the mountains with her mother, Irma. Emilie can't remember where it was or how they arrived there. It was winter. The place where they stayed belonged to some relation or other. She remembers a man's clothes and hats, hanging on large iron hooks.

Every day, before breakfast, she and Irma had to bank up a huge pot-bellied stove. Its fire tore into wood like a famished animal tears into a bone. When you opened its little door, it would roar at you like a tiger.

On the ice-blue mornings, Emilie and Irma climbed onto a luge they'd found in the woodshed and went flying down a steep slope, and came to a stop in a silent grove of trees, where the only sound was the soft drip-drip of the snowmelt from the pine branches. Emilie remembers some inquisitive little creature – a roe deer or a chamois? – arriving in the grove and staring at her and she stared back. Then, they would tug the luge up the hill once more, in preparation for another flying descent.

What else did they do? Emilie can't remember. So when Erich comes and asks her if she'd like to go to the mountains, this is all she can recall – the famished stove, the man's clothes and hats, the luge, the silent creature on its delicate feet. 'I don't know,' she says.

He produces a picture of a large hotel, the Hotel Alpenrose.

He tells her it's in Davos, and they are going to stay there for five days.

She stares at the hotel, with a view of the mountains behind. She wants to say that it looks too grand for them, but Erich has anticipated some protest from her and cuts her off. 'Roger Erdman has been to Davos,' he says, 'and he's stayed in this very hotel. He tells me that if we're ever going to try to be happy again, this is a good place to start.'

It feels to Emilie like a different world – one to which only the rich could belong.

In their hotel room, net curtains move gracefully at the windows. There is a jug of peonies on the dressing table. The bedcover is silk damask. Emilie hangs up her few summer dresses in a grand wardrobe which smells of camphor.

They go out onto an ironwork balcony, decorated with pots of red geraniums, and stare up at the mountains and breathe in the sunshine and the scented air. They see a huge bird, which might be an eagle, turning in the empty sky. Erich has brought along a camera, borrowed from Roger Erdman, and he takes a picture of the view. He wants to include the eagle in the photograph. He turns the viewfinder this way and that, but can't manage to capture the bird.

It's late afternoon on the day of their arrival and they're both hungry. They stroll down a quiet street and hear the sound of a little orchestra. It comes from a café where, in a small space behind the tables, elderly couples are dancing. They go in. Emilie stares at the dancers and is touched by their grace. All are in their seventies or eighties and yet they keep perfect time to the steady beat of the music. They hold their elbows high and keep their backs straight.

Erich and Emilie sit at a table and order lemonade and apfelstrüdel. They don't talk, but eat and drink and watch the dancers. The music holds them in a fragile spell. And Emilie finds herself thinking, I don't want to grow old – as old as these people – without having lived a proper life. She raises her head and looks at her husband. She's almost surprised to find him still there. She's become so used to wanting to be alone, it's as though she expected, every day, to look up and find him gone. But he hasn't gone. He's sitting calmly by her side, finishing his lemonade and lighting a cigarette. Sunlight from the café window touches his cheek and puts glints of chestnut into his brown hair.

After a while, she says, 'Can we dance now?'

Erich says nothing. He puts out his cigarette. Then he gets up and bows to her formally and holds out his hand and she takes it and they move onto the dance floor. The other dancers nod to them and say 'Grüezi' and they reply 'Grüezi, grüezi to you all', and the dance band mellow their sound into a slow sweet number for the young strangers who have joined the throng.

They hold themselves as upright and as correct as the others. Erich leads Emilie with a firm hand round her waist. And Emilie thinks, if we could just go on like this, in this slow, formal dance, go on and on like this, without the need to speak, without the need to pause, then in the end – if an end had to come – all might be well.

She lets her head move forward, closer and closer to Erich, until her cheek is resting against his.

Davos.

Emilie knows it's where people still come to be healed of a disease that is killing them. She knows also that many of them die. There's a big graveyard lower down the valley, which she would like to visit.

She lies awake in the large bed, while Erich sleeps. She looks at his face, half seen in the shadowy room, and understands, in a way she has not understood before, how tired he is, how sorrowful, how damaged by what happened to them, but also by the work he's trying to do, to help people who have been driven from their country and from almost everything that was beloved to them.

She whispers to herself, 'He is a good man.' She wants to go and tell the Jewish refugees who throng Police Headquarters, 'This man will help you. You're lucky to have found him. He will help you, where hundreds of others might turn you away.'

Then she wakes him. She knows this is unkind; he needs a sound sleep. But she has to tell him, then and there, that she *does* understand what's happening in the world, she's not really an ignorant girl, she knows about suffering – other people's suffering, far worse than her own. She wants to say that she's sorry.

Erich holds her close to him. He strokes her hair. He begins to weep, and he weeps for a long time.

# Liebermann

## *Matzlingen, 1938*

On August 18th a directive comes from the Swiss Justice Ministry in Bern that all German, Austrian and French Jews attempting to get to the safety of Switzerland after this date are to be sent back.

Roger Erdman says to Erich, 'This probably means an end to these people arriving in Matzlingen. They'll be picked up and turned around long before they get this far.'

Erich says, 'I don't think it necessarily means an end. The IF here is very active and well supported and word of this will have gone out to the border crossings. Some may get through, Roger. Then, what are we supposed to do?'

Roger Erdman picks up a pencil and holds it between his hands, as though measuring something in the opposite corner of the room. 'Speaking as a policeman,' he says, 'I will have to follow the Justice Ministry directive. Speaking as a man, I can't follow it. Resolve my dilemma if you can.'

The arrival of Jewish refugees (those who crossed into Switzerland before August 18th) continues for a while, then slows, then stops. Every day, Roger and Erich look out into the foyer where the men and women used to wait and sees only empty benches. They imagine a convoy of exhausted people, carrying flimsy bags and bundles, cradling their children, being escorted back over the border into Austria, and from there being sent to camps, or – rumour has it – taken away to be killed. Roger says one morning, 'Thank God we're not at St Gallen, or in Basel, for that matter.

We'd be turning these people away. We'd be responsible for their deaths.'

But Roger Erdman is ill. He's taken into hospital for tests on his liver. The tests are 'inconclusive' and Roger tells Lottie that he's just suffering from strain and exhaustion. He goes home, but he has difficulty keeping food down and is ordered to stay away from work. He tells Erich that he's sorry to be 'shirking my duty', but adds, 'At least the problems of helping the Jews seems to be over, for now.'

But it's not over.

One morning, when Erich gets into Police Headquarters, he sees a man waiting on the benches. As Erich passes through the foyer on the way to his office, the man gets up and says, 'Herr Chief of Police, may I see you urgently? The IF have sent me. I must tell you my story, please.'

Erich calls the man into his office. He asks for a glass of water to be brought to him. He notes the man's worn boots and the exhaustion in his face. He tells him gently that he is not the Chief of Police, merely his Assistant.

'But have you got authority?' asks the man. 'I cannot tell my story more than once, sir. I am too tired.'

'I have authority,' says Erich. 'Herr Chief of Police Erdman is ill at the present time so I am acting on his behalf.'

The man gulps the water. He stammers out that the IF didn't treat him very well, offering him nothing. He'd been told the IF people would be his saviours, that he would be safe once he reached them, but he was wrong. 'They offered me nothing,' he says, 'because they're afraid.'

'Afraid of what?'

'Of the Bern directive about dates. My name is Liebermann. Jakob Liebermann. But I beg you, Herr Assistant Police Chief, don't send me away. My wife and my son are already here in Switzerland. My son is only four. They need me. I sent them on ahead. I thought there would be time enough for me to obtain some money and then follow them. And then the diktat of the 18th of August came out of the blue. I am here to beg you not to send me back.'

Erich examines Liebermann's passport. He notes that he is

thirty-six, the same age as himself. His profession is written down as 'Doctor'. He looks up and says, 'Will you tell me the date that you entered Switzerland, please, Herr Liebermann?'

Liebermann gets up and leans towards Erich, over the cluttered surface of the desk. 'I could tell you anything, *anything*,' he says, 'and you wouldn't know! But the mistake I made was to tell the IF that I crossed on the 26th of August. I came over the border at Diepoldsau – that marshy crossing. I have no visa. I thought the IF would turn a blind eye. Why do they exist, if not to help us? But they escorted me here. They told me my entry must be registered with the police, or I can have no future, no work in Switzerland, nothing, not even IF charity, that's what they said. They say I am a "Police Problem".'

Erich feels his own heart beating very fast. He wishes he could get up and walk into Roger's office and give the 'Police Problem' to him. But Roger Erdman isn't there.

He asks Jakob Liebermann to sit down. He hears a tremble in his own voice as he speaks. He reaches into his desk drawer and brings out the registration form that he must complete. He sets it in front of him, next to Liebermann's passport, but doesn't pick up his pen. He says, 'Tell me what kind of doctor you are.'

'Oh,' says Liebermann, 'well, I was in general practice. In Bludenz. I had hopes of becoming a surgeon. I would like to save lives.'

'Perhaps you will still do that – become a surgeon?'

'Sir, I will become *nothing* if you send me back! I will be dead. My boy will have no father! Look at me! I'm an honest man, a man who wants to do good in the world. I've committed no crime: only the "crime" of being Jewish. My son's name is Daniel. If you send me back, you're throwing me and my boy to the lions.'

Erich folds his hands together. He remembers that he himself might have been a father by now, the father of little Gustav, who would have been four months old. Supposing he, Erich, had died and not Gustav? Supposing Emilie were all alone with her child, driven from her home, driven from her country . . .

He picks up his pen. He says quietly, 'I am going to put down that your arrival date in Switzerland was the 16th of August. Tell the IF that you were confused about dates – between the 16th and the 26th. And there may even have been some confusions of language, as you speak High German and the IF people would have talked to you in Swiss German. Did they?'

'Yes, sir, they did.'

'Well, there you are. Confusions can sometimes arise. But go back to them and explain that we have sorted it out in this office. All right?'

For a moment, Jakob Liebermann looks dumbfounded. Then, he opens wide his arms. 'God will bless you, Herr Assistant Police Chief!' he says. 'God will give you a long and happy life!'

He leans over the desk and pulls Erich to him in an awkward embrace and Erich can smell the sweat of travel on him and feel the roughness of his unshaved cheek against his ear.

Erich tells nobody what he's done. Certainly not Emilie, who, since Davos, has let Erich resume their lovemaking, whispering to him that she wants to try again for a child, and Erich doesn't want to risk upsetting her. If, sometimes, he's afraid that he could be punished for disobeying a national directive, he tries to set this worry aside. He reasons that he disobeyed it *in only one case.*

He visits Roger Erdman, who is back in hospital. Roger looks very thin. His skin is waxy and white. He tells Erich that there is going to be an operation on his colon, and after that, the doctors tell him that he'll be well again. Then, he asks, 'How is everything at HQ?'

'All right,' says Erich.

'What about the . . . erm . . . August dilemma?'

'As you predicted, Roger, Jews no longer get as far as Matzlingen. St Gallen has to decide what to do.'

'What do they decide? Have you heard?'

'I've heard that the directive has been obeyed.'

Roger closes his eyes. 'I'm still not sure,' he says, 'what we would have done. But thank goodness the thing has gone away.'

But of course it hasn't gone away.

Through Jakob Liebermann, word has been passed to other Jews who have slipped into Switzerland after August 18th: 'Try to make it to Matzlingen. There's an Assistant Police Chief there who will falsify the registration form. He'll do it even without a bribe – because he is a good man. Go to him first, not to the IF. His name is Erich Perle.'

The registration forms that Erich has falsified pile up. Date of entry: August 14th. Date of entry: August 12th. Date of entry: August 9th . . . But as August becomes September and a date is set for Roger Erdman's return to work, Erich has to whisper to the Jews who come to him, 'I'll do it for you. Just this once. But pass the word, when my Chief of Police returns on the 30th of September, it will have to end. He will not sanction it.'

Roger has lost so much weight that his police uniform no longer fits him. He says to Erich, 'I look ridiculous. I look like an idiot in fancy dress.'

Erich tells him he must begin to eat well again and invites him and Lottie to dinner. Emilie says she will cook roast pork and knödel with red cabbage, followed by Nusstorte, her speciality dessert. They will serve a strong French red wine, which Erich can buy cheaply and in quantity from a former colleague at the Police Academy, who opines to Erich that 'wine smells of the earth and police work smells of the sewer'.

The table in the sitting room of the apartment at Fribourgstrasse 61 is set with a lace cloth. It's a warm autumn evening – too warm to light a fire in the grate – and the French windows are open.

In recent days, Erich Perle's heart has started to beat faster. He can't seem to control it. He's aware of it all the time – the thump of blood in his ears, an agitated ticking in his wrist – and he knows it's because he's afraid. He finds himself seeking out the familiar and the ordinary, to soothe this frantic heart. The gentle sound of traffic passing down Fribourgstrasse is reassuring, and he tells himself that nothing has changed in Matzlingen if the cars and scooters are going by at their usual, obedient pace. All that has changed is within himself. He is no longer the man he thought he was, the kind of man who reveres the laws of his country – his beloved Switzerland, whose moral code is unimpeachably high – and who would never break them. He's now a criminal.

He keeps telling himself that it all happened because of Liebermann, because of Erich's compassion for a man who only longed to join his little family, who – if he had been sent back into Austria – would have faced death. Wouldn't other men – even other policemen – have been moved to falsify documents, to break the law, to save a man who had done nothing wrong? Surely Erich's crime is rendered neutral by the saving of souls? Isn't it?

But he can't get his mind off what he's done. He wonders if he should have saved Liebermann alone, but sent all the others who followed him back to the border, steeling himself not to think about their likely fate. The particularity of Liebermann was what informed his decision. He was moved. He was weakened by his compassion for a man his own age, with a little son named Daniel. And surely one date falsification would never have been detected? But the stack of false dates is going to come to light, one way or another. Erich now understands that he's put his career – even his life – in jeopardy.

Before Roger and Lottie arrive for dinner, Erich opens one of the bottles of red wine. Emilie is basting the roast pork, in the kitchen. Erich stands by the French windows, drinking and smoking a cigar. He feels the wine begin to calm his heartbeat, so he pours another glass. By the time Roger and Lottie arrive, he has drunk four glasses very fast and has begun to be unsteady on his feet, as though the salon of the apartment had become a seagoing yacht, headed suddenly out of harbour.

But the sensation is not unpleasant. It feels to him that this altered Erich, this unsteady person on a drifting boat, has been relieved of the normal obligation to behave with decorum. He then thinks about the word 'decorum' and finds it ludicrous.

He says aloud that everybody's responsibility to behave well this evening has been nullified. '*Nullified!* Another stupid word! But it will serve.'

He sees Lottie look anxiously at Roger. He notices, as though for the first time, how very pretty Lottie Erdman is and he says to Roger, 'I hope that now you're well again, Roger, you're not neglecting Lottie.'

'What do you mean?' asks Roger.

'Lottie is a gem. She is a Rhinemaiden! I hope you're taking care of her.'

'Of course I am.'

'In every way. I mean in bed as well.'

Lottie blushes, touches her breasts in a flustered gesture, gives Erich a shy smile. Roger shakes his head with exasperation. 'I'll forgive you for saying that, Erich, because I think you've had quite a lot of wine already, but what Lottie and I do in bed is none of your concern.'

Erich fumbles to relight his cigar, which has gone out. '*Concern!*' he says, choking on the first puff. 'Very far from a stupid word! On the contrary, a thoughtful word. But where does "concern" begin and end? My friends, that is *the* great question of our times: how far are we to go, in showing concern for our fellow human beings? We strive for indifference. As members of the police we are *taught* to feel it. But is not indifference a moral crime?'

At this moment, before Roger or Lottie can attempt any reply to this, Emilie comes in to say that the dinner is ready. The aroma of the roasted pork now perfumes the air. Erich loves pork. The crunch of crisp pork crackling in his mouth, releasing the fatty juices within it, has, he thinks, an almost sexual pleasure about it. But tonight he feels a sudden dismay at the idea of the four of them sitting round their comfortable table, gobbling pork and knödel. He thinks of Liebermann and his little family (who would never have eaten pork in their lives) and wonders where they are and if the IF have helped them, or if they're starving in the mountains somewhere.

He follows his guests obediently to the table. Emilie's cheeks are bright red from the heat of the kitchen and he thinks how this redness doesn't suit her and how, tonight, he would like to make love to the adorable Lottie Erdman. He gets an erection at the mere idea of it and sits down abruptly, covering his lap with a linen table napkin. He pours wine for Lottie, gazing, as he does so, at her large breasts and inadvertently spilling wine onto the lace cloth.

'Be careful, Erich!' says Emilie.

He doesn't apologise. He thinks wearily how many times he has had to apologise in his recent life and how tired he is of always being in the wrong. As he receives his plate of food, before he's touched a morsel of it, he blurts out, 'You should all know that, really and truly, I am fed up with thinking of myself as a criminal!'

They stare at him. Lottie looks anxiously at Roger. Emilie dabs her hot face with her napkin.

'Please start your supper,' she says.

'Or not,' says Erich. 'Don't start it! Don't let yourselves enjoy the crackling. Think of the crunch of it as bones breaking. Human bones . . .'

Roger puts down his knife and fork. He says calmly, 'What is the matter, Erich?'

'I told you,' says Erich. 'I'm tired of my actions being criminalised. I did what any man – any man who has an ounce of compassion in his heart – would do. If you'd been there, Roger, you would have done it. But you didn't see Liebermann. You didn't see his sorrow. Why should he be made to abandon his family?'

'Who is Liebermann?'

'A doctor. A Jew. With a wife and child already in Switzerland. He missed the entry deadline by eight days. Eight days! And the IF thought I would send him back into Austria – send him back to die. I expect they could hear his bones crunching! But they reckoned without me. They reckoned without Erich Perle, the criminal!'

There is silence in the room. Steam from the plates of rich food still rises. And Erich then realises abruptly that he is going to be sick. He stands up and lurches out of the room, but doesn't reach the lavatory and vomits in the hallway.

Lottie goes very white. Emilie gets up to go to help Erich. As she reaches the door, Roger says quietly to her, 'I understand what he's done. I understand.'

# Theft

## *Matzlingen, 1939*

For several months, he seems to be safe, but then in May 1939 two security officers from the Justice Ministry in Bern arrive at Matzlingen Police Headquarters.

Why two? Erich wants to ask. Did somebody tell Bern that this man, this loyal Assistant Police Chief, might be violent, might need restraint?

He is taken to the Interrogation Room, walking past the benches where the Jews sat and waited to learn their fate. It is hot and airless in the room. Erich wipes sweat off his brow and asks for a window to be opened, but one of the Justice Ministry men says, 'There's no need. This won't take long.'

Heat seems to exacerbate the too-fast oscillation of Erich's heart. Sometimes, there is an accompaniment to the blood-beat and this is an aureole of pain, spreading across Erich's chest and up into his throat, threatening to choke him. Now, he wants to loosen his tie, but he knows that he must remain 'correct' in front of these officials.

He waits. Then, he sees arrive in front of him, on the scarred wooden table, a stack of refugee registration forms, bearing the falsified August dates and his signature beneath.

'There you are,' says the older of the officers. 'Will you confirm, please, that it is your signature on these forms?'

Erich stares at the forms. He can remember how his hand always shook as he signed them. Images of the people begging him to help them filter through his mind: women with huge, terrified eyes, girls on the threshold of beauty, grandfathers cradling young children to their chests, men weeping with joy and disbelief when the false dates were written in . . .

Erich clears his throat. Sweat runs down his back.

'Yes,' he says. 'This is my signature.'

'Good,' says the younger man. 'We told you this wouldn't take long. We are here to inform you that, as from this moment, you are suspended from the Police Service. Your crime is the falsification of entry dates into Switzerland of Jewish refugees, to which these forms bear testimony. You may take your personal belongings from your desk, but no police property, of course. We can only add that you may eventually be prosecuted, for Criminal Infringement of a Justice Ministry Directive. This prosecution is currently under consideration. Meanwhile, your pay and your police pension are forfeited, and the minister himself wishes us to convey to you his extreme displeasure.'

Erich thinks of Jakob Liebermann opening wide his arms and saying, 'God will bless you, Herr Assistant Police Chief! God will give you a long and happy life!' and how he, Erich, knew, as he signed Liebermann's form, that this was exactly what he had just signed away – the blessing of God, the long and carefree life . . .

'Please may I ask you one question?' says Erich quietly.

'Certainly. Go ahead.'

'How do you know that these dates are false? Who told you that I falsified them?'

The security officers exchange glances.

'That information is classified,' says the older man. 'All you need to realise is that you have put your country in danger by deliberately flouting its laws.'

'I did not intend to put my country in danger. I was concerned with saving human life.'

'Admirable, in most circumstances. We all have kind hearts, do we not? But Germany will no longer tolerate an open policy in Switzerland towards Jewish refugees. We risk being punished for it by a German invasion. This would be the end for our unique and beautiful land. And people like you will be held responsible. Oh, and by the way, at the end of the month you and your wife will have to vacate your police apartment on Fribourgstrasse.'

'Where are we to go?'

'I've no idea. That's up to you. You will be given two weeks' pay. This was urged upon us by your superior, Herr Police Chief Erdman, and we did not object. We are reasonable men. We suggest you use the money very wisely. But none of that is our responsibility.'

Erich is escorted back to his desk. His police badge is removed and immediately he misses the heaviness of it, as if the metal somehow protected his sick heart. He looks towards Roger Erdman's office, foolishly nurturing some hope that Roger would intervene to save him, but Roger is not in his room.

Outside his own office, in the Communications Room, he can hear the sound of typewriters and quiet conversation: police work going routinely on, as though nobody has noticed what is happening to Assistant Police Chief Erich Perle – nobody has understood that his life is ending.

It is not yet 10 a.m. when Erich leaves Police Headquarters. At the bottom of the steps, he pauses and looks back at the heavy door with its decorated ironwork grille and at the flagpole above it, from which the Swiss flag hangs limp in the May sunshine. And he thinks how much he has loved what these things symbolised. That is the word for it: *love.* Walking in through that ornate door with pride every single morning, as if the door *belonged to him.* And so comfortable in his profession that he sometimes caught himself boasting about it, just as he had boasted about it to Emilie on the day he met her at the Schwingfest.

He carries a few possessions in a paper bag: a photograph of Emilie in Davos, a half-full box of cigars, a desk calendar, a tarnished inkstand.

He begins to walk away from the building. He's still wearing his police uniform. He smiles bleakly to think that even the men from the Justice Ministry baulked at sending him out into the street wearing only his underpants. And he feels grateful that he has been left with this one substantial relic of all his years of service and thinks how sincerely he has deserved this. Yet he knows the world in which people deserve things or do not deserve them is passing away. Europe is at war. Fairness is now becoming a word without meaning.

He can't imagine what words he is going to use to tell Emilie what has happened. He thinks that the right words probably don't exist. He wonders how long it will take for Emilie to realise that they have fallen into poverty in a single day.

She stands by the unlit fire and the sunshine of the May morning bathes the room with flat squares of light.

She wants to say to Erich, 'The man I married was Assistant Police Chief Perle. He told me his age and his rank on our first meeting. How can I be reconciled to any other man but this?'

He looks pathetic to her, standing there with his paper bag – large and foolish. She knows that what is expected of her – what she even expects of herself – is sympathy and comfort, yet she can't bring herself to move from where she stands, facing him, with her fists tightly clenched.

'Well,' she says, 'I hope the Jewish people are satisfied. It was for them that little Gustav died and now it is for them that you've sacrificed what remained of our lives.'

She sees Erich open his mouth to argue with her and then change his mind, and she thinks, good, it's correct that he doesn't try to refute this, because that is the plain truth of it: he put Jewish lives before mine. He cared more about helping strangers than he cares about me.

She wants to walk out of the apartment, walk out into some other life and never return. Yet she thinks, why should I be driven out? Erich should be the one to go. I will stay here and tend my scarlet geraniums and read my magazines and buy French patisseries from the Café Emilie. I will go on as though nothing has happened . . .

But when Erich tells her that they will lose the apartment, she lets all her pent-up anger spill out. She tears at her hair. She falls to her knees and beats with her fists on the hearthrug. She grabs a cushion and rips open its seam and hurls feathers all over herself. She begins scratching her face.

*

Emilie travels to Basel, to the house of her mother, the house with the water pump in the yard, where the grass grows too long in summer and where wolves can sometimes be heard howling in the woods nearby.

Nothing is said about when she will be coming back.

She leaves a few clothes in the wardrobe and an old silver hairbrush on her dressing table. When the taxi arrives to take her to the station, Erich is not there to say goodbye.

Erich finds a small apartment on Unter der Egg. A flower stall just setting up on this road cheers his spirits. The rent is low, but a high deposit is demanded, a sum of money that will take almost everything that remains to Erich.

Though he's uncomfortable about this, he feels he has no choice but to borrow money. He believes that Roger Erdman will lend him the sum required. For Roger feels guilty about what has happened. He's admitted this. He has told Erich that, had he not been in hospital, but there in the office, seated in front of Liebermann, he might have done exactly the same thing. 'We can't know,' he has said to Erich, 'until the moment arrives what choice we are going to make.'

On a Sunday afternoon, Erich walks to Roger's apartment on Grünewaldstrasse. The door is opened by Lottie, whose hair looks wild and who is dressed in a silk peignoir.

'I'm sorry,' says Erich. 'I'm disturbing you.'

'Oh no,' says Lottie, yawning, 'I was just taking a nap, after eating too much chocolate. Roger is in Zurich. It's ridiculous how decadent I become when he's away!'

'I'll leave you in peace – to your decadence! I only came to ask a favour of Roger.'

'No. Come in, Erich. I'm glad you're here. I want to tell you how angry I am about what's happened to you. Come in and I'll make coffee.'

She doesn't dress, but only brushes her hair. She sits beside Erich on a small sofa to pour the coffee and he can smell sweat on her body and chocolate on her breath.

'You must tell us what we can do for you, Erich,' Lottie says. 'Really, we would do anything.'

A clock with a silvery chime strikes four. In the silence that falls after the chimes have ended, Erich remembers the night of his 'confession' and how he'd felt desire for Lottie Erdman. And now, he knows that he's troubled by her again – her abundant blonde hair, her over-large bosom, the wholesomeness she exudes, the delight she seems to take in showing off her body.

He drinks the coffee, but it's too hot. He knows he must hurry it and leave before he does or says anything that he will regret. Lottie yawns again. One side of the silk peignoir falls off her thigh. She makes no attempt to adjust it, and Erich, unable to resist glancing down, realises that she's wearing no panties.

'I heard,' says Lottie, 'that Emilie has gone to stay with her mother.'

'Yes,' says Erich.

'Never a very good sign – going back to the mother,' says Lottie. 'Does it mean your marriage is over?'

'I don't know,' says Erich.

Lottie turns and looks at him. The silky peignoir falls further off her lap.

'Well,' she says, 'given that I'm in such a decadent frame of mind, and given that both Roger and Emilie are so very far away, would it be very wicked to have a little fun? Nothing serious, you know. Just something to take our minds off the world and its ton of sorrows. You're a very handsome man, Erich. I've always thought it. I have dreams about you sometimes, extremely sexy dreams, but of course I never tell Roger. I wait till he's gone to work, then go back to bed and masturbate. Isn't that a hilariously wicked thing to confess?'

Erich can't speak. He knows he should stand up and say goodbye to Lottie and walk out of the apartment. To fuck Roger Erdman's wife would be a disgraceful thing for him to do. But it seems that Lottie – in her *déshabille*, with her chocolate breath, with her face shiny from sleep, with her provocative talk about masturbation – is blithe about everything, as though making love with Erich right now might be the most reasonable, natural and innocent thing in the world.

She gently lifts Erich's hand and puts it between her legs and holds it there, and with the very first touch of him she closes her eyes. At this, all resistance to her is lost. Erich is almost immediately on his knees and his mouth is where his hand was and the smell and taste of Lottie Erdman, on this hot Sunday afternoon, feels more overwhelming to him than the smell and taste of any woman he has ever known.

He stays until dusk. The scent of Lottie is all over his body, but he doesn't want to wash it off. As he leaves, he says, 'Now I'll think about you all the time.'

# Pearl

## *Basel, 1939–40*

Winter comes to the house with the water pump in the yard. Wearing fluffy blue slippers and a woolly dressing gown, Emilie works the pump handle, up and down, up and down, till the tin basin underneath it is full of water. All the while she is doing this, she is cursing. Inside the house, her mother, Irma Albrecht, waits for the water to be brought in and heated, so that she can wash herself.

They are living a sorry life. Basel is a prosperous city, but here, a few kilometres from it, there is poverty. Their nearest neighbour is a pig farmer who feeds his animals almost nothing except food thrown away in household bins. Quite frequently, the animals die of poisoning, or choke to death on a piece of cardboard or the key to a sardine tin.

Emilie's mother chides this neglectful man, but Emilie feels as much pity for herself as she does for the pigs. Irma uses her, as she was always used before she escaped to Matzlingen, as a servant. She has to clean the dilapidated house, do the washing, wind it through an ancient mangle and hang it in the yard. She has to make the beds and scour the tin bath. Her food is meagre.

More and more, as winter comes on, Irma takes to her bed. She orders Emilie to massage her back with a special lavender oil, to ward off muscle fatigue and lung ailments. Emilie's arms ache as she rubs the white, mole-flecked skin. There is a kind of torture in the task, because the sight of Irma's body, just on the threshold of being old, repels her. She dreads becoming like her. But Irma makes her keep on and on. 'Don't pretend you don't know how to do this properly!' she says. 'Rub harder. Do you want your mother to die of winter illnesses?'

Yes. She does. Emilie would like Irma to die. Then, the neglected old house could be sold and she would have money of her own, enough, perhaps, to start a little business in Basel: a flower shop or a small café, with rooms above it for her to live in. She would buy stylish clothes, meet other men, divorce her disgraced husband and marry again. She would conceive another child. She would *have a future.*

All there is now, however, is a succession of days, devoid of all pleasure, devoid of all joy. Irma goes back and forth to church. Emilie reads her magazines. She loves to hear about the lives of film stars. She fantasises about becoming the lover of Charlie Chaplin, caressed by his moustache, seduced by his beautiful eyes. She walks in the woods, listening for the sound of wolves. She digs up carrots and turnips from Irma's garden to keep them both alive. She bakes bread.

Sometimes, in the freezing nights, she dreams about the apartment on Fribourgstrasse: the warmth of it, the sunlight at the French windows, the scarlet flowers. Erich isn't in the dreams, but now and then a pale shadow passes between the window and the door, as though born of sunlight, swiftly fleeing away, and she knows what this is: it is her lost Gustav, her lost son.

Once in a while, Irma and Emilie take the bus to Basel. Irma puts on her best burgundy-coloured coat and hat. They walk down Freie Strasse, past the faded façade of the painted Rathaus, and go into a tea room off Marktplatz, where Irma orders chocolate cake and tea. She never pays for it. When the bill comes, she signs it and gives it back. Emilie has no idea how this arrangement was agreed upon, or how it will end. The café owners, Herr and Frau Mollis, seem forever polite and resigned to Irma's scrawled signatures.

In the café, Emilie looks out for Jews. She's been told that a lot of French Jews are now living in the Basel area, but no one is talking French in the tea room. When they go out into the busy town again, she hopes to see some Jews lying in the street, drunk or destitute, perhaps too weak to beg?

On the corner of Martinsgasse there is a jewellery shop, and when she looks in there one day she sees what she thinks of as a recognisably Jewish face staring back at her, a prosperous-looking man in his fifties, tugging at shirt cuffs secured with heavy gold cufflinks, and she wants to go into the shop and tell him, I lost everything because of you. I want you to know this. I want all of you to know it. I had a beautiful life and now I have a life of poverty and misery – because of you.

But Irma drags her on past the jewellery shop. 'It's time to go home,' she says. 'I need my enema.'

Always, after the cake-eating, there is the ritual of the enema. Irma's body is so used to a poor diet of bread and vegetables that – even though she gobbles the cake like a greedy infant – she believes that 'special arrangements' have to be made to accommodate anything rich or fatty. 'That,' she says, 'is God's punishment.'

So then she has to disappear to the outside lavatory with her rubber tubing and her enema pump and wait in there, in the bitter cold, until her bowels are free of everything they now contain, so that they're ready to 'process' the cake. After that, she is so weak, she has to lie down in bed. Emilie is ordered to bring her broth. Emilie dreads that the next thing to be asked of her will be to administer the enema. And refusing Irma's requests is as impossible now as when she was a girl. The requests are laced with venom. If you refuse, you're bitten by a snake. You could die a fearful death.

Snow falls in the new year, 1940, and Switzerland grows silent, as though listening, in terror, for the sound of advancing armies. The pump in the yard has to be bound with sacking, to stop it freezing. Round the sacking, Irma ties an ancient fox tippet, ragged and scarred. Now, when Emilie looks out at the pump, she imagines a wild animal in the yard, rearing up in terror at finding itself there.

More and more, Emilie dreams of Charlie Chaplin and the palm-lined boulevards of Hollywood, far away, where the war could never, ever reach. She dances with Charlie beside a floodlit swimming pool. He says to her, 'Ah, Emilie, you are just the right height for me. Let's fly over the rainbow together.'

But how long can it be endured, this life with Irma? Emilie

tries not to think about this. For what's the point in thinking about an end to your present sorrows, when you're a prisoner of events, a prisoner of time?

Sometimes, far down the valley, Emilie can hear the voices of children, building snowmen, playing on luges, and she thinks what a joyous sound this is, and how, by this year, 1940, her little Gustav would have been talking and laughing and how she would have had his own small sleigh made for him and how she might have borrowed a docile pony, to pull the sleigh along.

Once again, Emilie and Irma are heading for the town. Irma is wearing her burgundy coat and hat. Emilie suggests going to a different café – just to see if Irma is prepared to pay for their tea, but Irma says crossly, 'Certainly not. That is the only cake God will permit me to eat.'

So they take their usual table by the window. Irma and Emilie eat the chocolate cake and drink the milky tea. Irma cuts her wedge of cake into slices larger than usual and crams these into her mouth. Her thin cheeks bulge out. And Emilie recognises how, in some sad way, her mother *lives* for this, for these five or ten minutes of filling herself with chocolate. A moment of compassion for Irma slides into her heart. She wants to touch her shoulder or stroke her hand, but she holds back from these gestures.

When the cake is finished and Irma asks for the bill, what arrives is a stack of bills, perhaps thirty, or more, signed by Irma, but never paid. They are brought to the table by the café owner, Frau Mollis, who pulls out a chair and sits down.

'I'm sorry, Frau Albrecht,' Frau Mollis says, 'I think we have been very patient with these bills. But you see how many there are now. I am going to ask you to settle them today. That way, you will be free to enjoy your tea and chocolate cake again in the future. I will accept a cheque, if you do not have the ready money.'

'Oh,' says Irma. 'Well, of course I don't have the ready money. How much is owing?'

'Ninety-two francs and ten centimes.'

'So you're pernickety about centimes?'

'I'm just telling you what you owe.'

'I think it's far too much. All that for cake! Ridiculous.'

'You can examine the bills if you want to. My husband and I have added them up very carefully. That is the sum owing.'

Irma stares at Frau Mollis. She shakes her head, as though a mortal insult has just been aimed at her. Then, she reaches up and takes the long hatpin out of her hat and holds it out to Frau Mollis. On the end of the hatpin is a large pearl.

'Here you are, then,' says Irma. 'If you insist, I'll give you this in payment. It belonged to my grandmother. It was bought for her in Paris at the turn of the century. It's worth far more than ninety-two francs and ten centimes.'

Frau Mollis takes the pin. She looks confused. She doesn't examine it closely, but just holds it in her hand.

'I can't accept this,' she says. 'As I've said, I will take a cheque . . .'

'Well,' says Irma, 'I can give you a cheque. But there is no money in my account. Which would you like – a worthless cheque or a valuable pearl?'

Frau Mollis gets up, leaving the pile of bills on the table. She disappears into the kitchen at the back of the café.

Irma sniffs and shakes her head again. 'Very stupid,' she says. 'These are very stupid people.'

Emilie is silent. She remembers the pearl hatpin. As a teenager, she'd found it one day in a drawer in her mother's room, and – among the detritus of old combs, spilt face powder, cigarette ash, tweezers, nail files, pills and clumps of cotton wool – she had thought it an object of wonder. The pearl was so large. Surely no oyster could have produced such a thing? And how had it been attached to the pin?

Thirteen-year-old Emilie had taken one of the steel nail files and with the pointy tip had begun, very carefully, to scratch away at the pearl. At its base, where the pin went in, a tiny flake of pearly substance had fallen off. Underneath this, the pearl had been grey. And Emilie had thought that real pearls were *nothing but themselves* all the way through and that this greyness was something else, which was false.

She'd wanted to tell her mother, in case she didn't know, that the pearl wasn't real, but this would have involved admitting that she'd been prying into her personal possessions, that she'd seen all the secret mess of powder, of tangled grey hair in the combs. Yet, ever since, when Irma wears the pearl hatpin in her burgundy hat, Emilie remembers the little speck of pearlised coating that fell off and that still lies, perhaps, in Irma's drawer, invisible among the cigarette ash.

Frau Mollis returns to the table with her husband. It is he who is now holding the hatpin. He clears his throat and says, 'Frau Albrecht, I'm sorry, but we cannot accept this pin. Next time you come – and you know you are always welcome in our tea room – please bring the requisite cash sum to settle your bills.'

Other people in the café have turned to stare. Irma hesitates for a moment, ready to argue with Herr Mollis, but then changes her mind and snatches the hatpin out of his hand and stabs it angrily back into her burgundy hat.

Emilie knows they will never go back to the tea room, and they never do.

She lies in her narrow bed. She thinks how, throughout her life, Irma – for all her piety – has behaved in ways which are shameful. And she wonders how this began, this heedless treatment of other people.

In another drawer, containing winter scarves and darned gloves, Emilie once found a photograph – faded and bent – of a man Irma said was 'responsible' for Emilie's birth. She didn't refer to him as 'your father', but only as the 'man responsible'. His name was Pierre. He had come to Basel from Geneva, where he'd worked in a hotel. He wanted to 'better himself', Irma said, but could only get café work in Basel, and when he found out that Irma was pregnant with his child, he disappeared from one day to the next. Perhaps he went to Paris, where he'd dreamed of owning a nightclub?

Emilie has looked several times at the photograph of Pierre – a sleek and handsome man on the outside, but a coward and a cheat in his dealings with women, leaving Irma Albrecht with a lifelong fury that never abated.

In the darkness of the winter night, Emilie finds herself comparing her husband to her absent father. She begins to see something important, which she had never before considered: Pierre was like the false pearl on the hatpin, with a beautiful sheen to his body, but a soul of dross. Erich, on the other hand, is *himself through and through.* He did what his heart told him to do and was prepared to take the consequences. He is a man who can't lie to himself, can't follow a path he believes to be wrong. And she herself now glimpses a narrow road that winds back to him – to his forgiveness and his love.

# Folly

## *Matzlingen, 1941*

Erich has aspirations to be a teacher. He believes that all his disciplined and careful work in the police has fitted him for this new métier. He would like to teach history – to get to the truth of things. He begins to borrow history books from the library. Surrounded on every side by the war, he knows that Switzerland must cling fast to its neutrality and develop in its children an understanding of *why* their country is the way it is.

He applies to four schools in Matzlingen, but none of them want to risk hiring a 'disgraced' police officer, with a trial pending. He has wilfully broken the law. He is rudely reminded that 'criminals and children must never be allowed to mix'. He wants to protest, but he knows that minds have been made up. Fear of a German invasion is a daily agony for the country, seldom talked about, yet always felt. Nobody is going to listen to him.

He's taken on at the tram depot. He works a night shift with a much younger man called Erlen. Their job is to supervise the cleaning and maintenance of the trams between one and six in the morning and oversee their first despatch into the town. Erich is paid a scant wage for all these long, night hours, but he has to live somehow. He has to eat. He has to pay the rent on the apartment on Unter der Egg. And there is one bonus attaching to working nights: his days are free for his visits from Lottie Erdman.

Lottie Erdman haunts his waking and sleeping hours. It's as though he's been searching for Lottie all his life and now he's found her – his perfect lover. The sight, smell, touch and taste of Lottie are like a drug to him. Always, he wants more. When she leaves him, and he staggers about the apartment on legs weak from sexual exertion and lack of sleep, he counts the hours, or days, till he's going to see her again. All night, in the cold depot, he sighs over the fact that she's not his wife – and never can be. She's the wife of his friend. And when he thinks about Roger making love to her, he feels a pain in his heart and groin so acute it sometimes makes him wonder whether he's on the brink of some catastrophic collapse.

Lottie understands how obsessed he is. Sometimes, she can treat him like some wilful Cleopatra, making him wait, making him beg. And the more she does this, the more he wants her. And he wants her in every way, not caring if he hurts her, enthralled, in fact, by the idea that he can hurt her in the very midst of pleasure. He knows he's half mad in his yearning, with all restraint abandoned. It's the kind of folly that could kill a man.

Of Emilie, he hardly thinks. He imagines her sometimes in her mother's house, trudging between the empty hillside and the broken-down door. He marvels that he fell in love with such a person. How did it ever come about? Only because of a beautiful summer day at the Schwingfest. Because of a kiss. Because she was a virgin. Because she'd set her heart on him. But thinking of her now, he can barely remember any days or nights when he was happy with her.

After one afternoon with Lottie, an afternoon so potent he knows he will never forget it, he sits down and writes a letter to Emilie. He suggests that 'in the light of all that has happened' that they apply to get divorced. And when this is written, he feels consoled, as though a divorce from Emilie would enable him to marry Lottie, have children with Lottie, stay with her to the end of his life.

But before Erich has posted his letter, Emilie returns.

She returns in the middle of an afternoon. Erich is sleeping. Lottie had been with him since nine o'clock, but had left at mid-day. The bed is still scented with her perfume, the sheets still damp and tangled from their lovemaking.

Erich hears the knock at the apartment door, but turns over

and tries to sleep again. He hears footsteps retreat. Then he hears the door opening and the voice of Ludwig Krams, the teenage son of the concierge, calling out, 'Herr Perle, I saw you come in. You must be there. I have a lady here who says she's your wife.'

Erich sits up. He's naked in the bed. He tugs on a pair of trousers and a vest and goes into the small living room, where he sees Emilie standing near the door. Ludwig Krams is smiling his idiot smile. 'Your wife,' he says, putting his hand in front of his mouth, to suppress laughter. 'You didn't tell my mother you had a wife, Herr Perle!'

'Please leave us, Ludwig,' says Erich.

Ludwig says, 'I almost laughed. I know that's impolite. I'll go now.'

He turns and walks out of the apartment. Emilie hasn't moved. She is standing with clenched fists, staring at Erich.

He dismays her. His hair is long and wild, his chin unshaven, his lips raw, his neck scarred with red bruises – the kind of bruise which people who know about sex call something else, but Emilie can't remember what the word is. She's come back to say that she's sorry, that she's reconciled to the loss of their old life, that she wants forgiveness for the way she abandoned him so hastily. She wants to say that in recent times she's been thinking very deeply about the man she knows him to be, true to himself, honest, compassionate and kind. But, facing him as he is, stinking like a fox, she can say none of these things. All she can stammer out is, 'I suppose there's a woman with you. Is there?'

'No,' says Erich. 'There's nobody here. Come into the kitchen. I'll make tea. And we can talk.'

She sets down her suitcase and follows Erich to the kitchen. She notes the dirty dishes piled in the sink, the grime on the cooker. She notes that there is no kitchen table, but only a hinged shelf, on which there are the remains of breakfast, set out for two people, and a half-drunk bottle of schnapps. And at the sight of this, she thinks, I am too late. I was away for too long. He has replaced me.

She stands silent by the shelf, while Erich clears away the breakfast. Tired from her journey, in shock to find herself in this unfamiliar apartment, inhabited by two people, she begins to weep.

Erich ignores this, while he sets a kettle on the stove to boil. Then he takes the cork out of the schnapps bottle and passes it to her. 'Have a sip of this,' he says. 'It will steady you.'

She drinks the fiery schnapps, searches for a handkerchief, and stammers out, 'You've made another life, haven't you?'

'No,' says Erich, reaching up for two teacups.

'I mustn't blame you. You probably thought I wasn't coming back . . . You had no reason to believe –'

'Listen to me,' says Erich. 'I'm going to tell you the truth, so that we get it out of the way. I pay a whore from time to time. I work nights at the tram depot, so when she comes, she comes here early in the morning, and afterwards we have breakfast – because I treat her in a civilised way. Then, she leaves. All right? I pay a whore. Once a week perhaps. It's just an arrangement. We fuck, we have breakfast and she leaves. But now that you're back –'

'Do you want me back, Erich?' Emilie sobs. 'I know I did everything wrong, and I wouldn't blame you . . . But I still love you. I had to come and tell you this, at least. I love you very much.'

The word 'love' snags at Erich's heart. It's the word he uses so often to Lottie, all the while knowing that he will never be allowed to express that love as he wants to express it, as her husband, as the only man in her world. Hearing it from Emilie, he feels that she has somehow *stolen* it, and this chokes him with sadness.

He spoons tea leaves into a yellow, chipped teapot, biting his lip. He has barely looked at Emilie, but now he stares at her. She is his wife. Lottie Erdman, his voluptuous angel, the woman he makes love to three or four times a week, is not his wife. His wife is Emilie, who stands drinking schnapps and weeping and talking about love. This is she, the woman standing in front of him in a dress too large for her, with a body so thin, so sorrowful and starved, it seems barely alive.

Erich wants to cry out. He stuffs a fist into his mouth.

*Somebody save me from this!*

*Somebody save me!*

While she finishes her tea, he puts clean sheets on the bed. She doesn't see him holding to his face the semen-stained sheets that smell of Lottie's body and make him want to howl like a wolf.

He hears her washing up his dishes in the kitchen. He remembers how clean she kept the apartment at Fribourgstrasse 61, how she scented it with flowers. Then, he remembers her ripping apart a cushion and covering herself with feathers and tearing at her ugly face . . .

He goes into the kitchen and says to her, 'I really don't know how we're going to live together, Emilie. I'd been imagining that we would never try to be together again.'

'I know,' she says. 'I thought, after I left, that I couldn't live with you any more. But I want to try, Erich. I owe you this. I know the old, lovely life we had is gone, but we can try to make something together, can't we? Can't we?'

'I don't know,' he says.

'I was so unhappy in my mother's house. And I began thinking of you all the time. I thought about our time in Davos. Do you remember? The tea dancing. Our view of the mountains. Don't you remember?'

The afternoon sun is now coming in through the kitchen window and falling on Emilie's hair, making it look shiny and golden, scant though it is. She reminds Erich of a rodent – a rat or a squirrel – who, in certain configurations of nature's light, might suddenly arouse your compassion.

'I remember,' he says.

That he works nights means they never have to share a bed. Emilie gets up at half past six, when he returns from the tram depot. They drink tea together and then he gets into the bed and falls asleep. She moves about the apartment, tidying and cleaning. From the flower seller on Unter der Egg, she buys scented wild narcissi and bunches of spring violets.

She walks around the town, making enquiries about work. Erich has told her that he's in debt. She has promised him she will find work as soon as she can and she has hopes that she will be taken on at the newly opened cheese co-operative, making Emmental. 'From now on,' she has said to her husband, 'we will share all our burdens.'

But there is one burden he will never share with her.

On the night of Emilie's return, in the cold light of the tram depot, Erich Perle composes the only erotic love letter he has ever written in his life.

He puts it in an envelope and gets Erlen to write the address in his uneducated hand, so that Roger won't recognise Erich's writing. Erich is now ashamed of the envelope, but not embarrassed by the letter, which begins *Lottie my darling, my most precious of all beings*, and is signed *from your grieving Werther, your steadfast Dante, your persecuted Abelard.* He knows he sounds like a schoolboy, but he doesn't care.

He tells Lottie that, despite Emilie's return, they will find a way to go on with their love affair 'even at the risk of everybody finding out about it' because without her, he feels as though he's slowly dying. He proposes coming to Grünewaldstrasse, early in the morning, after Roger has left for Police Headquarters. He asks her to send him word about which day he should come. He imagines her putting on the silky peignoir she wore the afternoon they first became lovers.

Emilie goes into the spare bedroom in the apartment. There's no bed in it. It's stacked high with unopened boxes of books and forgotten knick-knacks from Fribourgstrasse. It has a square window, looking down on a yard and in the yard is a cherry tree in full bloom, a thing of such beauty, it makes Emilie gasp. She sees an elderly resident, Herr Nieder, come out of the building, walking with his stick, and pause by the tree. He reaches out an unsteady hand and touches the white blossom.

Emilie turns back to the room. In her mind, she removes all the boxes, and sweeps the floor. She buys a rug. She puts curtains at the window. Then, with tender care, she places a child's cot in the room and a soft toy – a rabbit or a bear – in one corner of it, keeping watch.

She knows these imaginings are futile. Erich doesn't touch her any more. He shows no inclination to want to touch her. But she remembers what a sensual, needy man he is. At the long-ago Schwingfest, she seduced him with one kiss. She reasons that it's only a matter of time before he will take her back into his bed.

And this is what she wants now. All her anger with Erich has gone. What she longs for is an ordinary, companionable life with the man she married. And sooner or later, a child – a boy of course, to replace her lost Gustav. And she imagines lifting this baby in her arms and taking him to the window and showing him, far below, the white cherry tree in the yard.

Then, Irma's voice begins to echo in her head: 'It's folly to go back to that Jew-lover! He may be handsome, but you can never trust him again. He'll cheat on you, just as Pierre cheated on me, and you'll be left alone, like me, with a child you never wanted.'

# Two Sundays

## *Matzlingen, 1941*

Emilie gets the job at the cheese co-operative. Though the manager, Herr Studer, looks at her thin body critically, doubting she's strong enough for all the lifting and stirring that it entails, she reassures him that she's tougher than she looks. She tells him how she carried great basins of water from a pump to a tin bath in a house near Basel. This puts a secret smile on the manager's bird-like face. He likes seeing women struggling with heavy work; it makes them both desirable and pitiable. He gives Emilie the job.

She's paid more money per week than Erich earns at the tram depot. And, in her mind, this gives her a little power over him. It is she who buys the food they eat, sometimes supplemented with small gifts of chocolate or cigars for Erich. She watches her husband closely as he receives these. He always thanks her politely, but there is something about them which seems to make him sad.

On certain mornings, perhaps once a fortnight, he doesn't come home at half past six and Emilie supposes that he's making visits to the 'whore' with whom he once had breakfast and drank schnapps.

Emilie thinks about this as she begins her work at the co-operative, housed in its draughty shed. She imagines Erich and the woman, warm and easy with each other in some scented room, and she wishes it were not so. But she's biding her time. She's taken all the boxes out of the small bedroom and unpacked them, arranging the books and knick-knacks around the apartment. Erich makes almost no comment about this. He just stares at these things, as though he'd never seen them before.

Erich looks at his life and knows that he's more unhappy than he's ever been.

The only place where he can make love to Lottie is in the Erdmans' apartment at Grünewaldstrasse, but she won't let him visit her too often, terrified that they'll be discovered. Once, driven mad by his need of her, now so seldom satisfied, he suggests that they run away together.

'Run where?' asks Lottie. 'There's war everywhere but here.'

'South America,' he answers.

Lottie's bright laugh rings out, the laugh he loves so much. But now it sounds as though it's mocking him. Already, he's imagined them – Erich and Lottie, Herr and Frau Perle to all the world – in some sunlit glade, with the wind from the high plains sighing sweetly all around them, and birds he doesn't recognise in the tall trees. But Lottie laughs at his dreams. She's Police Chief Roger Erdman's wife. She reminds him patiently that she will never leave Roger.

He goes mournfully back to Unter der Egg, glad that Emilie's at work, that he can at least be alone. He lies in a hot bath, where Emilie's stockings hang on a string above him, and washes the smell of Lottie from his body. He rests his head on the back of the bath and closes his eyes. He asks himself if he can stand to go on with the life he's living. Though his police revolver was taken from him, he has a gun in his wardrobe – the rifle every Swiss household is obliged to keep, in case the need for self-defence arises – and Erich wonders whether he would ever have the courage to shoot himself. He remembers that it's surely difficult to commit suicide with a rifle, and yet the thought that he *could* do it comforts him.

Erich crawls into bed and falls asleep. As always, Lottie is there, at the edge of his dreams.

On Sundays, he drinks.

Emilie cooks her famous roast pork with knödel, and they sit side by side at the kitchen shelf, sharing the meal and drinking red wine.

It is Sunday now and Erich, having eaten well, sips his wine greedily and feels his body and his mind to be free of pain. He knows that this freedom from pain won't last, but he's grateful for it, while it does.

'Wine,' he tells Emilie, 'is nature's consolation: the only one.'

'There used to be others between us,' she says.

He ignores this, but when she gets up to clear the plates, he looks at her and notices that she's wearing a clean summer dress and that she's set her hair into soft curls.

He gets to his feet. The only way that this can be done, he thinks, is to do it now – right now – with the help of the wine – and to hope that a distant memory of how it once was comes to his aid. He grabs Emilie's hand and leads her to the bedroom and pushes her down on the bed. He knows that she won't protest. He's known for some time that this is what she wants.

She's naked underneath her dress and this excites him enough to allow him to penetrate her. She tries to kiss his mouth, but he turns his face aside. He breathes heavily. The room spins. He remembers how easy this used to be between them, but now, already, he can feel desire fading. Yet he tells himself that he has a duty here, on this one afternoon, to complete the thing, that if he can make himself do this, then his life with Emilie – his life so starved of Lottie's love – will become more bearable. He thinks how, in the future, it could be something to taunt Lottie with: 'I make love to Emilie again now. She's begun to excite me, like she used to do . . .'

He looks towards the bedroom door. He conjures Lottie. This is the only way he can get hard again. Lottie stands in the doorway watching him make love to his wife. She's excited by it. All that is strange and contrary in sex excites Lottie Erdman. So she's come here to take part. She murmurs Erich's name and lifts up her skirt and begins to touch herself. And to see her do this has always aroused him more than he has ever admitted to her. He closes his eyes. Lottie whispers to him that this is a beautiful thing, to see him moving inside another woman, that in moments, she's going to come. So then, for Erich, there is no Emilie beneath him. There is no room, no daylight, no sound. There is only the taste of the wine in his throat and the pulsing of his heart and his beloved Lottie in her shameless delirium.

From here, it's an easy, beautiful ride. When he finishes he cries out and lets his body fall into darkness.

Emilie's pregnancy is confirmed in the autumn. When she learns about this, she weeps with joy. The doctor tells her that the baby will be born the following June.

She asks Erich if he's happy about becoming a father at last. He looks at her as though she'd just uttered a foreign word that he doesn't understand.

'Happy? Not particularly,' he says. 'I lost the knack of happiness when I lost my job.'

'Well,' she says, 'you should have thought about that before you sided with the Jews.'

'Please don't talk like that,' he says. 'It's hateful.'

'I think I have the right,' she says, 'considering everything that happened.'

'You don't have the right. It's in the past now.'

'It's not in the past. The threat of prosecution is still out there. A summons to court could arrive at any time.'

'It might, but it hasn't come yet. And anyway, there's nothing I can do about it.'

'Wrong,' she says. 'We can talk to the people at the Israelitische Flüchtlingshilfe. They must speak up for you. Who knows if it wasn't they who betrayed you?'

'It wasn't them.'

'How d'you know?'

'It couldn't have been. Why would they have done that? It was their people I was saving from death.'

'Who was it, then? Roger Erdman? Someone betrayed you.'

'Not Roger.'

'Very likely the IF, in my view. To save their own skins. So if the summons comes – or *when it comes* – they should behave with decency and send someone to the Justice Ministry in Bern, to plead for you.'

He tells her he's already been to see the IF and that they can do nothing, but she doesn't believe him.

The following day, after work, she goes to their cramped offices. She knows she smells of cheese, but she doesn't care. She climbs a set of narrow stairs, holding onto her pregnant stomach, as if believing the baby needs comfort, to find itself in such a place. She enters a large, threadbare room, stuffed from floor to ceiling with box files and bundles of paper tied with string. An elderly Jewish man sits behind a high desk, his head bent low, as though he were in the habit of hiding from the world.

When Emilie begins on Erich's story, the man looks confused. 'I don't know who you're talking about,' he says.

'I've told you: my husband. Herr Erich Perle. He was Assistant Police Chief here in Matzlingen in August 1938. It was because he agreed to falsify dates of entry on registration forms that hundreds of Jews were able to stay in Switzerland.'

'I've never heard about that. It was before my time working here.'

'Well. You're here now, sir. Among all these files in this room, there will be a record of this.'

'You expect me to go through a thousand files?'

'I am expecting you to help me. I am carrying a child. If my husband is sent to prison, I will be destitute.'

'Prison? Sent to prison?'

'He was sacked from the police force and had his pension and everything taken away from him. He was told that he could still be prosecuted and incarcerated. So I am here to say that we are expecting the IF to speak out for him, to go to Bern, if necessary, if the summons comes.'

The man rubs his eyes. Then he puts on a pair of spectacles and stares at Emilie. They confront each other, face-to-face. Somewhere, down the far end of the room, Emilie can hear the click-click of typewriters and the sound of a person with a choking cough. The man waits for the cough to subside, then he says, 'I suppose you have heard what is being done to Jews in Germany and Austria?'

'Yes. I have heard. Or, at least, I have heard rumours. That is why you must help my husband. He saved your people from a terrible fate, but at the price of his own life.'

'What d'you mean, "at the price of his own life"?'

'He has never recovered from the loss of his position. He works nights in the tram depot now. That was all he could get. He wanted to be a teacher, but no one would hire him. We lost our apartment – everything. He walks though his life like a dead man.'

The old man shakes his head, as though to dismiss as unimportant everything Emilie has just said. Wearily, he takes up a pen, pushes his glasses further up his nose, and asks, 'What was your husband's name again?'

Emilie saves up to buy the cot and the rug. She buys a tin train.

She looks at the child's room. She knows it's still too bare, not welcoming enough for her new little Gustav. She makes lists of the objects she would like to find for it. In March, she calls on Lottie Erdman to ask her to come with her to the bric-à-brac stalls one Sunday morning, to look for these things.

When Lottie opens her apartment door and sees Emilie there, resplendent now, in her sixth month of pregnancy, her face pales and she has to sit down on the nearest chair.

'Are you all right, Lottie?' asks Emilie.

'Yes,' says Lottie. 'Sorry. I get dizzy spells sometimes. I don't know why.'

# Heartbeat

## *Matzlingen, 1942*

Lottie sends a note to the tram depot. She asks Erich to meet her at an out-of-the-way café, where no one will recognise them. There is snow on the ground.

In the café, Erich still feels chilled after his night at the depot, and orders hot chocolate.

Lottie says, 'I'm not going to have anything comforting. Today is going to be hard, but we just have to bear it.'

She's dressed in a black coat with a fur collar. Her blonde hair is partly concealed by a black fur hat. He thinks, this is how Anna Karenina looked to Vronsky – before he tired of her, before the spell was broken. He wants to reach under the table and put his hand on her cunt.

She begins to talk, but he's not really listening; Lottie is just too perfect in the early-morning light, her skin so fine and soft, her blue eyes strangely glittering with tears. He could take her now, right there on the hard bench, not caring about anything in the world except being inside her and hearing her cry out his name.

But now she's telling him that he *has* to listen to her. She tells him that the love affair is over. She's made up her mind. With Emilie pregnant, she's decided that she wants to have a child, too – Roger's child. She wants to commit to Roger and to a family. 'The rest,' she says, 'is folly. We've always known this. And it has to end.'

Erich stares at her. Her beauty is like a weight on him, suffocating him, pinning him down to the earth.

'Why did you put on lipstick?' he asks.

'What?'

'Why did you paint yourself up, to tell me that you don't love me any more?'

Lottie takes off her fur hat and shakes her golden tresses loose.

'I never did love you,' she says. 'I never said that. I just liked what we did.'

'*Liked*? Is that the right word? You just *liked it*?'

'Yes. It was just animal sex, Erich. Animals don't even have the words to say if they're "liking it" or not: they just do it. They meet and the moment comes and they have to do it. And we were like them. We didn't think of anything but satisfying ourselves. Over and over again. Like pigs. We were pigs.'

Erich's hand trembles as he lights a cigarette. The waiter brings his hot chocolate and a glass of water for Lottie. The smell of the chocolate now sickens him. He can't look at Lottie any more, it's too painful. He looks down at the wooden floor, where the butts of cigarettes from last night's drinkers still lie, and he thinks how shabby the world is and how tired and old and full of discarded things.

'Listen,' says Lottie gently, 'I don't mean to imply that I'll ever forget us, Erich. The things we did! When I'm ancient, I'll probably remember them and wonder if it was true. And it's not like that with Roger. It's much more ordinary and quiet. But the thing is, I do love Roger. I've never stopped loving him. You've always known that. I've never lied to you about that. And when I saw Emilie, pregnant, I knew that this was what I wanted, to have children with Roger, lots of children. I don't want my breasts to be sex objects any more; I want to suckle my babies.'

Her breasts. Why did she have to mention them? He used to lie on her and suck like a child, loving the way the nipples hardened as she became aroused, even imagining that some beautiful dewy substance came out of these pert nipples, to nourish him and bind him to her – bind her forever, because he knew he would always need her. Lottie Erdman. His only love.

He gets up and stubs out his cigarette. He casts a last look at her in the harsh morning light of the poor café, to etch her there in his mind: her smooth cheeks, her scarlet lips, her pale hand clutching the fur on her coat collar. Then, he turns and walks out into the street, where a light snow is falling.

In the seventh month of her pregnancy, Emilie gives up her job at the cheese co-operative. The manager, Herr Studer, is courteous and says he will take her back whenever she feels ready to work again. She is given a large slice of Emmental in what Herr Studer calls a 'presentation box'. As she leaves, he kisses her cheek.

Emilie begins to count the days remaining before the birth: sixty days, forty days, thirty days . . .

She sees the doctor as regularly as she can and the doctor lets her put his stethoscope in her ears, to hear the baby's heartbeat. And this moves Emilie to say, 'I know it's a boy. We're going to call him Gustav. Like the one I lost.'

'Ah. You lost one?'

'Yes. At five and a half months, but this one is strong, isn't he? He's going to be all right?'

'As far as anyone can tell.'

'I think the heartbeat sounds strong. He won't be small and thin, like me, but tall and well made like my husband. I know he will. Or perhaps I just want it? Do you think that wanting things can make them happen?'

The doctor takes the stethoscope away. 'If I really believed that,' he says, 'I wouldn't bother being a doctor.'

But he laughs, and Emilie thinks, now that I'm going to be a mother, and hold my boy in my arms, I can bear anything.

She thought that Erich would be cheered by the thought of a son being born. But when they talk about the forthcoming birth, he just smiles a wan smile. He says the name, over and over: 'Gustav . . . Gustav . . .' It was his father's name.

There is something wrong with Erich. Some nights, he can't get out of bed to go to the depot. There is no telephone in the depot, so Emilie has to walk there, through the dark streets, to tell Erlen that her husband is ill. And she feels sorry for Erlen, alone in the vast shed, with his mops and pails of freezing water. Sometimes, she takes him a slice of Nusstorte. He says to her, 'Tell Herr Perle he's going to get sacked, if he keeps missing nights. The bosses are hard men.'

When she passes this on to Erich, he just closes his eyes. Emilie reminds him that, without the cheese co-operative and without the job at the tram depot, they would be destitute, but he doesn't seem to give this his attention. All he wants to do all the time is sleep.

She tries to care for him as best she can, calling on her reserves of compassion to fight off anger. He cries real tears in his sleep. When she asks him what it is that's tormenting him, he says it's sorrow for the state of the world. He says he believes the invasion of Switzerland is 'only a matter of time. And then, everything we've known will be destroyed.'

Emilie can't let herself think about this. She urges Erich to go to work. She tells him – for the third or fourth time – that the arrival of little Gustav will be the thing which helps him to recover his peace of mind. But when she says this, she sees a flash of his old anger in his eyes. 'You know nothing, Emilie,' he says. 'You know nothing.'

The pains begin on the 2nd of June. First, they come in a dream: a dark-faced goblin clawing at Emilie's womb with his scaly hands. But then she wakes and the pains arrive again, so she knows this is real now: it's Gustav tearing at her, asking to be born.

It's four in the morning, and on this night, Erich *has* gone to work. It will be another two and a half hours before he gets home. Emilie breathes deeply, trying to stay calm. She packs a small suitcase and dresses herself in a loose dress and coat. She washes her face and cleans her teeth. 'Do everything right,' she instructs herself, 'everything in the right order.'

Next, she goes down and bangs on the door of Frau Krams's apartment, and after a long wait, Frau Krams comes shuffling to the door. Her hair is in curl papers and her gnarled feet bare. Emilie apologises for waking her and asks her to summon an ambulance.

Frau Krams tugs on a robe and lights a cigarette. She sits Emilie down in her parlour and goes to the telephone in the hall. After a moment, Ludwig Krams comes into the parlour, tugging a blanket with him. He sits opposite Emilie and giggles. 'I thought it would be the other one,' he says.

'What?' says Emilie.

'I thought it would be the other lady he'd get into trouble. They were always at it in the mornings. I used to go and sit on the stairs and listen.'

Emilie regards Ludwig calmly. She feels sorry for Frau Krams having an imbecile for a son. She says, 'The *other lady*, as you call her, was a whore – a prostitute. But even so, I don't think you should have done that, Ludwig,' and then turns away from him.

'Always at it . . .' he says again, but his voice tails off as Frau Krams comes back into the room. She puts the kettle on. She finds a plaid rug and places this round Emilie's narrow shoulders. She sends Ludwig away.

'What's he been saying?' she asks.

'Nothing,' says Emilie. 'Nothing I didn't know.'

They wait. The pains come and go. Emilie tries not to cry out, but to continue keeping her breathing steady. Her forehead beads with sweat. She digs her nails into her palms. Frau Krams says, 'I hope for your sake, Frau Perle, that it's a girl. Boys are nothing but heartbreak.'

'Well,' says Emilie, 'if it's a girl, we don't have a name. What's your name, Frau Krams? We could use that.'

'Helga,' says Frau Krams.

'Helga?' says Emilie. 'Well, it's a bit ordinary, but it would do. I'm not naming any child of mine after my own mother.'

They just have time to sip a cup of hot tea, then Emilie is taken away in the ambulance. She wishes Erich were with her. She asks the ambulance men if they can get a message to the tram depot and they say they will try. They give her oxygen to breathe and the feeling of the pure oxygen going into her lungs is as beautiful as breathing the air of Davos.

And it feels cosy and safe in the ambulance, with the sweet oxygen and the two medics to care for her. She wishes the ambulance could stop somewhere quiet and that Gustav could be born here and put gently into her arms by these men she already trusts with her life.

But they arrive – too soon – at the hospital. She says goodbye to the ambulance men. She's wheeled into an elevator, then out again and into a room blazing with white light. A midwife peers at her over a mask. Emilie's legs are hoisted up and her feet hung into stirrups. Now, suddenly, she is anxious, frightened of the pain, frightened that her body is too narrow to push the baby out. Tears start at her eyes. She calls Erich's name.

She looks round the small, floodlit room. There is a cluster of people at the end of her bed. Emilie was unaware of them coming into the room, but there they are. They pass quiet instructions to each other. She is told to push and push again. The pain is so severe, she thinks she may pass out and she thinks, do children ever understand what we go through to bring them into the world?

Perhaps she does pass out. She's not sure. Time seems to stop and then start up again. And when it restarts, there is her baby, her boy Gustav, alive and screaming, wrapped in a green rag and laid on her breast.

# Beginning and End

## *Matzlingen, 1942*

The baby is very small. His little limbs are thin. He seems to cry all the time from hunger. He even cries at the breast.

Erich sits on the bed, watching Emilie trying to feed his son. Even in her maternal state, her breasts, which had grown large during her first pregnancy, are meagre. It's clear to Erich that Gustav is slowly dying from lack of sustenance. He snatches him off Emilie's breast, and carries him round to the pharmacy, where he lays him down on the counter and takes off his clothes.

'Look!' says Erich. 'Look how thin and weak he is! He needs milk.'

The young woman pharmacist examines Gustav, while other customers, who have come into the pharmacy for headache pills or stomach settlers, wait in bemusement and mild irritation.

'My wife,' says Erich, 'she's trying to breastfeed him, but I don't think there's anything *in her breasts*!'

Without commenting on this, the pharmacist takes baby Gustav away and puts him on a pair of scales. She moves weights around, then picks him up again and wraps him in his shawl. She hands him back to Erich. 'You're right,' she says. 'He is underweight.'

She gives Erich a large carton of powdered milk and a glass bottle with a rubber teat.

'Lovely Swiss milk,' she says. 'Give him two-thirds of the bottle every four hours. Bring him back in one week, or take him to your doctor.'

As he goes out, one of the female customers, waiting in line for some simple medication, says to him, 'You know he must have the breast as well. Or else your wife will get depressed.'

She is depressed.

When Erich gives Gustav the bottle, she sees on the infant's face an expression of bliss, whereas, on the breast, he's restless and agitated. And she knows she's clumsy with him. She can't seem to get him entirely comfortable in her arms. He kicks and screams. But when Erich picks him up, he goes quiet.

Her nights are purgatory. Erich is at the depot and she's alone with her child, who wakes her every hour with his screams. Sometimes, she lets him scream. She's so tired, she can doze through the horrible noise. She tells herself that nothing bad is happening to him; he's just a bit hungry, or wet, or just plain bad-tempered. And she needs her sleep. How will she get through the day of constant feeding and nappy changing unless she can get her rest?

She expected to feel joy. She remembers how much she longed for this baby. She imagined motherhood would cure the sorrows of the past and make her contented and proud. But it isn't like that. She nurtures the terrible thought that this Gustav is the *wrong* Gustav; the baby she lost was the rightful son, with whom she would have found a thrilling maternal bond.

When she runs into Lottie Erdman in the street one day, she says, 'It's not what we think it is, having babies, Lottie. It's more hell than heaven.'

Lottie looks at her with sadness. 'I envy you, nonetheless,' she says. 'Roger and I are trying for a baby, but it doesn't seem to happen.'

Emilie looks at Lottie, whose prettiness she has always admired and envied. And she notices that Lottie's hair has lost its shine and that her face looks pinched.

'I thought it would be different,' Emilie says. 'I can tell you, Lottie, because I can trust you. I thought I would feel an overpowering love for the child, but I don't.'

Lottie hesitates a moment before asking, 'Does Erich feel love for him?'

'Yes,' Emilie says. 'He seems very fond of him. When he comes home at six thirty, he feeds him a bottle and changes his nappy, then takes him into bed with him. I go and stand in there and watch them sleeping a perfect sleep – and this just makes me feel inadequate and sad.'

Lottie nods. Then, she reaches down into the pram and touches Gustav's face. 'He looks more like you than Erich,' she says.

All night, at the tram depot, Erich worries about his son. He sees how, between mother and baby, there's a peculiar chemistry of alienation. Emilie seldom kisses Gustav, or holds him close to her heart. When she changes his nappy, she's rough with him, pulling his little body this way and that, sometimes cursing as she cleans him up.

He tells himself that childbirth is an ordeal he gets nowhere near to comprehending, so women are bound to take time to recover from it and, in this slow recovery, their behaviour might be erratic or strange. He just has to pray that Emilie will grow closer to Gustav as the weeks and months go on. But the feeling that his baby is *in danger* when he's alone with Emilie won't quite leave him. It's as though, one morning when his shift at the tram depot ends, he will rush back to Unter der Egg to find Gustav dead.

In the midst of this unease, he gets the one thing he wasn't expecting: a summons from Lottie. He's sitting on a bench in the depot, reading it by cold strip light, but, as he reads, it's as though a golden luminescence suddenly envelops his whole being. His heart begins to beat so wildly, he feels it might break apart inside him, killed by astonishment.

> Erich,
>
> Often – so often in my dreams – you and I are in that café and I am telling you that I never loved you. But what I said was not true. I just said that thing about 'pigs' to make our separation more bearable – to enable you to walk away from me.
>
> Erich, I do love you – so much. The thought that we will never make love again is too unendurable to be borne. I keep hoping that I will be cured of my need for you, but every day, it gets stronger.

I know I have no right to ask this of you, especially now that you have your son and must stay at Emilie's side, but I want you to come to me. Roger is in Geneva. Will you be my lover again? And will you . . . God, I hardly dare ask this of you . . . I am so shameless . . . but will you give me a child? I am thirty-two years old. Roger and I cannot make a child, it seems. The love we make together is too weak. But I know that you and I, in that delirium we share – if we took no precautions now – could make one with perfect ease. I would look to you for nothing afterwards – no hint of parental responsibility, I swear. It would be 'Roger's child'. And only you and I in all the world would know that it was the angel of our desire . . .

It is deep night in the depot, a scent of autumn on the winds. Erich reads Lottie's letter over and over until he knows it by heart. He understands that what she's asking is audacious, the kind of grand deception that only a woman as wanton as Lottie Erdman would think up, yet he also knows that he's immediately on fire for her scheme and that he would go to her this very minute, if he could. And now that she's summoned him, he can't delay. His need of her returns as a terrible compulsion that he must satisfy at once, or die.

As soon as the six o'clock light begins to show, Erich walks to a telephone kiosk and calls Frau Krams, asking her to give a message to Emilie, to tell her he has been summoned to a meeting by the bosses of the tram company at eight o'clock and will not be home until later in the morning. 'Remind her,' he adds, 'to give Gustav his milk.'

When the shops open in Matzlingen, Erich goes into a cheap clothier's and buys new trousers, shirt, shoes and jacket. Then he goes to the public baths and washes and steams all the stink of the tram depot off his body. After this, he puts on his new clothes and visits a barber's, to demand a shave and a haircut. When he catches sight of himself in the barber's mirror, he sees that he's smiling.

Now, it's half past nine and Erich is walking down Grünewaldstrasse – his old, beloved walk to Lottie's door. Only now does he realise that he no longer has Lottie's letter; he must have left it in the baths or in the telephone kiosk or in the clothier's changing cubicle, but he can't go back to search for it, his longing to reach Lottie is too urgent. He prays she will be waiting, hoping he would act just as he has acted, and come to her at once, out of breath, even, from the haste with which he has run to her. He tries to imagine which dress she will be wearing.

Tired from her night, after being woken by Gustav five times, then by Frau Krams with her message, Emilie sits by the gas fire, still wearing her nightdress, and drinks coffee and smokes. Gustav is at last asleep in his cot and Emilie thinks she may go back to bed for a while. The apartment needs cleaning, but she will do this later. Sleep is what she craves.

She climbs into bed and is gone, almost at once, into a strange dream of Irma and the pearl hatpin. Irma is dancing round her small parlour in the house near Basel, with the pin, stabbing the air, crying out that she will 'have her revenge on life'. Emilie cowers in a corner, knowing that it's only a matter of time before Irma stabs her with the pin. She was the unwanted child. It's upon her that Irma's 'revenge' will fall.

There's knocking at the apartment door, loud and insistent. Emilie at first thinks it's part of her dream of Irma, but then she wakes and tugs on a robe.

There's no sound from Gustav's room, but whoever is at the door is calling her name: 'Frau Perle! Open the door. Police!'

So then Emilie thinks it's come at last, Erich's summons to the long-postponed criminal trial. She goes cold. She opens the door a crack and sees two police officers standing there. They say nothing for a moment, then ask her politely if they can come in.

'It's the trial, is it?' she says. 'Is it the trial?'

They say nothing, but shake their heads, no. They come into the untidy parlour that stinks of cigarette ash and ask her gently if she would like to sit down.

'Sit down?' she says. 'It's bad news, is it? It's about the trial.'

'No,' says the older of the two men. 'It's nothing about a trial. Please sit down, Frau Perle, and we will tell you.'

Emilie sits on the very edge of a frayed brown chair. The

policemen also sit. Then, they tell her that her husband, Herr Erich Perle, was found dead in the street at 9.35 that morning.

Emilie gapes at the policemen.

*Found dead in the street that morning?*

*Found dead . . . ?*

After a moment, she says stupidly, 'In the street? Erich couldn't have *died* in the street . . .'

It was a street, they inform her – Grünewaldstrasse. 'He was,' they say, 'on the steps of the apartment building inhabited by Police Chief Erdman. This may have been a coincidence, or he may have been intending to visit him. The cause of death seems to have been his heart.'

Emilie finds that she can't speak. She wishes herself back in her dream. Her mother she could overcome, but this – this 'death in the street' – is quite beyond what she can confront. Perhaps it is not true? Perhaps the policemen are not really there?

She turns her head this way and that, looking round the room for clarification. Is this happening or not happening? The room gives up no clues. So she waits for a sign, for something to occur which is present and real. And eventually that sign comes, in the form of an all-too-familiar sound: in his little cot, Gustav is crying.

# Part Three

# Hotel Perle

## *Matzlingen, 1992*

By the age of forty, Gustav owned a hotel in Matzlingen. He understood that the métier of hotelier was perfectly suited to his fastidious disposition. He took pride in the cleanliness of the place, and in providing the small necessities of human existence which helped to make life bearable: good central heating, beds both soft and wide, hairdryers for the ladies, comfortable chairs in the dining room, an open fire in the lounge . . .

His one act of vanity was to name the hotel after himself – the Hotel Perle. He understood that this name somehow made the hotel sound grander than it was, when in fact, in the Michelin Guide to Switzerland, it only merited a small house symbol, designating an establishment *assez confortable*, but of no special renown. Yet Gustav felt pride in it. His devoted Italian chef, Lunardi, concocted food that managed to be both interesting and consoling. The two men understood that when people travel, they often also long to be at home again, and so this was what they tried to provide for the guests of the Hotel Perle: a home from home.

Gustav was now fifty. He lived by himself in an apartment on the top floor. From its windows, he could see the River Emme and an ugly block of apartments built on the site where once the old cheese co-operative had stood. He felt glad that the cheese co-operative had gone, so that he didn't have to think of his mother coming home, smelling of Emmental and using this smell as a reason for never hugging or kissing her son.

Yet he thought about his childhood very often. It always

brought on a feeling of sadness which seemed absolute and complete – as though no future sorrow would ever touch him again in this way. The sadness gathered like a grey twilight around the idea of his own invisibility: the way the boy Gustav had kept on trying to push himself into the light so that his Mutti would see him better. But she had never seen him better. She'd remained half blind to who he was.

He'd believed, when he bought the old Gasthaus Helvetia and transformed it into the Hotel Perle, that Emilie, who, in a life deprived of luxury, had never ceased to yearn for it, would be proud of him. But this didn't seem to be the case. She'd admired the Biedermeier furniture he'd chosen for the lounge and she could occasionally become pink and breathless over some rich dessert Lunardi had made, 'especially for your mother, boss'. But she had never congratulated Gustav on starting up the hotel. In fact, she had told him that she didn't like coming there. It reminded her of her lowly job as a chambermaid at the Gasthaus Helvetia. She said, 'Your father rescued me from all that, and I'm sorry, Gustav, but I really have no wish to return to it.'

Gustav wanted to say that it was ridiculous for his mother to conjoin in her mind the comfortable new hotel, on which he'd lavished such infinite care, and the old gasthaus. There was no resemblance between the two – only that the roof and the outer walls still existed, but even these had been repaired and cleaned. He wanted to remind his mother that the rooms of the gasthaus had had narrow beds and linoleum floors and thin curtains which let in the light. The breakfasts of stale bread, weak coffee and rubbery Emmental had been a disgrace to Swiss cuisine. The public rooms had been dingy, the toilets smelly and stained. Whereas, in the Hotel Perle, wherever the guests might walk, they would find things to please them: flower arrangements in the hall, soft rugs beside the beds, bathrooms brought to a scented shine . . . But it was pointless to go on. If he ever began listing these things, Emilie would turn away from him, as though she couldn't hear a word he was saying. At these moments, with her pointy nose in the air, she would remind him of some terrified creature – a bat clinging to the wall of its cave – distressed by his human noise.

Yet he hadn't been able to give up on her. He knew that, in spite of everything, he still loved her. In some part of himself, he'd always believed that his mother couldn't die before she'd learned to love him. As he'd got older, he'd tried to teach her how to do this, before it was too late, but he hadn't succeeded.

When Emilie became frail, he asked her if she would like to come and live in the hotel, so that he and his staff could look after her. But the question appeared to wound her.

'I suppose,' she said, 'you're ashamed of me because I never had a kitchen table. Is that it?'

Gustav stared. He worried that his mother's mind was becoming as fragile as her body.

'I don't know what you mean, Mutti,' he said.

'I mean that you stop at nothing.'

'I still don't know what you're trying to say.'

'You stop at nothing in your shaming of me. With your Michelin-starred hotel! You would have preferred to have had Adriana Zwiebel as your mother, I know. With her money and her designer handbags. And instead you got me, and you've been ashamed of me all your life.'

Gustav stood very still. He found himself wondering whether there was any truth in what she'd just said.

'You don't deny it. You see?' said Emilie, and her thin hands were bunched like a boxer's, ready to hit out.

'I do deny it,' said Gustav. 'And the hotel has no Michelin star.'

'It's got a Michelin something or other. And twelve bedrooms! And I have no table to eat off, and that's a cause for shame in your eyes.'

Gustav went to her and put his arms around her, trapping her boxer's hands. He kissed the top of her grey head. But immediately, she pulled away from him, as he knew she would – as she always did.

He had been close to her only once. It was when they went together to Basel. He was sixteen years old.

They travelled there for the funeral of Irma Albrecht, Emilie's mother, whom Gustav had never met. In the train going to

Basel, Emilie said, 'You never met her because she was a horrible woman.'

After the funeral, to which nobody came but them, Emilie told Gustav that they had to stay on, to clear out Irma's old house in the hills and see if they could sell it.

When Gustav saw the house, all broken down, with a lavatory in a tilting hut in the garden, he said he couldn't imagine anybody wanting to buy it.

'You're wrong,' said Emilie. 'A developer will buy it. Basel is a growing city. People are eyeing up the surrounding land.'

On their second day, Emilie made a fire in an old brazier where Irma used to burn her garden debris. Gustav helped her to haul all Irma's clothes out of her cupboards and throw them onto the fire. Even her hats were burned. In one of these, Gustav found a pearl hatpin, but when he attempted to take this out of the hat, Emilie snatched it from his hand and threw it into the flames. 'The pearl isn't real,' she said. 'The pearl is a lie.'

While all the clothes were burning, Emilie began on the bedding and the rugs, as though she believed that everything Irma had ever used had become contaminated. As Gustav helped her to carry these out, the old pig farmer, who had been Irma's neighbour, appeared, cradling a baby piglet in his arms.

'I saw the fire,' he said.

'Yes?' said Emilie. 'All this is worthless stuff.'

The farmer held up the piglet. 'I'd like a blanket,' he said. 'They get cold, the little ones.'

Gustav watched the shadow of a smile cross Emilie's face. He thought that perhaps the idea that her mother's bedding was going to furnish a pigsty enthralled her.

'By all means,' she said. 'Take what you want.'

The old man handed the piglet to Gustav and he noted how the texture of its skin looked smooth, but was in fact as rough as sandpaper. The animal squirmed and shivered in his arms, while the farmer began sorting through the blankets. He shook his head in bewilderment.

'These aren't worthless, gnädige Frau,' he said to Emilie.

'They are to me,' she said.

'Fetch a barrow, can I?' he said. 'Make my bed cosy with these. Give you the piglet in exchange.'

Gustav expected his mother to accept this. One of the few things she was proud of in her disappointed life was her successful cooking of roast pork. But now there was an unfamiliar look of compassion on her thin face. 'We don't want the piglet,' she said. 'You fetch your barrow.'

The pig farmer took everything away. The baby piglet scampered back and forth by his side as he collected two barrowloads of rugs and blankets. When they were all gone, Emilie laughed and said, 'Perhaps he and the pigs bed down together. Nothing would surprise me in this world.'

The fire in the brazier had burned low. On top of the ashes lay some roses, made of thin metal, from one of Irma's hats. Emilie looked at these and announced, 'That's what she was like. You tried to crush her, but some part of her stayed whole. My life will be better now that she's gone for good – well and truly gone. Perhaps I'll be kinder to everybody, including you, Gustav.'

As dusk was falling, they started on the larder. Emilie said, 'We can give all the bottles of sauerkraut to the pig farmer, for the swill bucket.'

Irma's sauerkraut was lacto-fermented from cabbages she'd either grown or bought cheap in bulk from the local vegetable market. Emilie and Gustav counted thirty-four bottles of it, labelled and dated. The cabbage inside some of the oldest jars from the 1930s had turned a deep chestnut brown. They emptied everything out into a tin basin, large enough to bath a baby in. Emilie said, 'I expect I was bathed in this thing. Rinsed like a cabbage.'

It was dark, now, in the larder, almost night. Gustav felt sick from the smell of the fermentation and was about to suggest that they should stop, when he noticed one last bottle in a corner of the larder shelf.

He picked up the bottle and saw that it was full of banknotes. He stared at the money. Then he carried the jar to the window, where a rising moon provided a sliver of light. He unscrewed the lid and he and Emilie put their hands in, like children's hands into a bran tub, and pulled out rolls of fifty-franc notes, secured with rubber bands. It was difficult to calculate how much money was there, but they knew it was a lot.

Later, they counted out more than fourteen thousand francs. 'Well,' said Emilie, 'I could probably buy a whole tea shop in Basel with this, but I won't! I'm going to put it into a savings account and half of it can be for you.'

Gustav used his share of the money to put himself through catering school in Burgdorf. And he often thought, later on, that without the fifty-franc notes hoarded by his grandmother in a sauerkraut jar, and without the money got from the sale of her crumbling house, he would never have had the life he wanted and been able to establish the Hotel Perle. He came to wish that he'd retained some souvenir of Irma Albrecht, but he had nothing, not even a metal flower from a Sunday hat.

# Anton

## *Matzlingen, 1992*

Some dreams endure.

Anton Zwiebel said of his own dream of becoming a concert pianist that the word *endurance* was ironically appropriate to it, because it entailed so much suffering.

After the first piano competition in Bern, at which he'd come last in his group of five finalists, Anton had subjected himself to eight or nine further competitions, where once again he'd done well enough in the heats to reach the final and then faltered when he had to play on a grand stage. He had never once been declared the winner, nor even the runner-up.

Adriana took Anton to the doctor, to try to find a cure for what she said were just 'nerves'. He was prescribed calming drugs of different kinds and differing strengths, but none helped him to conquer his terror on the concert platform. He still played badly when it came to the moment of needing to play well.

He sometimes raged about being 'tested' in this way. It was Gustav who had to listen to his anger. Anton said, 'It has to be you, Gustav. I can't let my parents see me behaving like a wild dog. I've already let them down enough. They paid tons of money for lessons with Herr Edelstein and yet more for competition entry fees, and they expect results. Whereas you –'

'You're right,' said Gustav. 'I don't care if you win or not. All I mind about is that not winning makes you unhappy.'

One day, when Gustav and Anton were both eighteen and went to the ice rink after school, Anton said that he didn't want to skate, he wanted to talk. So they sat in the rink café, drinking beer, while the skaters kept gliding and turning and jumping and falling at their backs, and Anton said, 'I can't go on with this dream of fame. It's killing me.'

They talked for a long time, getting drunk on beer. Anton said that he'd never abandon music, it was too important a part of his life, but that he had to give up competing. 'I just want to play the piano, because playing the piano is a beautiful thing to do,' he said. 'I played Beethoven's "Moonlight" Sonata over and over the other evening, when my parents were out at some dinner. And I know this is a schmaltzy piece, but each time I played it, it moved me more and more and I played it better and better, until I was crying and playing at the same time. The keyboard was soaked, but I didn't care. I felt I was transfigured, or something. And that's when I thought, *this* is what I want – to be moved by my own playing, but not have to be on a stage and move a thousand other people. I know you'll understand.'

Gustav looked at Anton's face, bright pink from the cold of the ice and from the emotion welling up inside him. He reached out and put the back of his hand against Anton's cheek.

'Of course I understand,' he said. 'I'm glad you've decided this. I was beginning to be afraid for you.'

'Were you? But there's one other thing facing me, Gustav. How am I going to tell my parents? Especially my mother. How am I going to tell her that all her hopes for me are going to be crushed?'

Gustav turned and looked out at the skaters and he thought how the ice rink had always been a place of laughter and joy, and the laughter he could remember best was Adriana's.

'I'll tell her for you,' he said. 'If you want me to. I can explain it.'

'Isn't that asking too much of you?' said Anton.

'No.'

'She might accept it better, coming from you. She knows you always see into the heart of things.'

'Perhaps . . .'

'But she may get upset, Gustav. If she does, just put your arms round her.'

*

Gustav went to Fribourgstrasse on an early-summer afternoon, when Armin was at his office. Sunlight filled the room. Adriana was pruning her geraniums. He asked her for a drink of water.

He sat down with Adriana on one of the chintzy sofas and she took his hand in hers. 'You know I'm always delighted to see you, Gustav,' she said, 'but something tells me that you're bringing me bad news. Am I right?'

'Yes,' said Gustav. 'And I hate to be doing this to you and to Armin, but Anton's counting on me.'

Adriana let go of Gustav's hand. 'Has he got a girl pregnant?' she said. 'Is that it?'

'No. Not as far as I know.'

'Well, then, you'd better tell me what it is.'

Adriana let Gustav speak and didn't interrupt. He tried to explain Anton's feelings *as though he were Anton.* And he found that this wasn't difficult, because he knew these feelings so well. As he talked, he felt his face grow pink with emotion. He almost felt that he might cry.

When he'd finished, Adriana lit a cigarette. She smoked and said nothing for a while. Then, she leaned forwards with her elbows on her knees. She said, 'I had another child, Gustav. A little girl we called Romola, who died at the age of one. Anton will barely remember her. But Armin and I . . . of course she's with us in our thoughts all the time. And I suppose that all the hopes we may have had for our two children we've put onto the sole survivor, our beloved Anton. It's in our nature to strive, to want to see our children succeed, and what more wonderful thing could there be in the world than to become a famous pianist? Music is so important in a human life. It finds a space inside us that nothing else touches.'

Gustav was unsure of what he was expected to say. He began thinking about Romola and the day at the rink when he and Anton had cut their arms with skate blades, to mingle their blood and swear their secrecy. He could remember the pain of the cutting and the strange feeling of Anton's blood pooling in a slit in his arm.

After Adriana had smoked some more in silence, she put out her cigarette and said, 'I've imagined it so many times, Gustav – the moment when Anton would conquer his fear and begin to perform on a world stage. He has the talent to do it. We all know that he does. But now you're telling me that day is never going to come?'

'Yes. I'm telling you. That day is never going to come.'

'I can't bear it, Gustav!'

'I know it's hard. But perhaps you knew what Anton was feeling all along and this is really no surprise to you?'

'I *didn't* know! Armin had some anxieties about it. I told him he was being pessimistic: I told him Anton would conquer his fears in time. But I was wrong. And I should have seen it. We paid enough for medication. I'm his mother and I've been obtuse. I've pushed too hard and made Anton suffer. And now all our dreams collapse . . .'

Adriana began to weep. Gustav remembered what Anton had said about putting his arms round her, so he moved closer to her on the sofa and held her and she laid her head on his chest and allowed herself to cry. Gustav stroked her hair and said, 'You mustn't think Anton blames you in any way. He doesn't. He said to me, "We were all in this folly together." That was the word he used – folly. And he included me in that. Because he knows . . . well . . . he knows how much I love him. I love you all, Adriana. I wish I had a family like yours.'

When he found that this was what he'd said – this thing about love – Gustav couldn't suppress tears of his own. He and Adriana clung together, rocking and crying. The moment was so intense, it created in Gustav a feeling of overwhelming sexual yearning. He lifted Adriana's face and held it close to his and she whispered his name, Gustav . . . He kissed her mouth. He expected her to pull away from him, but she didn't. She returned the kiss and Gustav's head swam. He thought that he might lose consciousness. He knew that what he was doing was pure, exquisite sin.

He forced himself out of the moment and back into the sunlit room, where the white net curtains moved lazily at an open window. He drew back from Adriana and laid her head gently against the sofa cushions.

'I'm sorry,' he whispered. 'That was wrong of me. Will you forgive me? Please forgive me and don't hate me, Adriana. And please don't tell Anton.'

Adriana looked at Gustav tenderly. She wiped away her tears.

She stroked his burning face. She said, 'That was a beautiful kiss, Gustav. And we all love you very much. I hope you know that. Anton and Armin and I, we love you very much.'

That autumn, Gustav went away from Matzlingen, for the only significant time in his life, to begin his catering course at Burgdorf.

Anton Zwiebel became a piano teacher.

During Gustav's first vacation from his college, he went to a pupils' concert at the junior school where Anton worked. He saw not only how hard the young children tried with their music, but also how clearly they loved and worshipped Anton. After the pupils had played, they would rush to Anton's side and open their arms to be hugged by him. Gustav saw him as a kind of Pied Piper of Hamelin, with all the enchanted children clustered round him. And he thought, I am one of them; I am enchanted, too. I will follow Anton wherever he leads me – even into a dark cave.

At fifty now, Anton had become head of the Music Department in the much expanded Protestant Academy of Sankt Johann, where once he and Gustav had studied. He was a handsome man with thick, curly hair, greying at the temple, a wounding smile and an infectious laugh which Gustav never tired of hearing.

Gustav knew that women were seduced by Anton and that he enjoyed, to some extent, his power over them. But Anton told Gustav that he never let himself fall in love. He said the idea of living with a woman was 'inimical' to him. He said that making music on the piano would always be the most important thing in his life and the idea that there would be 'this wife-person, this stranger' eavesdropping on his piano practice filled him with horror. Gustav reminded Anton that he always played for him and for his parents, not minding if he made mistakes in front of them, but he replied simply, 'You're not strangers.'

'But your wife would be?'

'Yes. In certain ways, I think she'd remain one.'

Gustav watched with attention Anton's repeated refusal to let any of the women in his life believe she *belonged* to him. They might stay a night or two at his apartment, which was near to that of Adriana and Armin on Fribourgstrasse, but seldom talked about them or let them visit the school. Sometimes, he couldn't remember the name of the woman he was currently sleeping with. He said to Gustav, 'Perhaps one day it will be different, but for the moment, it isn't like that, any more than it is for you, eh, Gustav?'

'No,' said Gustav. 'I've got no time for it. My heart and mind are taken up entirely by the Hotel Perle.'

# Pastime

## *Matzlingen, 1993*

The Hotel Perle was a place where guests mainly stayed a very short time – one night or two – on their way to somewhere else. For what was there to see in Matzlingen? A few elegant shops. A tile factory. The Protestant Church of Sankt Johann. Long ago, visitors had been shown around the cheese co-operative, to the fury of Emilie Perle, who didn't like being gawped at as she went about her arduous work. But now the cheese co-operative was gone. Matzlingen had become little more than a stopover place on the road to Bern.

Yet, just occasionally, guests booked in for a longer stay, attracted by the gentle walks in the surrounding valleys and by the undemanding insignificance of the town itself. And in the cold spring of 1993, one such client arrived.

He was English. His name was Colonel Ashley-Norton. He was in his late sixties and spoke good German, which, he told Gustav, he had learned 'at school and then in the war, when I was nineteen'. He appeared to Gustav like a caricature of a reserved English gentleman, with brilliantined white hair, a rosy complexion and a ridiculous little moustache, trimmed so close to his top lip, it resembled a worn-out nail brush.

When Gustav began talking to Ashley-Norton, he saw at once that this reserve concealed an emotional personality. The elderly man said, with a little choke in his voice, that he wanted to be in Matzlingen, 'in the middle of nowhere, with nothing much to see, so that I can be very quiet and solve the puzzle of what to do with the rest of my life'. He added that all he asked of this nowhere was that it be clean and with a fragrant valley nearby, where he could walk. He said that he knew, in Switzerland, he could rely on this.

It emerged that Colonel Ashley-Norton has been married for forty years to a woman he referred to as Bee, but Bee had let him down. He put his hand against his heart as he said, 'She let me down by dying.'

Colonel Ashley-Norton went on. 'She died on Christmas Day. In the interval between eating our Christmas pudding and going into the drawing room to watch the Queen's broadcast. She just sat in her chair and closed her eyes and died. Her heart stopped. And now I'm alone.'

Gustav was tempted to say that, having witnessed the long-drawn-out death of his mother, he thought this was a good way to complete a life – just closing your eyes and never moving again – but he didn't. He could tell that Ashley-Norton was still afflicted by talking about Bee. His bottom lip began to tremble. He snatched out of his breast pocket a paisley handkerchief and wiped his eyes. He asked Gustav for a tot of whisky.

When the colonel had downed the whisky, he said, 'You're going to find this very foolish, Herr Perle, but the thing which upsets me most, on a day-to-day basis, is that I've lost my gin rummy partner.'

Gustav asked, 'What is gin rummy, Colonel?'

'Oh yes,' said the colonel, 'I stupidly forget that this isn't universal, because it's always seemed so universal to me. It's a card game. Fairly simple, yet with a little skill attached to it, but without the need for perpetual vigilance, as in bridge. Bee and I used to play three or four times a week for years and years. It's a game that calms your nerves. I would even go so far as to suggest that it may help to regulate a human life, and make what is unbearable easier to be borne. And now I have no one to play with.'

'We play an obscure card game in Switzerland called Jass,' said Gustav. 'The cards are decorated and complex. The scoring is difficult. Perhaps, while you're here, you could teach me gin rummy, Colonel? Once the service of dinner is complete, I have very little to do, except make the rounds of the hotel before I go to bed. I would be delighted to learn.'

'Would you really?' said Ashley-Norton. 'That's very decent

of you. None of my friends in England wanted to stand in. They thought gin rummy was an infernal waste of time. I said to them, "That's the whole point of it. Wasting time changes the nature of time. And the heart is stilled." But nobody paid me any bloody attention.'

They played in a quiet corner of the lounge, after dinner. Lunardi sometimes came through from the kitchen and stared at them and shook his head, no doubt thinking that cards were 'an infernal waste of time', but perhaps recognising that Gustav was enjoying himself, because he took to making chocolate truffles for the two men to eat with their coffee and cognac. Ashley-Norton declared that the texture of Lunardi's truffles was 'beyond perfect'.

Gustav liked being in the lounge – a place where he'd seldom sat for long. The room was at the very centre of the hotel and, from his comfortable chair, he could listen quietly to the life of the establishment going gently on, then readying itself for the night. This attention he gave to his surroundings only distracted him very marginally from learning the card game and Ashley-Norton was a patient teacher.

On the first evening, the colonel won every single game, but he said to Gustav, 'This will change. Once you've learned the knack of placing cards strategically in the discard pile, for later picking up, you will start to win. It may take you a few goes at it, but what is exceptionally consoling about gin rummy – if the players are each moderately good or moderately bad at it – is that the scores have a reliable tendency to ebb and flow like tides. No player ever gets so far ahead in the arithmetic that disharmony occurs. You will soon see.'

And so this proved to be. Ashley-Norton had booked into the hotel for two weeks, but now he extended his stay into 'unknown time'. He asked only to keep the same room, of which he had become fond, and that the supply of chocolate truffles might not diminish. In the cool spring weather, he spent his days walking around the town and going into the valley beyond, carrying an alpenstock, looking for wild narcissi. His cheeks became even more rosy than they'd been at his arrival. He praised the cherry trees of Mittelland, now coming into flower.

*

One night, after once again talking about the cherry blossom he'd encountered on his walks, he laid down his cards, took a swig of his cognac and said, 'The only trouble about the trees is that they remind me of the road to Bergen-Belsen.'

Gustav paused in the game.

Ashley-Norton once again took out the paisley handkerchief that was always reliably there in his top pocket, and blew his nose. Then he said, 'Once you've witnessed that, it's like a film inside your head. You don't want to press the "play" button. But then something happens – like me seeing the beauty of those trees in your valleys around here, and smelling their scent – and it gets pressed. And now I'm having trouble sleeping again.'

Gustav asked him gently if he wanted to talk about what he'd seen. The colonel said, 'Talking about it helps the nightmares to go away, but I can't do it for long.'

He said it was a perfumed road, the road to the camp. All the cherries were in flower and the scent of the air was beautiful. And as the British soldiers passed through the villages, they saw children playing happily in the orchards. They saw animals and birds seeming to thrive on the farms, and ponds full of fresh water and windmills turning in the spring breeze. He said, 'We didn't believe we were going to see what we saw.'

Gustav refilled the colonel's glass with cognac, and when Lunardi came through to say goodnight, he sent him quickly away.

When Lunardi had gone, Ashley-Norton said, 'It's when I get to this bit that I can't go on. The thing is, Herr Perle, I was only nineteen. I'd been called up just a few months before. Some of the other chaps in the regiment, they coped with it better than I did, because they'd seen other terrible things. Shocking things. But nothing as bad as what we came across at Belsen, mind you. I'm not sure there can, on earth, be anything more terrible than that.'

He told Gustav he had been given a camera and told to take pictures, because rumours had reached the British Army of an extermination camp at Bergen-Belsen, and it needed to be documented for the courts – for all the reckoning to come after the war. He said the commanding officer gave the camera to him because he was reputed to be 'an arty type'. The officer instructed him to take as many pictures as he could and to leave nothing out.

'I began on the road,' he said, 'taking pictures of the trees and the geese and the children. Then, the first sign we had that something terrible was approaching was that the air was vitiated with an appalling stench. It grew and grew. All the chaps, even the senior officers, started to slow down. We honestly wanted to turn back. Some of the boys were sick in the ditch, before we even got there. I tied a handkerchief round my nose and mouth. I knew that we had to go on. I took a picture of my best buddy, Ralph Thompson, puking on a grassy bank.'

Ashley-Norton drank more brandy. He said he was unable to describe, any more, the horrors that he saw. He said they were really beyond words. What he wanted to talk about was the camera – 'the bloody camera!' – and how much he began to hate it round his neck and to hate pointing it at the stacked-up piles of bodies and then at the suffering inmates of Belsen, 'as if I were at some wretched seaside holiday, as if I were a stupid adolescent who takes up photography as a pastime!' He said that some of the prisoners even smiled for him and the women tried to rearrange their hair, but that half the time he could hardly see what he was photographing, he felt so sick and blinded by misery.

'The thing was, Herr Perle, if I hadn't had the blasted camera and the heavy pack of film on my back, I could have done more to help people. But I was instructed never to let any of this "equipment" be separated from my body, and this was an order I had to follow. You see why I hated it so? I felt that camera and that bag of film were dragging me down into the earth. We had feeding teams and delousing teams, and chaps sorting and washing clothing, and I could have helped with some of that. Not with the medical stuff perhaps, because I had no training. But I could have been of some bloody use, couldn't I, instead of taking bloody pictures?'

The colonel wiped his eyes. After a moment or two, Gustav said, 'In fact, you were probably doing the most important job that any of you could have done – bearing witness. Somebody had to do it.'

'I know. Somebody had to do it. And yet, you see, not really. Because the Americans arrived with cine-film. They took moving pictures. It's all there in the archives. They didn't need my photographs. But all the same, I had to sleep with the wretched camera round my neck. I said to Ralph Thompson, "I'm near to hanging myself with the strap."'

Gustav sat with Ashley-Norton far into the night.

When he told him he couldn't manage to speak any more about Belsen, he offered to accompany him to his room, because he knew the colonel would be unsteady from all the cognac he'd put down, and he dreaded the idea that he might fall and injure himself in the Hotel Perle. But he said he didn't want to go to bed and 'risk the nightmares'.

They sat in silence for a while. Gustav banked up the log fire that he liked to keep burning in the lounge every evening until the summer came round. He knew they were both too tired to begin another game of gin rummy, or even finish the one that was incomplete on the table in front of them, but he left the cards spread about where they were – as if they *might* begin it again any moment. And Gustav wondered, was that what some of the Jewish families had done when they were rounded up – let things remain just as they were in the apartments they were leaving, as though, by nightfall, they would be home again, in time to switch on the lamps and make supper?

Ashley-Norton lit a cigarette. This seemed to soothe him a little and he was strong enough to start a new conversation, asking Gustav to tell him about his life and how he'd come into the hotel business.

Gustav embarked on this. He knew that his own voice was shaking a little, but he pressed on, describing his time at catering school and telling the colonel how caring for people and objects had always counted very strongly with him, ever since, in childhood, he'd been part of a little team caring for silkworms in the kindergarten. This made Ashley-Norton smile and he knew there was much more that he could have told him about how he'd become the owner of the hotel and why the place was so important to him.

But then, drawn back to the terrible road to Bergen-Belsen, he found himself suddenly veering away from his own past and saying, 'My father was a policeman. He rose to quite a high rank:

Assistant Police Chief, here in Matzlingen. I think he liked his work, but he lost his job during the war, for falsifying documents that allowed Jews into Switzerland, but I've never really known the full story of why he dared to do this – or even if he did it at all and, *if* he did it, how he was found out. My mother often implied that he'd been betrayed. She always talked about my father as a "hero", but I don't know if he was one or not.'

Ashley-Norton was silent for a moment. Then he said, 'Are you really saying that you *don't know*, or just that you haven't made up your mind about it?'

'I'm saying that I don't know.'

'I see. Well, in this case, you must find out, Herr Perle. You must find out! One should not go through life not knowing the history of such a matter. How old are you? Forty-eight? Fifty? Isn't it time you got the truth out of somebody, before everyone's dead and gone?'

# The Zimmerli Moment

## *Matzlingen, 1993*

The claims which Ashley-Norton had made for the card game – that it slowed down time and allowed the heart a rest from its perpetual agitation – Gustav had considered to be the exaggerations of a person with a somewhat protected life. But after the colonel left Matzlingen, Gustav found himself dismayed by how much he missed the nightly gin rummy sessions.

The idea came to him to persuade Anton to learn the game. He wondered if Anton's restless nature would allow him to settle down to it, but he also knew that Anton was frequently bored by the evenings he arranged for himself. He'd said to Gustav, 'I'm quite weary of taking women out to dinner in restaurants and picking up the bill for the ridiculous desserts they like ordering – in return for baleful sex.'

But no sooner had Gustav decided to broach the subject of the card game with Anton than he came flying round, one early evening, with an agitated look in his eyes, clutching a copy of the *Matzlingerzeitung* and saying he had to speak to Gustav immediately 'about something which has disorientated me completely'.

Gustav was in the dining room, checking, as he always did before dinner service, that the *couverts* had been laid out correctly, that the glasses were clean and the tablecloths spotless and freshly ironed. Disregarding for a moment Anton's evident anxiety, he continued his task without hurrying. (Anything which prevented him from performing his role as the meticulous overseer of the hotel's strivings after perfection created in him a feeling of dismay and mild irritation. He also believed that, in a life where he had so often played servant to Anton's whims and desires, he should, from time to time, keep his friend waiting.)

'Hurry up, Gustav,' said Anton. 'There's something in the paper I need to talk to you about. I'll go up to your apartment.'

Gustav found him sitting in his own habitual chair, pouring himself a glass of whisky.

'Look at this,' Anton said, holding out the newspaper.

Gustav took the paper and sat down opposite Anton. The headline he pointed to read: FAME BECKONS FOR MATZLINGEN BOY. The short article underneath it recounted the *astonishing success of former pupil of the Matzlingen Sankt Johann Academy, Mathias Zimmerli, at the prestigious Tchaikovsky Piano Competition in Geneva. Zimmerli took first prize and is now expected to be offered concert opportunities worldwide.*

'Read the last sentence,' said Anton. 'Make sure you read that because that's the one which really kills me.'

Gustav put on his glasses. He coasted through praise of Zimmerli's *clarity of sound in the Rachmaninov Piano Concerto Number 4, a highly difficult piece for a young musician to master*, and arrived eventually at the statement Zimmerli made when accepting the winner's prize. After thanking his parents, Zimmerli said: *I also want to thank my piano teacher at Sankt Johann, Herr Anton Zwiebel. Without the patience and inspiration of Herr Zwiebel, I know that I would not be standing on this podium now.*

Anton had his face in his hands. Through the closed hands, he said in a choked voice, 'He did it, Gustav! The thing I couldn't do. Zimmerli did it. How old is he now? Twenty? Twenty-one? But he goes on to fame and I'm stuck in Matzlingen for all time.'

Gustav stared at his friend. That he could be so dismayed by the success of a former pupil surprised him. But that he could use the words 'stuck in Matzlingen' was shocking. Gustav had never questioned the certainty that he and Anton would live out their lives very close to each other in this town which had nurtured them. But now, he saw suddenly that in Anton's mind Matzlingen was just a place where he was 'stuck' and from which (it followed) he might one day be free. Gustav kneaded his chest, to try to calm the turbulence that he felt in his heart.

'Anton,' he said, 'surely, you've said to me many times in our lives that you made the right decision about your career . . .'

'I don't know about *right,*' said Anton. 'I made the *only* decision I could make, because it was impossible for me to go on trying to succeed at public performance. But you don't imagine I've gone through all these years without regret, do you?'

'You've never talked about "regret".'

'I may not have talked about it. That doesn't mean I haven't felt it. You saw for yourself, I had the talent to do it, but my mental and physical make-up just wouldn't let me go on.'

'I didn't know you were feeling sad about it, Anton. I never knew. Perhaps that was very unobservant of me.'

'Not sad. That's too sentimental a word. Just *unreconciled.* Because think of the life I would have had – in the capitals of the world! And now all this is laid at Zimmerli's feet. He'll have a dazzling public career, and I'll go on with the humdrum life of a teacher in a small town. But I tell you frankly, and without meaning to boast, Gustav, Zimmerli is no more talented than I was at his age. If I could only have conquered my fear . . .'

Gustav got up and refilled Anton's glass with whisky and poured himself some cognac. He knew that this was one of those moments when the course of things in a life's quotidian existence is suddenly altered. If anybody had asked him what the state of Anton's mind had been up until that evening, he would have said 'content', but now he saw that this contentment had been snatched away from him and might never be found again in quite the same way.

He sat down with his glass of cognac. He said, 'I've always felt that it's pointless to try to change the things we can't change.'

'I know that.'

'I guess we have to try to change ourselves to fit them. Is it possible that you can get any consolation from the knowledge that you've helped this young person in ways which perhaps nobody else could?'

'No,' said Anton. 'I'm not generous enough to think like that.'

Anton fell ill.

He ran a high fever and refused food. Adriana and Armin

took him into their flat and sat for long hours at his bedside. They brought in the family doctor, a medic so old he couldn't stand straight above the patient, but had to lean at an angle over him, which Anton found irksome. The doctor could make no definitive diagnosis and was sent away.

Gustav visited Anton every day, bringing soups and broths made by Lunardi. When he began to recover, he tried to start teaching him gin rummy. They played on a bed table which reminded Gustav of the hinged shelf in the kitchen at Unter der Egg. There had never been quite enough room for the plates and dishes and cutlery on the shelf and now there was not quite enough room for the cards on the bed table, and they kept sliding to the floor.

For a short while – because there was nothing much else for him to do – Anton seemed to take to the game and Gustav let him win as often as he thought he wanted to win. But one evening, he told him what Ashley-Norton had said about the game 'stilling the heart' and this seemed to vex him.

'I don't want my heart stilled,' he said. 'I want my heart to overflow with joy.'

Anton went back to his own apartment and summoned one of the women he'd been going out with. Her name was Hansi, which Anton said he considered a ridiculous name, but he told Gustav that sex might 'bring back his will to live'. He said Hansi liked to make love 'sitting on top' and that this suited him because he felt too lazy to adopt any other position.

Adriana and Armin and Gustav were now told to leave Anton alone, so they stayed away.

Adriana took Gustav's hand in hers, which was wrinkled and bony, but still semaphoring the world with scarlet nails. 'It's very unfortunate, this Zimmerli business,' she said. 'My heart bleeds for Anton. But what can any of us do?'

'Nothing, Adriana,' said Gustav.

Anton stayed away from school for the rest of the summer term and then he announced that he was taking Hansi to Davos.

When Gustav heard him say the word 'Davos', he felt inflamed by jealousy and sadness, and his heart once again began its horrible fast beating. To imagine his friend lying in some airy room, lit with the white light of the derelict sanatorium, with Hansi bouncing up and down on him, trying to bring him to an 'overflow of joy', made him feel sick and afraid.

He said to him, 'Anton, don't take her to Davos. Take her somewhere else.'

'No,' said Anton. 'Tell me why.'

# Frau Erdman

## *Matzlingen, 1993*

The summer season at the Hotel Perle was busy. After complaints from Lunardi that his overload of work was putting his health in danger, Gustav hired a sous-chef to help him.

The sous-chef, Vincenzo, was twenty years old, a wild boy from Torino, and Gustav had to concentrate on calming him, without taming his talent as a cook. When he suggested to Vincenzo that he should try to master himself and cultivate a more robust outside shell, 'like a coconut', Vincenzo laughed and said, 'That's a stupid idea, boss! Coconuts are hairy, but I'm as smooth as a gladiator.'

Though the boy was hard work, Gustav felt glad of this distraction – any distraction – which prevented him from imagining Anton sitting in the sunshine of Davos, or walking the secret pathway into the forest above. He'd told himself that the sanatorium would long ago have been demolished, to be replaced by hotels or apartments in this now fashionable ski resort, and yet so vivid was it, still, in his mind, he couldn't imagine it ever being dismantled. In his dreams, he saw Anton and Hansi walking hand in hand up the steep road under the pines and finding wild strawberries at the verge. Their lips became red. They passed the wild strawberries from mouth to mouth . . .

There were times when Gustav half hoped that Colonel Ashley-Norton might return to the Hotel Perle. He knew that he would even be willing to endure the old man's further memories of Bergen-Belsen, in return for his consoling company and the games of gin rummy. But he never appeared.

What returned to Gustav, however, was the remark Ashley-Norton had made about his own need to discover the truth about his father's life. But where did that truth lie? If his father really had been a hero, then why had Emilie kept none of his possessions, only the empty cigar box which had once contained Gustav's 'treasure'? If she had revered him for an act of bravery, why had she acted towards him just as she had acted towards Irma, seemingly burning or giving away every last item that had belonged to him?

It came to Gustav now, that perhaps there *had been* a secret surrounding his last years, one which Emilie Perle wished no one to uncover. He lay in his narrow bed, content with the feeling of the great *substance and weight* of his precious hotel beneath him, quiet and still in the night-time, but poised to move and come alive again in the morning. And he thought how secrets of great importance may slumber in this way, but one day be woken and brought into the light.

Gustav went down to the Matzlingen Police Headquarters, gave his name and occupation, and asked whether he could consult police records for the years 1938 to 1942. The duty officer looked at him suspiciously and said, 'Why do you want these, sir?'

'Very well, I'll tell you,' said Gustav. 'My father was Assistant Police Chief here in 1938 and he was dismissed from the force in May 1939. I need to know why this came about and how. My father died soon after I was born. Before I grow old, I need to know what happened to him.'

The duty officer said, 'What was his name?'

'Perle,' said Gustav. 'My hotel is named after him.'

Gustav was then told to put his request 'for sight of confidential records' in writing and was informed that he would be contacted, if authorisation came through.

'I'm his son,' said Gustav.

'I know that, sir. You've just told me.'

'I have a right to know.'

'Well, we will have to see.'

While Gustav filled in his request form, he glanced up at a display of framed black-and-white portraits of police personnel hanging above the reception desk.

One of these was a man he thought he recognised from years

past, someone who had come once or twice to the apartment on Unter der Egg. Gustav now asked the duty officer who this person was and the policeman replied, 'That is Police Chief Roger Erdman. A very good wartime Chief, by all accounts. A man everybody respected.'

'Is he still alive?' asked Gustav.

'I doubt that he is,' said the duty officer. 'This is 1993. But look in the telephone directory, Herr Perle. You might find him.'

There were nine people called Erdman listed in the Matzlingen Directory, none with the initial R beside the surname. One evening, Gustav sat down and began to telephone them, starting with Erdman, A.

When he got to Erdman, L, a woman's voice answered. Gustav asked to talk to Roger Erdman, and the woman said, 'Who are you?'

When he told her his name was Gustav Perle there was a breathless silence on the telephone line. Then the woman said, 'Gustav. Emilie's child. I saw you when you were a baby. Before and after your father died.'

'Oh,' said Gustav, 'you saw me? So are you Roger Erdman's wife?'

'Yes. Roger has been dead for a long time now. The war made him ill and he never truly recovered. But let me tell you something. Your father was a wonderful man.'

'That's what my mother used to say . . .'

'He was. Oh my God, I'm moved to hear your voice, Gustav. But why are you telephoning me?'

It was now Gustav's turn to be silent. It was difficult to admit that he was trying to ferret around for secrets, but he stammered that he had now passed his fiftieth birthday, but still knew next to nothing about his father's life and that he was now going to try to talk to anyone in the town who could remember him.

'Well,' said Frau Erdman, 'I can remember him. Come to tea with me on Sunday afternoon. I live on Grünewaldstrasse. I will tell you whatever you want to know.'

The apartment was large and lightless. Although this was a summer afternoon, heavy drapes were drawn across the windows.

At first, Gustav was puzzled by this, but when he sat down with Frau Erdman and allowed himself to look at her carefully, the reason she'd chosen to live in this strange penumbra became clear to him. It was obvious that she'd once been a beauty. Adriana Zwiebel had said to him one day that beautiful women, as they age, 'become afraid of harsh light', and he felt certain that Frau Erdman preferred the darkened room, lit kindly with soft, yellow lamplight, to the glare of the summer day, so that those vestiges of her beauty which remained could still be seen.

At his arrival, she'd greeted him with a kiss on his cheek. 'Gustav!' she exclaimed. 'You can't imagine how happy I am that you found me! You don't look like your father, but your voice is very similar. When I heard your voice on the telephone, my heart skipped a beat. For a moment, I imagined Erich alive again.'

'Well,' said Gustav, 'I'm very happy to have found *you*, Frau Erdman . . .'

'Call me Lottie. Will you? I don't want to be "Frau Erdman" to you. Please call me Lottie.'

Lottie Erdman's hair was piled up in a grey tangle on her head and secured with a tortoiseshell comb. Despite her age, it was still thick and Gustav could imagine that it had once been blonde and shiny and worn long, perhaps, or else in the plaits which would have been the fashion of her youth. Her blue eyes were puffy, but still shone brightly inside their pouches of flesh. Her breasts and stomach were large and her movement was slow.

She had made tea and bought *millefeuilles* from the French patisserie at the end of her road. As she lifted one of these fragrant concoctions to her mouth, she said, 'Gluttony is the last indulgence of most people's lives, Gustav. In my opinion, it is a much better vice than drink. Don't you agree?'

Gustav found her laughter infectious, almost like the laughter of a young girl. They sat and laughed together and ate the *millefeuilles*, and then Gustav said, 'I don't want to take up too much of your time, Frau Erdman . . .'

'Lottie. I have to insist on "Lottie". I want to hear you say it.'

'Lottie. I don't want to take up your time or pester you with questions, but I've lately begun to understand how little I know about my father's life, and –'

'I knew your mother. If she hadn't lost her first baby . . . then,

I think, everything might have been different between her and your father. I think that she never forgave him for that.'

Gustav gaped at Lottie. He put down his half-eaten *millefeuille* on its china plate. He opened his mouth to speak, but nothing came out.

'You didn't know about the other baby? Emilie never told you?'

'No.'

'Well, she never liked talking about it. I think she tried to put it out of her mind. But there was an accident in the apartment, the one they had on Fribourgstrasse. Erich was mortified at what happened. He struck out at Emilie – because he thought she didn't try hard enough to understand the work he was doing in the war.'

'He hit her?'

'No. He just . . . I don't know exactly . . . she was rushed to hospital, but they couldn't save the baby. Poor Emilie. She was distraught. She blamed Erich for her terrible loss. She left him for a while and stayed with her mother in some mountain house.'

'The house near Basel?'

'Yes. I think so.'

'I know that house. I went there. It was a terrible place.'

'Was it? Well, she stayed away a long time. Erich was certain she was never going to return. But she did – perhaps because that Basel house was so bad. But I think she had decided to try again with Erich. And in time, you were born.'

'I never knew. I never knew about the lost baby.'

'No? Well, that was how your mother was. She kept things to herself. Not like me. I spill everything out. Do you keep things to yourself, Gustav?'

'Yes. My mother was never really interested in what I felt or thought. So it's become a habit, to keep things hidden inside me.'

Lottie reached out and poured more tea into the fine china cups. Then she lit a cigarette.

'The baby was a boy. They were going to name him Gustav.'

Gustav put his hand to the area of his heart and massaged his chest. Then he said, 'That's odd. I used to . . . when my mother was alive . . . sometimes get the feeling that I wasn't completely *there* for her, that she was looking around for someone else and then disappointed when she discovered that all she had was me. I guess she would have loved that first little Gustav better.'

Lottie's puffy eyes began to shimmer with tears she was trying to choke back. She reached across the tea table and took Gustav's hand in hers.

'Gustav,' she said. 'Your father loved you. I know he did, because he was such a loving man. And nobody knows this better than me, you see. Now, I don't know what you came here to ask me, but let me tell you the one thing I am just not able to keep from you. Your father and I were lovers. It began when Emilie went away and he thought she wasn't coming back. Nobody knew. Nobody was hurt by what we did. And when your mother came back, I broke it off. I told your father I didn't love him, but that was a lie. I worshipped him. He was my world. He was the love of my life.'

The tears began to fall. Lottie let go of Gustav's hand and picked up a little linen table napkin and wept into that.

Gustav felt moved by the sight of her. He didn't feel angry with her, or with anyone. He knew that instead he felt *glad* for his father, irrepressibly glad that he had been the lover of this once-beautiful woman. And then he remembered something. He remembered Emilie telling him that Erich had died in Grünewaldstrasse. And this was where he was sitting, in the Erdmans' apartment on Grünewaldstrasse – perhaps on the very sofa where his father had sat and gazed at Lottie, or taken her in his arms.

'The day he died,' he said. 'It was here, on the steps of your apartment building. He was coming to see you, wasn't he? He was coming back to you?'

Lottie looked up at Gustav, her eyes brimming, her hand still clutching the table napkin.

'I will never know,' she said. 'I tried to imagine that was the case, because I'd written to him not long before. I was finding it impossible to live without him. But was he coming back to me that day he died? Or was he coming to tell me that he could never see me again? I would give anything to know, but I never will.'

It was night now, but Gustav couldn't sleep.

What he'd learned on this day had awoken complicated

feelings, but the most intense of these was a feeling of relief. He knew that Lottie Erdman's revelations had helped him to make sense of Emilie's failure to love him. It had made him see that, for all her protestations about Erich's heroism, she'd been unable to love him either.

# Hans Hirsch

## *Matzlingen, 1994*

Gustav had noticed that, in many people's lives, the 'crisis' which came in time to everyone, usually arrived in the fifth decade. But in his life and in Anton's it arrived later, in 1994, when they were both aged fifty-two.

What he thought of as 'the Zimmerli moment' was a kind of precursor to it, waking in Anton all his old longing for singularity and adulation. From that moment, he'd had dreams about Mathias Zimmerli. He was also forced to read in the *Matzlingerzeitung* that the young man was giving concerts in Geneva and Amsterdam. There were days, he admitted to Gustav, when all he could think about was Zimmerli's mounting fame and his own insignificance.

And then, something else happened.

It began near to Christmas, when, as tradition dictated, the Sankt Johann Academy staged a pupils' concert, organised by Anton. At the end of these events, Anton always entranced the parents with a short recital of his own. He'd discovered over the years that Beethoven's late sonatas, particularly Sonata 26, 'Les Adieux', and Sonata 29, 'Hammerklavier', were the ones which spoke to him most passionately, so it was often one of these which he played as the finale.

He practised these two sonatas over and over. He frequently invited Gustav to listen to them and to answer questions about technique and clarity, which Gustav wasn't equipped to understand. But this didn't bother Anton. 'I like you as an audience,' he said. 'I always have. You make me feel calm.'

Gustav was there, then, on the cold December night when Anton played the 'Les Adieux' Sonata. And he was able to recognise that this performance was exceptionally good, as if something extraordinary had inspired Anton on that one occasion.

The school always put on a buffet supper after the concert, but Gustav wasn't able to stay for this. The central-heating boiler at the Hotel Perle was giving problems and he had to return to make sure the plumber he'd managed to find at short notice had been able to fix it.

The night was very cold. Keeping the hotel warm at all times had always been high on Gustav's list of priorities. His memories of his freezing room at Unter der Egg, and the touch of his tin train, like ice under his fingers, still lingered in his mind. He couldn't bear the idea that his guests would suddenly discover that they were shivering. So he was relieved to find the boiler working when he got back from the concert. He paid the plumber and wished him a merry Christmas and New Year and then went up to his apartment to enjoy the cold meats and cheese he'd asked Lunardi to set out for him.

Near to eleven o'clock, Anton appeared. He was carrying a bottle of champagne. His eyes were bright and his cheeks were very red, as though he'd been dancing on ice.

'Indescribable news!' he said as he took off his coat and threw it on a chair. 'News I thought I'd never live to hear!'

Gustav waited. His worries about the boiler, together with the emotion of Anton's playing at the concert, had tired him. He didn't want to drink champagne at this time of night, he wanted to go to bed, but he let Anton pour out two glasses and hand one of them to him. Anton raised his own glass and said, 'To fame! That's what we're going to drink to. To fame!'

They clinked glasses and Gustav said, 'To fame, that fickle whore?'

'Yes,' said Anton. 'I'm fifty-two years old, but now I'm going to tame the whore at last. You don't believe me, I can see from your face. And it is really a bit extraordinary. I'm going to drink fast, to calm my overexcitement. And then I'll tell you . . .'

A man called Hans Hirsch had attended the concert. Hans

Hirsch was the uncle of one of the pupils taught by Anton. Gustav had never heard this name, but it was apparently well known in music circles. Anton described him as 'a ridiculously handsome impresario', working in Geneva, the owner of a classical recording label, CavalliSound.

During the school buffet, Hans Hirsch had approached Anton. He'd clutched his hands and congratulated him on his playing of Sonata 26. He then explained who he was.

'I didn't know at first why he was telling me all this,' said Anton, 'but then he suddenly said that the thing which excited him most about his career was making musical discoveries – of people nobody had heard of and bringing them to prominence. He looked at me very intently and then he said, "I won't beat about the bush. I believe I've discovered in you a talent quite overlooked. If you're willing, I would like you to come and play for me in Geneva, with a view to making some recordings of Beethoven sonatas. We could begin with one or two, but, if you're as good as I think you are, I see the possibility of eventually doing the whole cycle, all thirty-two of them." I couldn't believe I'd heard correctly, Gustav. I had to ask him stupidly to repeat everything he'd said. I thought I was in a dream and would wake up any minute. I'm sure you can imagine that?'

Gustav stared at Anton. The bright blood in his cheeks made him look young again.

Before Gustav could say anything, Anton went on. 'It wasn't a dream, Gustav! Hans Hirsch believes in me. He really thinks I can master all thirty-two sonatas. Isn't that the most amazing thing that has ever happened to me?'

Gustav closed his mouth, which he realised had fallen open, like the mouth of an old man confronting some long-buried terror. He took a gulp of the champagne and forced himself to say, 'I think it's extraordinary, Anton. That it should come like this, out of nowhere. It's quite extraordinary . . .'

'The thing that's so beautiful about it,' Anton went on, 'is that, when I play for Hirsch, I'll just be in a small recording studio – not marooned out there on a vast stage – and so I should easily be able to conquer my nerves. It'll be quite different from a concert platform, and yet, once the recordings are made, millions of people may hear them. Imagine that, Gustav! I'll be playing for millions.'

'Extraordinary . . .' Gustav said again, seeming to find no other word but this.

'And it falls so well,' said Anton. 'He wants me to go to Geneva next week, when the Christmas holidays start. He made a joke about my age and said, "I think we should not delay, *n'est-ce pas*? We must get you out into the world, before it's too late."'

'Next week?' Gustav mumbled.

'Yes!'

'But next week is Christmas. You and Armin and Adriana are going to come to the hotel for the meal –'

'Fuck Christmas. Fuck the meal. Come on, Gustav. I thought you'd be happy for me. Why aren't you happy?'

'I am happy. It's only –'

'Only what? You don't seem to be happy. Remember that day at the rink when I told you I couldn't go on with my public performances, and you were so supportive to me? Well, now it's all turning around and I need your support again, when things are working for me at last. I thought I could count on you.'

'You can count on me. I think it's a wonderful thing, Anton. It's taken me by surprise, that's all.'

'Surprises are good. They happen so seldom.'

'Of course they're good. And I guess this is a new beginning to your life.'

'That's right,' said Anton. 'It is. And I tell you, my friend, I *need* a new beginning. I know you're happy in Matzlingen, with the hotel and everything, but me . . . I've known for a long time that I'm slowly dying here. If all goes well, I'll be able to give up my job at Sankt Johann and never come back to Matzlingen again.'

The champagne now tasted acid in Gustav's mouth and he put his glass aside. He felt such an intolerable pain in his heart that he knew he had to try by any means, however cruel or inappropriate, to soothe it. He got up and went to the window and looked out at the clouded moon over the roofs of the town that he'd never left. Without turning towards Anton, he said, 'You mention that day at the rink. You'll remember, then, that I offered to be the one to tell Adriana about your decision not to go on with the competitions? And I did go, as you know. And Adriana began to cry. And then I kissed her. I've never told you this. I kissed your mother on the mouth with a passionate kiss.'

There was a long silence in the room, then Gustav turned and saw Anton staring at him. Gustav wanted him to feel shock and hatred, as much as he himself felt devoured by the news of the arrival of Hans Hirsch. But he saw no hatred in Anton's face and after a moment, Anton took another sip of his champagne and said, 'It happens all the time. Don't think you're special. My mother is a very seductive woman.'

# Three Movements

## *Matzlingen, 1995*

The new year began.

In Davos and the other ski resorts, the grand establishments were crowded, but the Hotel Perle was almost empty. In January, Matzlingen seemed a sad place. The roads were bad, with snow falling upon ice and frosting over, and another layer of snow falling upon that. The tram service had been brought to a temporary halt by the frozen tracks, and Gustav thought about his father, spending arctic nights at the tram depot, longing to be with Lottie Erdman, then running, running to her door and dying in Grünewaldstrasse, dying from his faulty heart just moments before he was able to take Lottie in his arms. He imagined the passers-by crowding round the steps where Erich had fallen, and then retreating in horror, calling out, 'The man is dead.'

Anton was in Geneva. He told Gustav in a letter that Hans Hirsch had rented an apartment for him, with a grand piano. Every morning, a colleague of Hirsch's, a talented accompanist, came round to the flat and Anton rehearsed two Beethoven sonatas with him, 26 and 29. The following Monday, he was going to attempt the first of the recordings, Sonata 26, 'Les Adieux'. He told Gustav in the letter that, to his horror and shame, he felt some of his old anxiety returning.

Gustav knew this sonata very well by now. The piece was divided into three movements: 'Das Lebewohl' ('The Goodbye' or 'Les Adieux'), 'Abwesenheit' ('Absence') and 'Das Wiedersehen' ('Return'). He always found himself moved by the slow, middle movement, 'Absence', but, in the light of how sombre and almost deathly this was, the final movement, whipped up to an overemphatic liveliness, felt wrong to him – as though it belonged in a different piece of music.

He supposed he felt this because absences – such as the one he suffered when Emilie was in hospital and he was all alone in the apartment at the age of ten – did not very often end in high-spirited joy; they ended in reproach: *they had to be forgiven.*

Enduring Anton's absence, which Gustav saw as a kind of rehearsal for an absence which would be permanent and final, he knew that all he could do was wait. He supervised the clearing of snow and ice from the hotel steps. He made certain that the fire in the lounge was banked up for the few guests who were in residence. He saw that these tasks were the mundane tasks of a servant and he thought that, for all his ridiculous pride in the Hotel Perle, this was what he was: a slave to other people's comforts and desires. But this, it seemed, was the life he'd chosen.

It was now Sunday evening. The next day, at ten in the morning, Anton would arrive at the CavalliSound Studios to make his recording of 'Les Adieux'. Gustav was certain that his friend wouldn't sleep at all that night. Gustav's resolution, then, was not to sleep either, but to keep some kind of distant vigil over Anton. Yet he knew that his thinking about this was shamefully divided. On the one hand, he was going to keep his vigil so that Anton's anxiety might be lessened and he would get some rest; on the other hand, his vigil was malevolent, willing him to fail.

To keep himself awake though this darkest of nights, Gustav decided to replay in his mind an episode in his life that he didn't often visit: the slow death of his mother. Thinking about it always caused him a storm of helpless crying, yet he would often emerge from this feeling purged and free.

Gustav had been forty-three when his mother became seriously ill.

A year or so before this, she'd taken a lover – the man who had been the manager of the Matzlingen Cheese Co-operative and who had apparently always nurtured romantic feelings for his 'sweet Em'.

Emilie didn't try to conceal the relationship, but boasted about it to Gustav. She said, 'I expect you thought, in my sixties, no man would look at me again, didn't you?'

Gustav had replied that he didn't have thoughts like these, one way or the other, but told his mother that if this man was making her happy, then he would be happy for her, too.

His name was Martin Studer. Emilie began bringing him occasionally to the hotel for Sunday lunch and Gustav would join them at the table. Studer was about seventy years old. His head and neck jutted forwards from his shoulders, like a vulture's head and neck. Sometimes, these seemed to be withdrawn and his neck would disappear into his shirt collar, and Gustav would wait for the moment when they would be projected outwards again. He was both fascinated and repulsed by this phenomenon. Studer had big, glittering eyes and long, claw-fingered hands, with which he now and then caressed Emilie's cheek.

But there was one thing which Gustav had appreciated about him: he admired the hotel. He would point out to Emilie the crispness of the white tablecloths, the fresh flowers on the tables, the good service given by the waiters, and of course Lunardi's cuisine. At first, when he mentioned these things, Emilie said, 'Oh, all the details you point out have very little to do with Gustav.'

Gustav refused to rise to this, but Studer reminded Emilie that ultimate responsibility for excellence, in any hotel, lies with the manager or owner.

And, in time, after she'd gobbled up a significant number of Lunardi's Sunday Specialities, Emilie was able to bring herself to say, 'At least you've kept standards high, Gustav. Not like in your schoolwork, eh?'

Then, one Sunday, Emilie was unable to eat. She sat at the table without talking, but nodding her head back and forth, as people much older than she was were inclined to do, as though their last task on earth was to agree with everything they have seen and heard in the world.

Gustav suggested to Studer that he took her home. He always remembered how Studer reached out one claw hand and began to stroke Emilie's hair. The poor man had only just finished his roast chicken and was no doubt looking forward to Lunardi's chocolate torte or his peach parfait, but he took a last sip of red wine, then got up obediently and helped Emilie to her feet.

'Come, Em,' he said tenderly. 'You're tired. We'll get you into bed.'

Gustav went with them as far as the front door. Suddenly, he saw his mother break away from Studer and stagger a few paces, to vomit into a flower bed. He started to go to her, but Studer held him back. 'I will take care of her,' he said. 'I'm sorry about the flowers. I expect you can hose them down. Your mother will be well again soon.'

She was never well again.

Tumours were found in her stomach and in her lung. She went into the hospital where she'd almost died when Gustav was a boy, and was given the new chemical drugs that were supposed to reduce cancers, but which had to thread their poison through every bodily system, and weakened and distressed the patients to such an extent that Gustav had found himself wishing, at moments, that they had never been discovered and put to trials.

For a while, Emilie's sufferings had abated, and she was allowed to go home to Unter der Egg. Gustav arranged for two of the hotel chambermaids to go into the apartment the day before she came out of hospital and clean it from top to bottom and put a vase of scented roses in her sitting room. Then he collected her from the hospital. She was clutching a small suitcase he recognised from years and years before. And it had been the sight of this old, worn suitcase that had begun, suddenly, to choke him. He couldn't drive out of the hospital car park. He rested his head on the steering wheel, and cried. Beside him, Emilie sat very still, saying nothing, paying him no attention. Then he dried his eyes and apologised and drove on.

Martin Studer was at the apartment. Emilie didn't want to get into bed, but sat in her habitual chair in the parlour, staring at the roses. 'I don't know how these got here,' she said.

'I had the hotel staff bring them,' Gustav said.

'Oh, of course,' said Emilie. 'I'd forgotten. You don't do anything for yourself any more, do you? You get the "staff" to do it. But that's no way to live, my son. It will all end.'

Emilie's hair, always so scant and thin, had fallen out, so she was wearing a wig. The wig was brown and thick, slightly curled, and didn't resemble her own hair at all, so it felt to Gustav as though Studer and he were sitting there with a stranger – a stranger who now appeared slightly insane. Studer's vulture neck moved in and out of his shirt as he peered, in sadness and perplexity, at his beloved Em. Gustav looked around the room and thought, nothing good ever happened here, not even the time when Anton came to tea and he put on the purple lipstick; it would be best if this building were torn down.

He made tea and Emilie drank some of this and then she got up and walked out of the room. Gustav and Studer heard her farting in the lavatory. They didn't look at each other. The farts kept piping out loudly. After a moment, Studer said, 'I fell in love with your mother when she was very young and came to work at the Emmental co-operative, but of course I could never declare it then. Now, it seems to me as if I've wasted my whole existence.'

Gustav often asked himself, what held Emilie to her life? She'd been so angry and sorrowful for so long, so impossible to love or even to please, that he'd imagined that, when she saw the end was coming, she might be glad of death's release. But, in her stubborn way, she fought death off. Perhaps it was for Studer's sake? Though he looked like a bird of prey, he was a kind and sympathetic man. One time, when Gustav went round to Unter der Egg and Emilie was clearly in terrible pain, Studer was cradling her in his arms, like a child. Her wig had fallen off, but this didn't trouble him. He was kissing her bald head and singing to her in a tuneless voice.

She went back into the hospital. The last time Gustav visited, she was in a small room, lit by a blue lamp, exactly like the one she'd been in when she'd caught pneumonia and he'd had to bolt his door against Ludwig Krams.

She was sleeping. She looked peaceful. A nurse came in and Gustav said to the nurse, 'How long has she got?' and the nurse smiled and said, 'I think she's ready.'

When the nurse had gone, Gustav spoke to Emilie. He

addressed her as 'Mutti'. He didn't know whether she could hear him or not. He said, 'You may be ready, Mutti, but I'm not. There is something I always thought I could teach you, and that was how to love me. But I never have. Have I?'

He paused here, waiting, or hoping, that Emilie might say something, but she slept on, unmoving. There was more – plenty more – that he could have said, but he knew that the time for saying it was long past.

Gustav lifted her hand and held it in his. The hand was very cold. He told himself to kiss her forehead and not cry, but to master himself and just walk out of the room, knowing he would never see her again, that the rest would be eternal absence, with no 'Wiedersehen' to come. Walking out of the room would be his only triumph – that he deserted her life before she deserted it herself and left him behind.

He went out and the door of the blue room closed with a click-click which reminded him of the sound which came from a cinema projector when an old movie was at its end. In the corridor, he met Studer, holding a bunch of anemones. The two men stopped to talk for a moment and then Studer went on his way towards Emilie. Gustav did not see his mother again until she was in her coffin, where, on her lipsticked mouth, he fancied he could glimpse the ghost of a smile.

It was very late now, near dawn. Gustav wanted the crying to come, the tears that would purge him, but his eyes remained dry.

# Never Knowing for Sure

## *Matzlingen, 1995*

Late on Monday night, Anton called Gustav from Hirsch's penthouse, where he and Hirsch were drinking champagne. Anton seemed to be yelling into the receiver, as though he were on some military campaign with a field telephone held to his ear.

'Ask me how it went!' shouted Anton. 'Ask me!'

'Yes,' said Gustav, 'I'm asking you.'

'Brilliantly well is the answer. Brilliantly well! Everybody's tremendously excited.'

Gustav said nothing. He thought how wearisome it was that human excitation so often expressed itself in a deluge of clichés.

Anton went on. 'The thing is, Gustav, I didn't get nervous. I felt a kind of euphoria about making the recording. I was high, but not anxious at all. None of that sickness thing. I must have had an angel watching over me!'

'That's wonderful, Anton,' Gustav forced himself to say. 'It's everything I hoped for.'

'And now,' said Anton, 'Hans and I are making plans – in between gulps of this amazing Dom Perignon we're drinking! One recording isn't enough. Hans wants to waste no time. I'm staying here to work with our accompanist on three more Beethoven sonatas. Then we can release a cassette and a CD on the CavalliSound label.'

Gustav was on the point of asking 'Who is Hans?' His mind had swooped back to Davos and the sanatorium game and the boy with the tambourine. But then he remembered that Hirsch's name was also Hans.

'I think the Sankt Johann Academy will be understanding, won't they, Gustav?' Anton asked.

'Understanding about what?'

'About my not coming back. Don't you think? They know it's my one chance. They'll have to hire a new music teacher for the January term.'

'You mean you're not coming back at all?'

'Not yet, anyway. Maybe never. Who knows what will happen once the CD is released. There may be offers of one kind or another. But for now I have to stay here in Geneva, for as long as the work takes. You could go and see the school for me, couldn't you?'

'Why me?' said Gustav.

'Because you're a diplomat. Look how everybody jumps for you at the hotel. You have the power to make people do things. D'you remember how, on my first morning at kindergarten you ordered me to stop crying?'

'Of course I remember. But this is different.'

'Why's it different?'

'Because it's something I don't want to do.'

'All right. But you'll do it anyway. You always do things for other people. I'm counting on you.'

When the call ended, Gustav lay down on his bed. The silence outside his window reminded him that he was in Mittelland, that quiet place in the middle of his country, where nothing much happened, from which the mountains kept their distance. But now, he thought, I'm in my own Mittelland in my life and everything is roaring at me and asking me to change the way I think about things, and this is going to kill me.

The next day, after a scant few hours of sleep, he set out for the Sankt Johann Academy, to talk to the headmaster about Anton. But when he came to within sight of the school, he knew that he was unable to perform this mission. He didn't even want to *think* about Anton, let alone make pleas on his behalf for his desertion of a job he had done for fifteen years.

He changed direction and walked towards Grünewaldstrasse. He suspected that Lottie's company would be consoling to him and that, in talking about Erich, the roaring in his head might be stilled.

Lottie was lying on her sofa, near an electric fire, reading a short story by Guy de Maupassant, in German. She said, 'I don't know whether the actual story is good or bad, but the German translation strikes me as shit.'

This made Gustav smile. He sat down opposite Lottie. He wished that Lottie would offer him a *millefeuille*, something creamy and outrageous in which he could find comfort.

Lottie looked over her spectacles at his anxious face and said, 'So what's the matter, Gustav? You look like a sad, grey donkey today.'

'Yes, that's about it: a sad, grey donkey . . .'

'Tell me what's happened, donkey.'

Gustav took a breath. He wanted to say, The person I love most in the world is about to leave me forever, but he knew these words were impossible to utter. Instead he said, 'I got a letter this week from Police Headquarters. You know I'd gone there to try to find out more about my father's dismissal and how it came about. But they say they can't discuss the case.'

'Why not? All the information must be there, on file.'

'It may be there, but they tell me it's classified.'

'*Classified*? Don't you just *hate* official jargon? I think they won't tell you what happened to Erich because they're ashamed.'

'Ashamed?'

'They know that what Erich did was moral and brave, not criminal. He never should have been left to suffer in that tram depot job. He should have been reinstated in his old job, but they didn't do it. Everybody was afraid – afraid of the German High Command and what Hitler might do to Switzerland. They let him die.'

'What I still don't understand, Lottie: somebody in Matzlingen must have reported what my father had done to the Justice Ministry in Bern. How would they have known otherwise? But who was it?'

Lottie closed her eyes. After a moment, she said, 'Perhaps the people in Bern accused the Israelitische Flüchtlingshilfe of falsifying the dates and it was they who said, "No, it wasn't us, it was Assistant Police Chief Perle." But maybe you should let it rest, Gustav. I think it can never be known for sure.'

'Everything – in the end – can be known, Lottie.'

'Most things. But perhaps not this. You must let it go.'

Gustav looked searchingly at Lottie. To escape his gaze, she'd picked up the Maupassant stories again and begun flicking through the pages, as if searching for her place in the book.

Abruptly, Gustav asked, 'Was it your husband?'

Lottie sighed. She set the book aside once more and said, 'Roger was an honourable man, Gustav. It was your father and I who betrayed him, not the other way around.'

'But if he knew my father was your lover?'

'He wasn't my lover then, in 1939. It began later, when your mother left.'

'And your husband's job was never under threat?'

'Everything was under threat. This was a perilous moment for Switzerland. Your generation has no idea . . .'

'We have an idea. But the Germans *didn't* invade. There must have been deals made, at every level.'

'Perhaps there were deals. Perhaps there were betrayals? But what is a betrayal anyway, Gustav? Are you sure you know?'

'No. I'm sure I don't know.'

'Well then?'

Gustav stood up. He knew that the conversation about Erich was over, for the time being, at least. Lottie would say nothing more. He went to Lottie's window, half shrouded by her heavy drapes, and looked down at the cold street, where snow was delicately falling. Then he turned and said, 'Right now, I feel as if I've been betrayed by my friend, Anton, but perhaps there's a sense in which I'm really the betrayer. Anton never asked me to feel the way I do.'

Lottie stared at Gustav. 'Wait a minute,' she said, 'slow down. I think we need a drink here. Wine or whisky? Or schnapps?'

'I don't mind.'

'Come on, Gustav. One *always* minds. Which would you like?'

'White wine. German wine, if you have it.'

Gustav watched Lottie get up and walk slowly towards her kitchen. He saw how her big thighs rubbed together as she moved and how she favoured her right leg. And he wished these things were not so. He wanted Lottie Erdman to be as she'd been for his father, with her golden hair and her eyes the colour of a delft jar.

When she came back with the white wine, she sat down and waited for Gustav to begin to talk about Anton. He sipped the wine, which tasted sweetly of apples and of elderflowers, and he thought that this was how he was going to live life from now on, savouring small pleasures and not looking beyond them for happiness that was more complete.

'So, tell me . . .' said Lottie, after a while.

But he found, now, that he didn't want to talk about Anton. He wished he hadn't spoken his name.

He looked at his watch. 'I must go,' he said. 'I have an appointment with the headmaster of the Sankt Johann Academy.'

Late at night, Gustav telephoned Anton. He wanted to tell him how courteously the headmaster at Sankt Johann had greeted the news that his principal music teacher had left Matzlingen with no warning. He wanted to say, people in this country behave with restraint, Anton. When they might be angry about something, they choose, instead, to be polite. They may not understand how certain things come about, or why, but they are accepting. They hold themselves together – in ways that you have never quite mastered.

But there was no reply from Anton's phone. Gustav imagined him out in Geneva somewhere, being feted and spoiled by Hans Hirsch. He thought how, all around Anton, would lie the beauty of the city, the marvellous place where he was going to make his home and make his career and come to money and fame. He pictured him walking down a wide boulevard, passing the windows of smart boutiques, his silhouette lit by the yellow lights of huge, whispering cars. And then he pictured himself as others might see him, alone in a hotel which had almost no guests at this time of the year and nothing to break the silence except the clanking of a passing tram and the sound – unheard – that emanated from him, the ceaseless and pointless braying of an old grey donkey in pain.

# Absence

## *Matzlingen, 1997*

Anton Zwiebel left Matzlingen for good in the spring of 1996.

Gustav arranged a farewell supper for him in the dining room of the Hotel Perle, with Armin and Adriana. Lunardi cooked a sea bass with fennel, followed by a vanilla *crème brûlée* with an apricot coulis. Adriana said, 'This day was supposed to come years ago, when we were all young.'

Gustav saw at once that Anton was distracted. It was as though he couldn't wait to get back to Geneva, as though all the decades he'd spent in Matzlingen were of such paltry account that he couldn't be bothered to give this dinner his attention. What he wanted to talk about was Hans Hirsch and the 'fantastic sound engineers' at the Cavalli studios. He said, 'Every time I walk in there, knowing I'm going to play well, it's like a homecoming.'

*Homecoming.*

When this word was spoken, Adriana and Armin stared at their son in dismay, but said nothing. Gustav looked away, out of an uncurtained window, at the still-wintery sky holding on to a pearly-green luminescence before it surrendered to the darkness.

Anton left the dinner early. He said he had packing to do. Gustav walked with him to the door of the hotel, then hugged him and said, 'Don't let me go from your mind, Anton. I'll think of you every day.'

'No you won't,' he said. 'You've got the hotel to run and I've got a career to make. Think of me once a month; that's enough.'

Then he walked away, past the flower bed where Mutti had

been sick, and out into the night. Gustav stood watching him go, then he returned to Armin and Adriana, who were clinging together, like the occupants of a boat in a storm.

Gustav ordered coffee and brandy. Armin said, 'That was a very nice dinner, Gustav. But I bet Anton didn't even say thank you.'

Adriana pulled away from her husband and turned to Gustav and said, 'Do you believe it can happen?'

'You mean what Anton wants – fame and success?'

'There's part of me which refuses to believe it. He was disappointed before.'

'Sometimes things come later in a life. And he can cope very well with recordings. It was only the terror of the concert platform . . .'

'All right. But from what I know of the music world, he will eventually have to perform to audiences. Won't he? Careers are only made like this, from recordings *and* performance – not from recordings alone.'

'He doesn't seem to have thought of that,' said Armin. 'Has he talked to you about it, Gustav?'

'No. But I think we shouldn't start worrying, Armin. At the moment, he's happy. We should let him enjoy what's going on now.'

Anton sent Gustav a CD of his first recording: Beethoven's Piano Sonatas No. 24, No. 25, No. 26 ('Les Adieux') and No. 27. In an accompanying note, he wrote, '*Geneva is the most wonderful city in the world. At night, sometimes, I go and stare at the lake and count my lucky stars I was given all this before it's too late.*'

Gustav sat in his apartment, listening to the music. He had no idea whether Anton's playing was exceptional or just ordinary. After a while, he got out his hotel accounts and began to work at these while the music went on and on. Then he took the CD out of the player and laid it aside. He kept working at the accounts, which, in the silence which followed the music, began to absorb him completely. But he felt hot and agitated. The accounts showed all too clearly that over the last year, the revenues had gone down and down. The hotel had begun to fail.

Gustav knew why. He recognised that he had been in denial

about it for some time, but now he had to face up to it: the place was becoming shabby. The dining-room walls were dirty. A smell of stale gravy clung to them. The carpet in the lounge was stained. And guests had begun to complain that it was 'no longer acceptable in the mid-nineties' to have to walk to a lavatory and bathroom along a corridor. All the rooms should be given bathrooms en suite.

Gustav saw that the cost of the redecorating could be easily borne, but that the building alterations to install new bathrooms would constitute a heavy expense. More than this, in some cases, no bathroom could be fitted into the existing room; in three cases, he would have to suppress adjoining bedrooms and knock through into them in order to accommodate the 'en suite'. This would leave the hotel with nine bedrooms instead of twelve, thereby reducing his potential profits by almost one-third. Worse still, he could see that to carry out the work properly, he would be forced to close the hotel altogether for a while; he couldn't subject his guests to the perpetual noise of hammers and drills.

Gustav worked until late on the accounts. At the moment, it was summer and the hotel was full. He decided that he would have to consult with his builders and then, if he could get some reasonable price from them for the work, consider closing the hotel for the winter months. It then occurred to him that in order to retain Lunardi, he would have to give him paid leave. And he could see that if he did this for him, then the other staff, even Vincenzo, would expect him to do this for them too. He saw that he was destined for a long period of financial loss.

He didn't sleep well that night, but the following day, which dawned very bright and clear, he drove out of Matzlingen into the long valley that curved along the River Emme. He parked his car and walked up towards a forested hill and looked down upon the town.

He sat on the warm grass. At the edge of the forest he recognised the familiar leaves and bright buds of a clump of wild strawberries. He turned away from these and stared down at the untidy conglomeration of apartment houses, offices and places of commerce that was Matzlingen. That all his life had been passed in this ordinary town now struck him suddenly as a sorry reflection on the person he was – so devoid of the spirit of adventure, so afraid to find himself in some other place, where he would feel lost, that he'd never looked – nor even wanted to look – beyond the streets and squares that were familiar to him.

Aside from Bern, Burgdorf, Basel and Davos, he'd been nowhere; he had never left Switzerland. Now and then, travel brochures had come his way through the post and he'd looked at shining photographs of Rome and Barcelona and the islands of the Aegean. But Gustav Perle had never felt any inclination to get on a plane and attempt to go to these places. Indeed, the thought of arriving in them, alone and lost in another language, filled him with nothing but terror. In common with many of his countrymen, he believed that Switzerland was almost certainly the best place on earth. He had the notion that travel would only make him suffer in ways which he couldn't quite imagine, but which nevertheless lay in wait for him.

Yet now that he was looking down on Matzlingen, sitting smugly in its green valley, a small, unlovely place where visitors were few, where no famous men or women had been born (aside from the young pianist Mathias Zimmerli), a place which only came near to rejoicing in itself through the ancient Schwingfests, where men drank beer and wrestled with each other in linen shorts, while the girls looked on in amusement – in other words, a place which could have been erased from the map with little or no lamentation – it made him ashamed to think that he had been trapped here for fifty-four years.

Feeling suddenly thirsty, Gustav got up and walked to where the strawberries grew and began picking them and cramming them into his mouth. As the beautiful tiny fruits began assuaging his thirst, he made a decision. It was not one he'd expected himself to make, but it seemed, at least, to contain no terror. Once he'd installed his builders in October, he would leave Matzlingen for two months, returning only in time for Christmas, when he knew Anton might come back to visit Armin and Adriana. He would go to Paris.

Gustav didn't want to travel alone. He decided he would take Lottie Erdman with him. He knew how much a trip to Paris would mean to her – how, indeed, it was beyond anything she could have dreamed of in what remained of her life. And the idea that Lottie Erdman was owed some *gift*, for the love that she had given his father, felt correct to Gustav.

And there was another consideration: dreading to find Paris dark and crowded and not much to his liking, he preferred to try to experience it through Lottie's eyes, to discover in it at least some fleeting wonder. He had the feeling that he would be unmoved by the colossal reach of the Eiffel Tower, by the broken limbs of the Venus de Milo in the Louvre, by the formal grandeur of the Jardins des Tuileries, but that Lottie would not be unmoved by these things. Her delft eyes, peering in rapture at all that he guided her to, would shine with grateful tears. She would clutch his arm or take his hand. She would say, 'Gustav, you can't imagine what this means to me. You can never imagine.'

Before leaving, he had to go over plans for bathrooms with his builders. He told them, 'I want these new bathrooms to be stylish and modern and warm. I want marble tiles on the floor and showers that are spacious and simple to operate. I want the Hotel Perle to become renowned for its luxury in this important area.'

The cost was daunting. Over the years, Gustav had managed to save money, but he now saw that a big slice of this would have to be put towards the refurbishments. And part of him wondered, is the Hotel Perle, of which I've been so ridiculously proud for so long (but inhabiting as it does an undistinguished street in a very undistinguished town) really worth all this terrifying expense? Will I ever be able to recuperate it?

He couldn't know the answer to this. All he knew was that he had to keep moving forwards in his life, not stay still to pine over Anton's absence, and that moving forwards sometimes entailed spending money. He thought frequently about his grandmother's store cupboard full of sauerkraut and the notes Emilie and he had found in the ancient jar. And it struck him as sad that Irma Albrecht had never moved forward, but had lived out her entire life in a broken-down house on a wild hill near Basel, amassing a treasure, note by note, in a grimy larder, but taking no pleasure from it, only the pleasure of depriving small tradesmen of what she owed them.

*

The evening before Gustav left for Paris, with the hotel already emptied of its staff, except for his *maître d'hôtel*, Leonnard, who had agreed to remain as a caretaker, there was a ring at the door.

There was already a notice on the front door explaining that the hotel was closed for refurbishments, so Gustav was surprised that anybody should ring the bell.

The early-October night was cold, so he came down quickly to see who was outside, and at once recognised a face that was dear to him, peering in through the grille. It was Colonel Ashley-Norton.

He ushered in the elderly man and shook his hand, which was freezing. A battered waterproof hat had been pressed onto his brilliantined white hair. From his nose, an icy droplet threatened to fall onto his nail-brush moustache. Gustav felt wretched that there were no fires in any of the downstairs rooms.

'Colonel,' he said, 'I'm so sorry. I'm closing the hotel for some restoration work. I leave tomorrow for Paris . . .'

'Yes,' said Ashley-Norton, 'I saw your notice. Bad timing, eh? I wanted to come back here in the summer and take up my marvellous valley walks, but I was trapped in England by illness. Too bad, too bad. I'm recovered now and I was hoping we could resume the rummy games this autumn.'

Gustav led the colonel up to his apartment, the only warm space in the building, and sat him by the fire. He'd eaten no dinner, so Gustav made him up a plate of cold cuts from his own small fridge and poured him a large glass of brandy.

'Capital,' he said. 'First rate.'

'I'm so sorry,' Gustav said again. 'I can't tell you how often I've thought about you and the cards and hoped you'd come back. Everything you said about the game being consoling and "stilling the heart" I found to be right. I taught my friend Anton how to play. You remember Anton Zwiebel? He's gone away now.'

'Oh, gone away where?'

'He lives in Geneva.'

'Geneva, eh? Nice city. Elegant in every particular. But Matzlingen . . . for some reason, I found this town to be very congenial. Not too smart. And just about the right size for me.'

He made up a room for Colonel Ashley-Norton. He told him

that the water was still hot so he could take a bath or a shower before bed, if he liked. He then telephoned the only other hotel in Matzlingen, the Hotel Friedrich, and booked him in for the following night.

'The Hotel Friedrich,' said the colonel, shaking his white head. 'Am I going to be all right there?'

'I hope so. It's the best I can do.'

'I bet their chef doesn't make chocolate truffles, eh?'

'I fear he may not.'

'Most delicious thing I've ever tasted, those truffles. And the other thing that happened here, Herr Perle,' he said. 'I always slept well. Always slept as though I was an innocent – almost as though I had no past I had to be ashamed of. Why? you will ask. Comfortable beds, I suppose, and that gentle clink-clank of the trams, but most importantly, the childish feeling that you were watching over me.'

# Interlude

## *Paris, 1996*

Long before Gustav and Lottie Erdman reached Paris, Lottie began to comment on the marvellousness of things.

Walking along the concourse at Bern airport, wearing a smart white woollen travelling coat and suede ankle boots, she kept pausing to wonder at the shops selling chocolate bears, Emmental cheese, Swiss sausage and aprons imprinted with the national flag. Then, on the plane, when Gustav ordered her a drink, she laughed with pleasure at the miniature bottle of whisky she was given. When she looked out of the window and saw the shadow of the plane borne across the clouds, she said, 'Look, Gustav! We're a cargo of angels!'

Gustav glanced at her profile, lit by the sunlight coming through the plane's window. She had had lilac streaks put into her grey hair, which she had swept into a neat chignon, and set off with gold earrings, and these things gave to her the shine of a rich woman. Gustav felt suddenly proud to be with her. He imagined how moved and amazed his father would have been if he had been able to take his beloved Lottie to Paris. He would have bought her new dresses and new French underwear. He would have spent hours in cafés, holding her hand.

Soon after arriving in Paris, Gustav saw clearly that the best time to visit an unknown city was in the autumn. He understood that everything which gives to a foreign metropolis its outward expression of hostility – the grey contours of buildings from which you feel you might be forever excluded, the pavements with their freight of hurrying strangers – was softened and made human by leaves falling and dancing in the wind. He felt that there was a sweet melancholy in an October rain, and on fine days, the cries of children kicking their way along the strewn sidewalks or across the gravelled walkways of the parks, searching for conkers and sweet chestnuts, sounded pure and lovely in the clear air.

He'd expected to feel lost in Paris, to experience the feelings of shame and stupidity of those who haven't worked out how to negotiate a place for themselves in a world they don't understand. But walking there with Lottie, both of them surprised at every turn by the great vistas the city suddenly revealed, gazing up like babies at the Arc de Triomphe on its hill of light, dawdling along the banks of the grey-green river, what gradually stole upon him was a feeling of lightness, as though he had been imprisoned in a tiny cell for a long while and was now suddenly released.

The flat he'd rented was in the rue Washington, about one hundred paces from the crowded sweep of the Champs-Elysées. The apartment was on the second floor. To reach it, you went up a wide staircase which at first reminded him of the staircase in Emilie's old apartment, except that that stone was carpeted – so that no melancholy echo sounded as you ascended or descended.

The rue Washington itself was undistinguished: a bar, a pharmacy, an optometrist's tiny shop. But the back of the apartment looked out over a cobbled courtyard, sun-filled in the afternoons, and in their first week, Lottie and Gustav spent long, spellbound moments gazing down in wonder at this. The courtyard, planted up with bay trees and box and tubs of geraniums going brown in the sharp winds of October, didn't belong to them, but nobody stopped them looking at it; it was there for all the residents of the building to enjoy.

'What I feel,' said Lottie one evening, as they watched the courtyard fill with shadow and the light in the sky turn an electric blue, 'is that we're outside time, Gustav. This bit of our lives is an interlude; it doesn't count in the measurement of days or hours. When we leave we'll be exactly the age we were when we arrived.'

Gustav thought about this for a long time. He saw how his life in Matzlingen – a life he would have said was far from unhappy until Anton left for Geneva – had had about it a low hum of *weltschmerz* which he had not been inclined to hear. He thus deliberately set about changing certain habits. He let the apartment become untidy and forced himself not to mind when Lottie left her clothes strewn about the rooms. And he quickly became reckless about spending money. He knew that this was ridiculous, a bit infantile, but he wanted to buy for Lottie the things his father would have bought her, if they had only had the time and the means.

They went to beautiful little boutiques in St-Germain-des-Prés and Gustav sat among shoes and rails of brassieres while Lottie disappeared behind curtains to emerge, like an opera diva, dressed in velvet skirts and sparkling low-cut blouses, her large breasts held up and her waist held in by a bit of female armoury she called a *bustier.* With her lilac hair, with her blue eyes ablaze with joy, Lottie appeared far younger than she'd looked when he'd first met her, and her great curvy body, he saw, was a source of admiration among the thin salesgirls who helped choose her outfits.

'Madame looks wonderful!' they would chorus, as yet another shimmering confection made Lottie want to dance about the shop like a child. 'Madame has a very special style!'

Then, Lottie would turn to Gustav and say, 'It's very expensive, Gustav. I don't need it.' And he would say, 'I think you do need it. I want you to need it.' And the salesgirls would let tumble forth a waterfall of giggles, assuming 'Madame' had a lover enslaved to her every desire.

But where was Madame to wear these astonishing clothes?

She saw an advertisement for a concert at the Salle Pleyel, and asked him to buy tickets. The programme was the Rachmaninov Concerto Number 4 and Mahler's Fifth Symphony, played by an orchestra from Jerusalem.

Gustav hesitated. It had become his habit to acquiesce with most things that Lottie wanted, but the thought of being inside a concert hall made him feel afraid. He'd decided he would live his life without ever going near one again. The beautiful Mahler symphony he thought he could endure, but he knew that, in the Rachmaninov concerto, terror for the soloist and memories of

Anton's struggles with a piece for which his pupil, Mathias Zimmerli, had become renowned, would make him feel physically sick.

'Lottie,' he said, 'let me buy you a ticket and I'll meet you for supper afterwards. We can go to that nice restaurant we found in the Places des Ternes.'

'Go to a concert on my own, Gustav?'

'Yes, why not?'

'Well, I don't think that's very nice of you.'

'I don't like concerts,' Gustav said. 'I find them hard to endure. I'm sorry.'

She let the subject go, but that night, feeling the weight of Gustav's melancholy on her, spoiling the mood of elation she'd been feeling, she dressed herself in a shimmering blouse and a velvet skirt and announced that she was going out on her own.

Gustav stared at her. Her lipstick was a fiery red. Her lilac hair fell in cascades around her shoulders.

'Going where?' said Gustav.

'I'm going to the Paris Bar on the boulevard,' she said. 'I'm going to see what happens.'

Gustav knew what she meant: she was going to see if she could pick up a man. Very often she talked about her continuing need for sex. She termed it a need, not a desire. Perhaps she'd hoped that she could recapture something of her lost love, Erich, if she could have taken Gustav to her bed. One evening, she'd attempted to kiss him, but when he pulled away, she said gently, 'Oh, I see. It's not like that with you. That's a shame, considering we're living together in Paris, but I understand.'

Now, she went out into the Paris night.

Gustav sat in the apartment, imagining all the dangers that could come her way. He felt he was to blame, for not being able to be her lover. He wanted to go to the bar and bring her back to safety, but who was he to decide what was safe and what wasn't? Who was he to spoil her chance of rapture?

The hours passed and Gustav didn't move, but only listened, with an agitated heart, to the bright sounds of the city, caught in its own enchantment, in its own overflow of beauty and desire. He fell asleep in his armchair and had a dream of the boy, Anton, bending over him in bright sunlight, in Davos, and kissing his lips. When he woke, it was early morning and he could hear Lottie snoring in her room.

She never spoke about what had happened to her and never went to the Paris Bar again. Though Gustav pressed her to tell him, she refused, saying he had no right to ask. And he found himself wondering whether, after all, there had been no man, no hungry stranger in the bar, and whether Lottie had only sat there on her own, sipping her new, favourite drink, Campari and soda, until the bar closed. And this image of her, wearing her dazzling clothes and with her lilac tresses curled, waiting and waiting but never being approached by anyone, made Gustav feel that he wanted to cry.

To banish this night from his mind, to resume his role of Lottie's benefactor, he agreed, after all, to get tickets for the concert at the Salle Pleyel.

Lottie took a long time to get ready for the evening. She at last appeared in a black, strapless dress with a white fake-fur jacket. People in the concert audience stared at her with frank Parisian disbelief. Most of them were dressed in drab winter coats or anoraks and scarves. November was beginning. Wearing a thin suit, Gustav shivered in the cold hall.

The young soloist was from Israel and held himself away from the piano in exactly the same position that Anton always adopted. Gustav was unable to look at him. He reached for Lottie's hand, but held it too tightly, only realising he was bruising her when she tugged her hand free. She stared at Gustav in the darkness. He was so cold that he was trembling.

On went the Rachmaninov. At a distance, Gustav could appreciate that the soloist was talented and so he made himself lift his head and look at him, but he tried not to see the young man from Israel, only his hands dancing over the keyboard and his feet in shiny black shoes pressing delicately up and down on the pedals. Lottie took off her fur jacket and handed it to Gustav and he wrapped it round and round his hands and held it close to his body, to warm it.

Memories of being cold began to tumble into his mind: crawling on his hands and knees, cleaning the grating of the

Church of Sankt Johann before any winter light was in the sky; going down to the nuclear shelter in the building on Unter der Egg and seeing the beds arranged in high tiers right up to the ceiling; walking in darkness to the hospital when Emilie had pneumonia; standing at his window with his tin train.

And he thought, this used to be my condition in Switzerland: being cold in the freezing air of Mittelland. I bought the hotel first and foremost as a refuge, as a place I could fill with warmth and homely light. And without it I would not have survived.

In the interval, Gustav gulped whisky and this warmed him a little. Lottie asked him if he wanted to leave. He wondered if he could sit through the Mahler symphony, with its heart-clutching fourth movement, which he couldn't listen to without thinking of Visconti's film of Thomas Mann's *Death in Venice.* The sufferings of the protagonist, Aschenbach, had always struck him as being an extreme version of his own. Mann had understood perfectly that a secret passion, unfulfilled, must lead inevitably to physical collapse and so, in time, to death. Gustav only had to wonder where and when that death was lying in wait for him.

He knew that Lottie wanted to hear the Mahler. He looked at her, with her breasts bunched up like bulbous veined orchids by the armoury of the black dress, and the eyes of the concert-goers upon her, and decided that he couldn't desert her. So they returned to the Salle. When the slow movement of the Mahler began, scenes from the Visconti film crowded into Gustav's mind. He couldn't remember the name of the English actor playing Aschenbach, but his sensual face and his marvellous ability to convey the pain in his heart with few words remained very present before his eyes. The moment which affected him the most was when Aschenbach visits a barber's to get his hair dyed black. The barber puts make-up on him and, in his vain attempt to look younger and more acceptable to his boy-love, Tadzio, Aschenbach descends into effeminate clownishness. Later, when the rain falls, the black hair dye begins to run down his face. Gustav had never been able to sit through this film without weeping.

He wanted to weep now, but he kept it down, just as he had kept it down as a boy. He leaned a little towards Lottie, so that he could feel her warmth and breathe in her perfume. She seemed rapt by the music. And Gustav told himself to curtail his self-pity and think only of her. The time in Paris was going quickly by. It had started so well, with such gladness and resolution, but now Gustav was beginning to spoil things with his misery. He knew that he had to try to make amends.

The park nearest to the rue Washington was the Parc Monceau, and on fine days, Lottie and Gustav enjoyed walking there in the late mornings, arm in arm, before deciding where they would like to lunch. This park was a favourite place for joggers, and these people amused Lottie – their expressions of self-satisfied determination, their way of showing off their lean bodies by pausing to do stretching exercises on the sandy paths.

They went to the Parc Monceau the morning after the concert. Lottie's mood was good. She giggled at the joggers. Then she began to admit how her own body had changed a little since arriving in Paris. 'It must be our walks,' she said, 'or all the stretching and bending I've done, trying on new clothes!' She told Gustav she had lost a little weight and the pain in her left leg, which had sometimes been acute in Matzlingen, had lessened. 'What did I do all day in Grünewaldstrasse,' she said, 'except lie on my sofa and read novels and drink wine and sometimes indulge my old habit of masturbation? I think my bones were seizing up.'

'It's good that the pain's lessened,' he said. 'We must hope it stays that way.'

'It won't stay that way,' said Lottie, 'unless we can move to Paris. Couldn't we do that, Gustav? As friends – as people who take care of each other. Couldn't we?'

Gustav turned to Lottie. Her face was very close to his, her expression ardent, beseeching.

'I have to go back to run the hotel,' he said.

'Why? Couldn't the hotel run itself?'

'No.'

'Put in a manager. Go back every few months to see how things are going.'

'I can't do that, Lottie. I wouldn't be happy with an arrangement like that.'

'Well then, sell the hotel. You'd have a lot of money then. You could buy us an apartment here. We could be happy.'

Gustav looked away from Lottie and around at the wintry park. Last leaves clung to the plane trees. The flower beds contained only a few bright dahlia flowers among damp and dying foliage. In these things, he could see the inevitability of their coming departure.

'It was you,' he said, 'who commented that this was an "interlude". Surely, it's a mistake to think that an interlude can translate itself into a permanent state?'

'I don't see why.'

'The hotel is my refuge, Lottie. I'm not ready to give it up. I've worked half my life for that. It's all I've got.'

'It's just a *place*, Gustav. This is a place, too. Just exchange one for the other.'

'What would I do here?'

'Why do you have to *do anything*? Couldn't you just *be*?'

Gustav didn't know what to say to this. He had the feeling that, no matter what he did or said from now on, Lottie would feel that he had failed her. He had failed her because he didn't love her in the way that Erich had loved her.

Tenderly, he took Lottie's arm and they walked towards the little carousel where, even on this November day, a few small children were being loaded into miniature metal cars and fire engines and aeroplanes that would begin to turn as soon as the music started.

They sat down on a bench and Lottie stared sadly at the children. After a while, she said, 'There's something I've never admitted to you, Gustav. When I wrote to your father, to ask him to come back to me, I told him I wanted to have his child. Roger and I had tried for a baby, but I didn't conceive. And I thought that with your father – if we took no precautions as we'd had to do before – it would probably have happened very quickly, our loving was so deep and potent. So you would have had a little half-brother or half-sister. Does that shock you?'

Gustav took Lottie's hand, encased in a soft suede glove, bought by him chez Chanel. He said that when it came to the question of human love, nothing shocked him and never would.

The carousel music began – an old accordion tune he

remembered hearing at a Schwingfest long ago. Round and round went the children, who held out their arms to their parents as they passed, most of them in greeting, but some in fear, as though begging for the ride to stop.

# Father and Son

## *Matzlingen, 1997*

It was many months before Gustav heard from Anton again.

When he went to see Adriana, she admitted that she was worried about him. Anton had apparently told her that he was 'pursuing things with Hirsch', but that the reviews of the first four Beethoven sonatas had not been 'what Hans hoped for', so they had postponed making further recordings until Anton had worked harder on his technique.

'My poor son,' said Adriana. 'I can't bear him to be disappointed a second time.'

'Perhaps you should go to Geneva and see how things stand?' Gustav suggested. 'You and Armin.'

'Armin can't travel any more,' she said. 'He has a prostate cancer.'

'Oh,' said Gustav. 'Oh . . .'

It was difficult for Gustav to imagine Armin Zwiebel being struck down by disease. He was a man, who, even as he'd aged, had always appeared strong. His frame, his voice, his appetites – these things had remained expansive and significant. His complexion had always been ruddy, tanned in summer; he had never paled as many old people pale. And that strange antipathy towards the world which often seemed to creep upon elderly people had never deranged Armin Zwiebel. His politeness towards strangers, his courtesy towards Gustav, his love for Adriana, to all of this he had remained true.

But Adriana told Gustav that Armin had been very

depressed, in recent months, by the international accusations against certain Swiss banks that, having received gold and other treasure from the Nazis during the war – treasure taken from Jewish families sent to the death camps – these banks had made 'insufficient effort' to trace the rightful heirs to this vast fortune.

'The bank that Armin worked for is not one of the accused,' said Adriana, 'but that the integrity of the Swiss banking system should be weakened in this way is very bad for the country. We always thought the banks behaved with absolute probity, despite their code of secrecy. We, the Jews, trusted them. We believed all that gold had been returned to its rightful owners, wherever they or their descendants could be found, but it seems this is not so. The banks enriched themselves with money that was not theirs. It makes Armin feel very ashamed. Ashamed of the banking system. Ashamed of Switzerland. These are terrible, unpatriotic things to feel. And I wonder if it isn't this shame which has allowed his illness in.'

Gustav listened carefully to all this. It was a subject much discussed by guests at the hotel and it seemed to make all Swiss citizens feel queasy, as though there was a new epidemic of some contagious illness to which they had already fallen victim.

He told Adriana that he had always believed absolutely that sorrows in one's life could weaken the body's ability to fight off disease. He said that his own father might not have died when he did had he not suffered the loss of his job and his self-esteem. 'Who knows,' he said, 'whether he might not still be alive now, and married to Lottie Erdman?'

'Lottie Erdman,' said Adriana. 'You took her to Paris. Why did you do that?'

'Because I wanted a companion. And because I feel that I owe her quite a lot. She loved my father far more than my mother ever did.'

'You know she has a bad reputation in Matzlingen. Even at her age. As a courtesan.'

Gustav smiled at the old-fashioned word. 'I didn't know that,' he said, 'or perhaps I did? Let her be a courtesan. It makes no difference to me.'

*

One afternoon, Gustav went round to Fribourgstrasse for tea. Armin was sitting in front of the fire, and he appeared shrunken to a man half the size he once was. When he saw Gustav's mouth gape, he said, 'Don't be alarmed, Gustav. We all have to die. I'll fit in my coffin better now that I'm a bit reduced.'

Adriana was in the kitchen making tea. Gustav sat opposite Armin and said, 'You can't die, Armin. It's not in my scheme of things.'

Armin laughed and said, 'I didn't think it was in mine. I thought people who died gave up too easily. But you know, Gustav, I've honestly had a very good life. I started poor, but everything came round. I know banking is now considered a corrupt occupation, but it never was when I worked in it and I always took pleasure in my job. What more could I have wanted? I married the woman I've always loved. It doesn't matter if I leave now.'

'It matters to us, the ones you leave behind.'

'I know. But what can I do? And, à propos, I was going to ask you a favour, Gustav. Will you look after Adriana when I'm gone? Give her some nice meals at the hotel? Come and visit her as often as you can. Make sure her finances aren't in a muddle. Can you do this?'

'Yes,' said Gustav. 'Of course I can. Willingly. But what about Anton? Surely he should be here with you now?'

Armin looked into the fire. After a moment, he said, 'Anton has gone elsewhere. I have to respect that.'

'Elsewhere?'

'He doesn't communicate much with us. He doesn't know how ill I am. His mother wants to tell him and beg him to come, and of course he would come. But I'm against it. I think Anton may be in rather a fragile place. We're not sure how well he is in his mind. I don't want to suggest anything that would bring about a crisis.'

Adriana came in with the tea. On the tray was a plate of small meringues and she gave one of these to Armin. 'The only thing I can eat,' he said, smiling, 'egg white and sugar. Where did the roast lamb go, and the cakes soaked with rum?'

They sat in silence and ate the meringues. Suddenly, Adriana said, 'Anton is composing now. I didn't tell you that, Armin. It was in his last message. He says Hirsch is encouraging him.'

'Composing?' said Armin. 'Isn't that fifty times harder than playing? Why's he gone down that road?'

'I don't know,' said Adriana. 'He only tells me half the story of his life. Perhaps he'll be good at composition.'

'Only with untold struggle,' said Armin. 'It could be the thing that kills him.'

'You don't know that.'

'I know Anton. He's taking a wrong turning there. I'm sure Gustav agrees.'

Gustav looked from Armin to Adriana, at a loss to know what to say. It hurt him to imagine Anton bent over sheets of composition paper, sowing lines of quavers and semiquavers, searching for illusive new musical forms and idioms, believing that the genius of Beethoven was lying like an undiscovered malady in him and trying to get it out.

'I can't judge,' Gustav said. 'I've never been able to predict what Anton was capable of.'

'Well, I have,' said Armin. 'And you'll see that I'm right, one day. Anton was capable of being a very good music teacher and that's as far as his gift went. I could have told you that years and years ago. In fact, I did tell you, didn't I? But you've all forgotten.'

Armin Zwiebel died in December. Gustav asked himself whether – strangely – it was this death that he had been waiting for.

Anton arrived the day before the funeral, then stayed to sit shiva for his father, with Adriana and Armin's brother, David, from Bern and his wife and daughter, Magda and Leah. During this time, as Jewish custom dictates, the family remained at home, the mirrors in the apartment were covered, candles were kept burning and the Jewish prayer known as Kaddish was said several times a day. The men were forbidden to shave for seven days.

On the last day of the shiva, Adriana called Gustav. He could barely hear her because she was whispering into the telephone. She said, 'It's breaking my heart, Gustav. Anton says he's going back to Geneva tomorrow. I said to him, you must stay and see Gustav, surely, but he says Hirsch needs him. Needs him for what? I suppose it's work, but he hasn't talked much about it, only about his compositions. So I don't know what to do, except to suggest you come round this evening. Will you come?'

Gustav hesitated. It had been distressing, knowing that Anton was at Fribourgstrasse, but that he, Gustav, had to respect his friend's commitment to the mourning rituals for his father. Though Adriana had often teased him about being 'one of the family', when it came to the great and final matter of death, he knew that he had no right to intrude.

After a moment, Gustav said, 'I'll only come round if Anton wants me to.'

Adriana was silent. Then she began crying. 'I don't know what he wants,' she sobbed, 'he's so distant with me, so closed down. Please come, Gustav. Something's happened to him, I know, but he won't talk about it. Perhaps he will talk to you.'

'I can't come, Adriana, unless he wants me to. I can't intrude like that.'

'I've told you, I don't know what he wants, and I don't think he does. But come for my sake. Our shiva is over. You two could go out to a café . . . Please, please say you will . . .'

When Gustav arrived at the apartment door, it was Anton who opened it.

His eyes looked bruised with tiredness. His seven-day beard, here and there flecked with grey, gave him the air of an old prophet of the wilderness. His body was thin, as if, in sympathy with his father's last sufferings, he'd been living on a diet of egg white.

Gustav embraced him, but Anton quickly pulled away. He said, 'Adriana invited you, I hear.'

They were still standing in the doorway. The light was subdued here and when Gustav looked at Anton, it was as if he was deliberately retreating into shadow, not wanting to be seen. But then he began to move towards the apartment door and said quickly, 'We won't stay here. We've got the whole Zwiebel family lumping about on sofas. Strangers all. Come on.'

Gustav would have liked to talk to Adriana, but Anton took

his arm and hurried him out of the apartment and down the stairs.

The December night was cold and Anton had no coat. Gustav took off his woollen scarf and wrapped it round Anton's thin neck and Anton led the way, pounding very fast, towards Marinplatz, towards a dark beer cellar they used to frequent when they were young.

They went down the familiar steps – always dark and damp and smelling of urine. Gustav saw that the cellar had hardly changed. The walls were stained brick and the lighting dim. The tables were painted black and lit with flicking tea lights. Anton ordered the strong Belgian beer he told Gustav he drank in Geneva. With his first sip, Anton downed a fistful of pills taken out of his pocket. 'Don't ask,' he said.

He waited, staring blankly at Gustav, as if he didn't want to speak until the pills had taken effect. Then he said suddenly, 'You've got fat. I never thought I'd see that. You were always so skinny.'

Gustav protested feebly, 'Not fat, I wouldn't say. That's a bit unfair. Just a bit *fatter*. I told you I had a spell in Paris. I sent you cards from there, but you never replied.'

'Oh, cards. Well, I never reply to those. They're never serious.'

'No one decrees that everything has to be "serious".'

'I decree it. I'm in a serious life now. Everything has to match up with it, or else I let it go.'

'What do you mean by "a serious life"?'

'I'll tell you what I mean, Gustav. You just have to swear never to repeat what I'm telling you to my mother. All right?'

'Yes.'

'I know you and Adriana are close. But you mustn't betray me.'

'You know I would never betray you. You're the last person on this earth I would ever –'

'I live with Hans now. I make music with him and I make love with him. It's all a very serious business.'

Gustav set down his large beer goblet. He noted how the candlelight, reflecting through the goblet, reminded him of the stained-glass pietà in the Church of Sankt Johann. He fumbled for a cigarette and lit it, hoping Anton wouldn't notice that his hands were shaking.

'You're shocked, I see. That's odd. I thought you of all people –'

'I'm not shocked.'

'Why are you trembling, then?'

'Surprise. Not shock. I thought you liked women.'

'No, you didn't. Not really. You knew I *tried* to like them – Hansi and those other poor slags. But when I met Hans, something else happened.'

'You love him?'

'Trust you to mention love, Gustav. But the word has no meaning for me any more. I'm *enslaved* to Hans Hirsch, that's all I know – because he's beautiful and because he has power over me. Thank goodness my father died. Armin always saw right through me. He would have known that what I've got is slavery, nothing more nor less.'

'How can you be happy with that?'

'I'm not happy. Or only as a slave knows no other happiness except the benign touch of his master. One day in ten, I feel it, and then it overwhelms me – when I make music that Hans admires, when we fuck all night. But he's not faithful to me. He's got lovers all over Geneva, because nobody can resist him. But what I figure is, we're grown up now, eh, Gustav? In fact we're almost *old*. We need to follow our desires before it's too late. Don't you think?'

Gustav looked at Anton. In the dim, trembling light, his features had taken on a haunted look, as though he'd stepped out of a painting by Goya. His eyes were huge and wild. He leaned close to Gustav and said, 'Don't let me down, Gustav. I'm counting on you to understand.'

Gustav took another pull on his cigarette, but suddenly realised, with terror, that he was going to be sick. He threw the cigarette into the ashtray, stumbled out from his seat and hurried towards the place where he remembered the toilet to be. There were two lavatory stalls, but both were occupied, so Gustav threw up in one of the urinals. He held onto the white porcelain. An elderly man came in and stared at him in disgust.

Gustav looked up at his own face in a stained mirror and saw that it was yellow, the very colour of the fat on an uncooked joint of beef. He reached for some paper towels and wiped his mouth. Then he tried to flush the vomit down the urinal, but it choked at the outlet. He stared, growing dizzy and confused, at this horrible sight. Then everything began to cloud and grow dark.

# Two Women

## *Matzlingen, 1999*

After Anton's revelation that he was the lover of Hans Hirsch, Gustav tried – by an act of will, by a desperate attempt at his old childhood self-mastery – to put him out of his mind. He never made contact with Geneva and Anton never made contact with him. Only in dreams, sometimes, did he see his friend's beloved face, and feel his old yearning for love return.

Yet Gustav's life went on in its calm, unvarying way. When he asked himself if he was unhappy, he discovered that he could find no deeper unhappiness in his own soul than he perceived in other people's. He refused to see himself as Aschenbach. He did not particularly want to die at fifty-seven. Yet there were times when he thought that two women, Adriana and Lottie – by their kindness and by their need of him – made him cling to existence only because they willed him to.

He decided to teach Adriana gin rummy. She came up to his apartment twice a week, after he had given her dinner in the hotel, and she was soon an adept at the game, falling under its consoling spell.

They played with a set of expensive but well-thumbed cards, which had been sent to Gustav from England. In the package with the playing cards had been a letter from a firm of solicitors named Montague and Lewis, located in Devon. This letter said:

Dear Herr Perle,

It is with regret that we are obliged to inform you of the

death of Colonel Reginald Llewellyn Ashley-Norton, DSC, at his home in Sidmouth on the thirteenth of January 1999.

Colonel Ashley-Norton put these cards into my hands before he died, with the express wish that I should forward them to you, in the event of his death. He wishes me to say that it was with this same pack that he used to play the game of gin rummy, with his late wife, Bee.

I remain, Herr Perle,
Yours very sincerely,
Jeremy Montague

Adriana was interested to hear about Ashley-Norton, and Gustav realised that talking about him – about the details he knew about the colonel's tranquil life in the south of England with his wife, Bee – had almost the same effect on him as playing rummy; it stilled his heart.

Gustav avoided telling Adriana that, at the age of nineteen, Ashley-Norton had taken photographs at Bergen-Belsen. He knew that both she and Armin had always disliked talking about the war, as if they, as Jews safe in Switzerland, felt guilty about the millions who had perished. Armin had once told him that he had a recurring dream about the camps. 'The terrible thing,' Armin said to him, 'is that I'm not an inmate in the dream. I'm one of the guards. I herd naked people to their deaths.'

Gustav and Adriana talked about Armin very frequently and this seldom upset Adriana, because, she said, 'I had a wonderful marriage. We both knew how lucky we were – in a world where couples have such difficulty staying together. We never had that difficulty. There was always harmony between us, and when I think about Armin, it's this that I hear deep inside me, a kind of melody, like a lullaby.'

And it was agreed between her and Gustav: they seldom discussed Anton. Adriana knew nothing about her son's relationship with Hans Hirsch; she believed Hirsch was just 'an arrogant impresario' who had now brought out two more CDs of Beethoven sonatas on the CavalliSound label 'but who doesn't bother promoting them'. This she and Gustav had talked about: the seeming failure of these recordings to sell widely and the lack of invitations to play in any important concert halls. Gustav suggested that this might be a good thing, given Anton's struggles with live performance, but Adriana once said wistfully, 'I remember being taken to the Grand Théâtre de Genève when I was a teenager. To see Anton giving a recital there would make my life complete.'

Gustav wanted to say, that day will never come, but this felt cruel, so he kept silent. He also told himself that he didn't know for certain that Anton, in his 'slavery', might not discover the ability to conquer his nerves and play in front of what he called 'the snarling tiger', but speculating about this was too painful to be endured for long.

They talked also about Gustav's life and Adriana often congratulated him on the refurbished hotel – its welcoming atmosphere, its warmth and beauty. But, aside from the hotel, there was very little to speak of in the present existence of Gustav Perle, so they drifted, sometimes, towards memories of the past. One evening, Adriana said, 'Anton was very lucky that he found you on the first day of kindergarten. You've shown him such loyalty, Gustav, and I don't know whether he has ever really paid you back.'

'Paid me back?' said Gustav. 'Well, I don't think of it in those terms. I love Anton. I have always loved him and that's just how it is.'

Lunardi teased Gustav that he only dined 'with old women now' because his other regular guest in the dining room was Lottie Erdman. Lottie was in her eighties.

Adriana ate very sparingly, but Lottie was always ravenously hungry and stuffed herself with food. She'd also taken to drinking more wine than in the past and this sometimes made her say things which both annoyed Gustav and broke his heart. One night, she declared that if she and Gustav had stayed on in Paris together, she would have been 'reborn'. She said that Erich understood what she was, a person of 'exceptionally perfected sexual skill', 'and who knows,' she went on, 'I might even have been able to work my magic on you, Gustav, and then we both would have been happy. But you wouldn't let me try. And now nobody in the world wants to fuck me any more, so what am I to do but kill myself?'

Gustav picked up her hand, where it lay upturned on the white tablecloth, waiting impatiently for dessert to be served, and brought it to his lips. He said that he thought the idea of suicide travelled with very many people through their lives, a companion who leaves only to return. But he reminded Lottie that if people do that companion's bidding, then, sadly, all hope of another *mousse au chocolat*, of a *baba au rhum* with whipped cream was gone . . .

Lottie hit Gustav's shoulder. She said she was weary of his teasing, that life was a serious business and that he should not forget this.

'I haven't forgotten it,' he replied, 'I'm just tired of being reminded about it.'

One autumn evening, when Lottie was due to dine with Gustav, she called him near six o'clock to say she wasn't feeling well and couldn't move out of her bed. In recent times, because she ate and drank so much, she'd become very fat and her legs had such difficulty carrying around this heavy load that they sometimes buckled underneath her. She now walked with the aid of a cane, and when she was with Gustav, he always took her arm, to guide her safely into her chair in the hotel dining room.

Gustav drove round to Grünewaldstrasse. He rang Lottie's bell, but there was no answer. He waited for a moment, then he called the concierge, Frau Richter, who had keys to all the apartments, and together they walked up to Lottie's floor. Gustav tapped on her door and called out, but there was only silence from the flat.

'I can open the door, Herr Perle,' said Frau Richter, 'but only if she hasn't put the safety chain on. Shall I do that?'

Gustav called out to Lottie again. He knew, from the Paris interlude, that she stuffed earplugs into her ears before she went to sleep. He told Frau Richter to open the door. The chain wasn't on, so he went inside. He asked Frau Richter to wait, 'in case there's some help needed'.

The autumn evening was cold, but Lottie kept the apartment very warm, and there was a fusty smell in it, as though nobody had lived there for a long time.

Gustav walked towards her bedroom and, not wanting to

make her afraid that an intruder had broken in, called out loudly, 'It's Gustav. I'm coming in, Lottie, if that's all right?'

Her room was hot, with an old-fashioned electric fire switched on and all the radiators turned to full heat. Gustav approached the bed, where Lottie lay with her grey hair spread in a tangle across the pillow. He touched her hand, where it clutched the billows of the duvet, and she opened her eyes. Gustav always marvelled that, in the folds of Lottie's fleshy face, these eyes were still a glimmering, watery blue.

'Gustav,' she said, 'what are you doing?'

'I won't disturb you. I just came to see if there's anything you need.'

'Sit down,' she said. 'Stay with me.'

'Shall I fetch a doctor?'

'No. You be my doctor. I wanted to come for supper at the hotel, but I can't move, that's all.'

'Have you tried to move?'

'Yes, I went to the bathroom, but I fell over. I had to get there on hands and knees. And getting back into bed was a comedy.'

'Are you in pain?'

'Yes, Gustav. I'm in pain. I've been in pain ever since we left Paris.'

Gustav didn't offer any comment on this. He called out to Frau Richter that she could go downstairs again and then he sat at Lottie's bedside, stroking her hand. He thought that she'd gone back to sleep, but she suddenly turned her head towards him, her eyes wide open, and said, 'There's something I'd better tell you, Gustav. I could have told you years ago, but I didn't want to. But now I think it doesn't matter any more, so I'm going to tell you: it's about what happened to Erich.'

Gustav waited. He wondered whether he *wanted* to know the thing she was about to tell him, or whether it wasn't better for certain knowledge to remain hidden, so that the mind could conjure its own stories from out of the past, stories it could bear to live with, stories which, in time, took on their own reality and seemed to become true.

'Are you listening?' asked Lottie.

'Yes.'

'Well, first of all, the thing you have to remember was that in

1939 everybody was afraid. We believed that the Germans could invade and then our world would end.'

'I know that, Lottie.'

'No. You can't know it – not like we knew it: that terrible fear of what was going to happen. And fear of that extreme kind affects how people behave.'

'Yes. I know.'

'You keep saying you know, but you *don't*, Gustav. Unless you lived through that, you have no right to say "I know".'

'All right.'

'You asked me once who "betrayed" Erich, but I took objection to that word, because it wasn't like that: it was just events unfolding in due time, as they had been bound to unfold.'

'Go on . . .'

'Well, when the Justice Ministry in Bern had put out its rule that no more Jews could enter Switzerland after the 18th of August deadline, they assumed that the police and the IF would be vigilant about enforcing this. But they realised, after the deadline had come and gone, that the number of Jews coming in was still going up, so they sent Justice Ministry officials to the various branches of the IF all over Switzerland – to question them. Perhaps they learned of a high concentration of Jews coming into Matzlingen, I don't know. But those people from Bern came to the IF here and asked them if they'd falsified dates of entry. The IF was apparently threatened with closure and confiscation of its funds. But it *wasn't* the IF who had falsified the dates – they hadn't dared to do it! – so of course they put up their hands in innocence and said, "If anybody has falsified dates, it must have been the police."'

'When was that, Lottie? Before or after Roger came back to work?'

Lottie took Gustav's hand and brought it to her lips. 'Now listen to me,' she said. 'And don't be tempted to judge anybody too harshly. All right? Promise me that you won't judge?'

'I'll try not to.'

'Well, it was after Roger was back from the hospital. He knew what your father had done, and he knew where the stack of forms was. And, in time, he got the visit he'd been dreading, from the Justice Ministry. They'd assumed it would be Roger's signature on the forms. They told him they were ready to strip him of his post there and then, if the dates had been falsified by him. Roger thought about trying to withhold the forms – to say they'd been mislaid, or I don't know what – but he was terrified, Gustav. Can you see how terrifying that was for Roger? He had to choose between saving himself and telling the truth about Erich. Yet it wasn't even a choice, because Erich's signature was on all those documents. Everything would have come out. So this is why you can't talk about "betrayal".'

Gustav sat very still. He was finding the heat in the room oppressive. Lottie stared up at him, her eyes suddenly brimming with tears. 'I've got to remind you, Gustav,' she said after a moment, 'Roger did not betray Erich. It was we who betrayed Roger – Erich and I. The only real betrayal was our passion. I hope that now you can get all this straight in your mind.'

They began drinking whisky.

Gustav had been hungry when he arrived at Lottie's apartment, but now his appetite had faded. The whisky tasted good and he liked the feeling of his brain becoming muddled. He thought he understood, at last, in his long sober life, why people drank – so that knowledge and reality would give way to something kinder, to a refashioning of things into a version of themselves in which they performed a dance of sudden grace and beauty. And who would not want to bear witness to this dance?

The only thing which now troubled Gustav was that he was getting an aching back from the hard bedside chair. When Lottie saw him shifting around uncomfortably, she reached out and said, 'Just get into bed with me, darling, and have done with everything.'

*Have done with everything.*

It made him smile.

He took off his jacket and shoes and climbed in beside Lottie. The heat of her body was so intense, he was afraid to go near it, but she pulled him to her and kissed his face.

'Gustav,' she said. 'Gustav Perle.'

They slept for a while and then Gustav woke, needing to piss away all the whisky he'd drunk. He was sweating all down his body, and wondered whether he'd caught some illness from Lottie.

The room was in darkness. Gustav groped his way to the lavatory and stood there for a long time, trying to cool down. He could hear rain on the frosted window glass. He wanted to get into his car and drive back to the hotel, to be alone to ponder the things Lottie had told him. But deserting Lottie in the middle of the night felt like a shabby thing to do.

He went back into the overheated room. He tiptoed to the window and opened it a little and breathed in the cool, wet air. Then, by the little light coming in from the street he could suddenly see that there was something lying on the floor, a bulky shape, folded almost into a square, like a bale of cotton. And he knew it was Lottie.

Gustav put on one of the bedside lamps. Lottie had fallen onto her knees and her back was bent over her knees and her head was on the hard floor. He knelt beside her and talked to her gently and then tried to lift her up. But as soon as he touched her, he knew that she was dead. Through all her magnificent flesh an unmistakable chill had spread.

Gustav stopped trying to lift Lottie up. He just stayed kneeling beside her, with his arm round her, holding her close to him until the morning arrived. The thought came to him that now he was in roughly the same position that he had had to adopt in the Church of Sankt Johann, cleaning the metal grating. Except that, then, he had had a hassock to kneel on and now there was no hassock, just the thin rug that lay beside Lottie's bed. And he understood that now, more than ever in his life, there was nothing and no one to cushion him from the hardness of the earth.

# The Wrong Place

## *Geneva, 2000*

Adriana called Gustav from Geneva. She told him that Anton had been admitted to a psychiatric hospital there, in the wake of 'a complete nervous collapse'.

'I'm with him now,' she said, 'but they won't let visitors come very often. They think it's better if he has complete rest, while his medication is sorted out.'

She then began to cry. 'If you could see him, Gustav . . . So thin. And he's torn out great hunks of hair from his head. And he was cutting himself. He's got scars all up his arms. And the mad things he says . . .'

Gustav's first thought was, I can't go there, I can't see this. Anton has to remain the way he was in my mind.

But then Adriana said, 'The only moment of hope I've had is when he asked for you.'

'He asked for me?'

'Yes. He said only you would understand that he's in the wrong place.'

'The wrong place?'

'I don't know what he meant. He wouldn't explain. Will you come, Gustav? I can get you a room at the hotel where I'm staying.'

Gustav fell silent. He hated the idea of going to Geneva. He didn't want to be pitched into suffering of this intensity. He didn't want to see the ways in which Anton had mutilated himself. He felt furious that, after all that had happened, Anton could expect this of him.

He heard Adriana blowing her nose and then she said, 'I understand how difficult this will be for you. It's difficult for me, I promise you. But this thing about being in *the wrong place*; I think only you will be able to make sense of it. We can't let him die, Gustav! You've got to promise me you'll come. Will you? I beg you.'

Gustav put Leonnard in charge at the hotel. He took a train to Bern, then another to Geneva. On both the trains, he fell asleep. He didn't want to contemplate how he would get through the next bit of time.

It was an autumn day. There was bright foliage in the grounds of the Marburg Hospital, where crows strutted about on the lawn, under a fine blue sky. Among the crows was a single Canada goose. An elderly hospital resident was feeding the birds, but as they clustered round, she kept sending the goose away. 'Go away, goose!' she muttered. 'Come here, crows! Didn't you hear me, goose? Goose, go away!' And Gustav thought, yes, that is how life is always arranged, with one living thing being chosen over another, and the loser sent away to hunger and solitude.

Adriana and Anton were sitting on an iron bench. Adriana was reading to Anton from the Geneva newspaper, *Le Temps*. She was stylishly dressed, as ever, but Anton was wearing a faded hospital gown, with one of Adriana's shawls draped over it. His feet and legs were bare.

Gustav walked towards the bench and Anton turned and saw him. At once, Anton got up and stretched wide his arms, and when Gustav reached him, he clutched him in a tight embrace. 'Help me,' he whispered, 'help me. You're the only one who can.'

Gustav sat down on the bench with Anton and Adriana. Nobody spoke. Part of Gustav's attention kept returning to the old woman and the strutting crows. The goose was now standing apart.

After a moment, Adriana got up. She told Anton that she was going to leave him with Gustav and come back tomorrow. Anton replied that he hoped he wouldn't be at the hospital tomorrow. Adriana looked at him with sadness. Then she kissed his head, where a patch of hair had been torn out, and walked away.

Anton pulled his mother's shawl more closely round his body. Gustav asked him if he was cold.

'No,' he said. 'I know the winter's coming, but I don't feel the cold of the air. I only feel the storms inside me.'

Gustav stared at Anton's arms, scarred red where he'd slashed them. He imagined, for one terrible second, that all the wounds had been made by skate blades.

'You don't have to look at me,' Anton said. 'I know I look like a freak. But you have to help me. If you don't help me, I'm lost.'

Gustav waited. He took Anton's hand and held it in his and stroked it, like he used to stroke Lottie's hand when she talked about suicide.

Anton's eyes closed for a moment, as though the stroking soothed him. Then he said, 'Listen, Gustav. Are you listening? I have to go to Davos. You have to get me there. I can't be in Geneva and I can't go back to Matzlingen. You've got to get me to the sanatorium in the woods. What was its name?'

'Sankt Alban.'

'That's it: Sankt Alban. We left a tambourine on one of the beds. I need to go there now.'

Gustav waited, in case Anton had more to say, then he answered, 'I'm sure you can go to Davos, Anton. Provided we can find a hospital there which will take you . . .'

'No, no,' he said. 'Not a hospital. I need to go back to the Sankt Alban Sanatorium. I need to find the tambourine.'

'I don't think those things will be there any more, Anton, neither the tambourine nor the sanatorium.'

'Why not? We healed the dying there. Don't you remember? We laid the beds on the balcony. And the sunlight was strong and white. It will all be there.'

'It was a ruined place, Anton. Even then, it was a shell. It was only us who made it come alive.'

'So we'll make it come alive again. I need to wipe out time, you see. I need to get back to the place where I can start everything afresh. At first, I couldn't think where I could go. My world has shrunk so much. I can't stand to be anywhere. But then I remembered Davos and Sankt Alban. So you fix it up,

Gustav. Right? And you have to come with me. I need you to answer when I bang the tambourine.'

Gustav waited a moment, then he said, 'I'll do my best to fix it up, Anton. But I have to know what I'm fixing in you first. You have to tell me what's happened to you.'

Anton shook his head. 'This is what everybody asks,' he said. 'What's happened to you? What's happened? But I don't want to talk about it. I *refuse* to answer that question. I just want to arrive at Sankt Alban and begin everything again. I'm depending on you, Gustav – only on you, out of everybody in the whole world! But if you can't fix it for me, tell me now and you can fuck off out of this place, whatever it is, and never see me alive again!'

'This place is a hospital, Anton,' said Gustav calmly. 'A very good hospital. If you stay here, you'll get well.'

'No, I won't. I'll kill myself. I thought you were my friend, Gustav. I thought you'd be on my side.'

'I am on your side. Goodness knows, Anton, I've been *on your side* for over fifty years! Can't you recognise that, by now?'

'Fifty years? Have we lived that long?'

'Yes.'

'Are we old?'

'Almost. We're getting that way.'

'That was probably why Hans betrayed me. I got too old.'

'Hans Hirsch betrayed you?'

'People make promises. But they're never kept. Everybody in the world betrays us – and then we betray ourselves. We cut our flesh . . . But if I can get to Davos, with you, and think myself back in time, when things were ordinary and safe, then I might have some hope of life.'

This phrase, *hope of life*, Gustav seemed to hear from a great distance, as though it came echoing through the sky. And he thought, Would my own existence have been happier, if I'd never known Anton Zwiebel? And he felt, at this moment, that it would have been.

Although Emilie Perle had schooled him well in how to love without being loved in return, he could now see how this state of lovelessness had made him obsessive in his quest for superficial order and control. He looked over at the old woman who had succeeded in separating the crows from the goose, and he wondered if he didn't, after all, resemble her in a mortifying way, wanting everything to be part of some category or other and never letting things be how they truly yearn to be. He saw that the goose was now sitting on its own on a concrete pathway, pecking at its own feathers.

Gustav stayed with Anton until the light began to fade and a nurse came out and called Anton inside. She led him away and he went obediently, without saying goodbye to Gustav or turning round as he disappeared from sight.

The following day, Adriana and Gustav went to see the director of the Marburg Hospital. When Gustav told him about Anton's expressed desire to go to Davos, the director said, 'Well, it's almost certainly delusionary. He's much better off here.'

Adriana said, 'I'm sorry, Herr Director, but why shouldn't Anton be moved to Davos, if that's his wish?'

The director gave Adriana one of those condescending smiles which, Gustav had often noted, seemed to be the speciality of people high up in the medical profession, and said, 'Davos was once a place renowned for its management of tuberculosis, as you probably know. But today, it's a winter sports resort. And the near association of illness is suicidal to tourism. So as far as I know, there are no suitable clinics in Davos to treat Anton's condition. I can enquire, but I'm not hopeful. The Marburg can help him, but you must understand that he's on a long road. We hope he will recover, but this will take time.'

'You *hope*,' said Adriana. 'You mean you're not certain he'll recover?'

'No. In cases like this one can never be certain. We do our best. But we're not helped by the fact that there seems to be nothing that Anton wants to *do.* He refuses all group therapy, becoming abusive if he's forced to participate in this. We've asked him to tell us how he'd like to pass the time, but –'

'Music,' said Adriana at once. 'He's a wonderful musician. I'm surprised you haven't heard his name.'

'Sorry, no,' said the director. 'What instrument does he play?'

'Piano. He's made recordings for the CavalliSound label. Beethoven sonatas.'

'Oh yes? Good for him. But of course we couldn't have him playing the piano here. It would be far too disruptive for the other patients.'

The next day, Gustav went to see Anton in his small room. He was lying on his bed, tugging at his hair. 'Shall I start packing, Gustav?' he asked at once. 'Have you arranged the travel to Davos?'

'No,' said Gustav. 'Davos has changed, Anton. It's a ski resort now. There's no clinic there which could look after you.'

'I don't want to go to a clinic,' said Anton, reaching out and clutching Gustav's arm. 'I told you. I want to go to Sankt Alban. I don't need shrinks and all that shit. You could look after me. All I need is that mountainside and a bed on a balcony and a view of what is to come.'

'What do you mean, "a view of what is to come"?'

'There is a road, Gustav. You know there is. Just this one road we have to take. We have to become the people we always should have been.'

Gustav stared down at Anton – his thin face, his bright and hectic eyes.

'I don't know what you mean,' Gustav said.

'Yes, you do. You knew what we should have been, but I was the one who resisted. Except that one time, at Sankt Alban, when I was the dying boy and you saved my life with a kiss. Now, you have to save it again.'

# Allegro Vivace

*Davos, 2002*

The money Gustav got for the sale of the Hotel Perle was substantial – far more than he'd ever thought it could be worth. It was bought by a Swiss hotel chain, as a profitable 'boutique diversification', and all the staff were retained, all except Lunardi, who refused point-blank the offer made by the new management.

'No way, boss,' Lunardi told Gustav. 'I'm not working for any fucking *chain*! Especially not if they're calling this a stupid "boutique". What kind of nonsense is that? I'll take my luck in one of the grand hotels in Bern or Zurich. Make some proper money at last, eh?'

But when Lunardi and Gustav parted, they both wept.

'Not like you, boss, to cry,' said the now elderly chef, wiping his eyes with a dishcloth. 'Me, I'm Italian, so of course I cry. This is a sad day. The end of so many years. But you. This is not so Swiss, my friend, is it? Where's your famous self-mastery now?'

Anton and Gustav were now both sixty years old.

They lived together in a large, isolated chalet Gustav had bought in the hills near Davos. It was the kind of solid, comfortable house, with some land attached to it, that Gustav realised he had sometimes dreamed of. On the wooded pathway that led up to it, he planted wild strawberries. From this path could be heard the carillons of Davos, ringing out the passing hours.

The bedroom shared by Gustav and Anton gave out onto a wide, south-facing wooden balcony. On summer mornings, they took their breakfast out there, among tubs of scarlet geraniums. In the winter, they embarked on gentle cross-country ski walks among the silent trees, and watched old movies by the fire. They grew their own vegetables and kept a few goats and chickens. Anton said that the sound of chickens stilled his heart and that working on the vegetable patch made it strong.

And he was strong, now. Lying in the dark, Anton had eventually told Gustav, bit by bit, about his life in Geneva with Hans Hirsch and how, with Hirsch, he'd always felt judged and scrutinised 'just like I was judged and scrutinised when I played on the stage of the Kornhaus'. He'd reached for Gustav and gripped his shoulder with great force and said, 'I can't lead a life in which this happens to me ever again, Gustav. So please, I beg you, my beloved friend, don't let me go back there.'

'Why would I?' Gustav said, pulling Anton close to him with rough urgency. 'If we had our lives again, I'd barely let you out of my sight.'

Adriana lived with Gustav and Anton. She was given her own large room and bathroom at the back of the house, facing into the hillside. Gustav worried that this room was dark, but Adriana said, 'Sometimes it is, but I don't mind that, Gustav. I don't mind it at all. You and Anton need the sunshine, you still need all that white light. But I'm happy with the grasses and wild flowers growing outside my window. When you're old, shadow can be comforting.'

From Fribourgstrasse, they'd shipped most of Adriana's furniture, including the grand piano, on which Gustav had heard Anton play 'Für Elise' so long ago. When they'd first moved in together, Anton hadn't wanted to go near it. He said that he didn't think he'd ever play again, because playing reminded him of so much that had terrorised him in his life.

The piano fell out of tune and Gustav asked Adriana if they should get rid of it. But she said, 'No. Not yet. I think if we do, then there will be a big gap in the room and Anton will look at the gap, one day, and remember that something beautiful was once there.'

One morning in summer, when Gustav woke up, Anton wasn't in their bed and Gustav could hear music. Anton was playing the piano.

Gustav crept to the door and listened and he caught a glimpse of Adriana, on the other side of the large room, listening too.

The piece Anton was playing had begun with some rich, sonorous chords and now leaped into a new motif, played *allegro vivace*, which immediately brought to Gustav's mind the image of a fast-running stream, rushing over stones and fallen branches, then slowing very gradually, but still keeping its energy and its momentum, as if it had found a calmer channel and could now flow on, unimpeded, towards the sea.

Anton seemed unaware that anyone was watching him. His body was held in its accustomed position, leaning out from the keyboard, and on his face Gustav saw an expression of great joy.

Later, when the three of them were taking their breakfast on the balcony, Adriana said, 'We must get the piano tuned, Anton. But what was that piece you played this morning? I thought it was lovely.'

'Oh,' said Anton, 'it's just a fragment I composed in Geneva. I composed it in one terrible night, when I understood all the wrong turnings my life had taken and where I wanted to be. It's unfinished, as you could tell, but I might begin work on it again now. I called it "The Gustav Sonata".'

## *Acknowledgements*

I acknowledge with gratitude the debt I owe to Mitya New's book, *Switzerland Unwrapped: Exposing the Myths* (I.B. Tauris, London, 1997) for revealing to me the story of Paul Grueninger, Police Chief of the Canton of St Gallen in 1938, as narrated by his daughter, Ruth Rhoduner. Some details from this story have been used in constructing the invented life of Gustav's father, Erich Perle.

I also want to thank the small, heroic band of 'first readers', whose comments and suggestions helped me refine the book from first draft to final MS: Vivien Green, Penny Hoare, Clara Farmer, Gaia Banks, Jill Bialosky, Roger Cazalet, Neel Mukherjee, Richard Holmes, and most especially Bill Clegg, whose perspicacious intervention helped to turn a pumpkin into a coach.